A TEMPTATION

Mary E. Buras-Conway

Copyright © 2015 Mary E. Buras-Conway
All rights reserved
First Edition

PAGE PUBLISHING, INC.
New York, NY

First originally published by Page Publishing, Inc. 2015

ISBN 978-1-68213-465-8 (pbk)
ISBN 978-1-68213-466-5 (digital)

Printed in the United States of America

To my mom

Mrs. Ellen T. Dinapolis (1926–2011)

This is what you always wanted me to do.
Just wish you could be here to see it. Miss you every day.

THE DISCOVER TRILOGY

Book One

In the dark recesses of your mind they lay
Waiting to control your unconscious thoughts.
They worry you by day
And mercilessly haunt your nights.
Is there no end to the scenes
Of these wild and wicked dreams?

—M. B. C.

PROLOGUE

I always wondered why I was so different from my girlfriends. I mean, I liked boys. A lot. I had quite a few boyfriends—boys that were friends, that is. But I just didn't feel any overwhelming need to explore even the most innocent of sexual interests.

Oh, I've been kissed. After dates. At dances. And, actually, I dated often. But no one ever pushed my buttons.

When I was nineteen, I was so worried about my underdeveloped hormones that I decided to talk to my grandmother. Who else would know me better than the woman who raised me? And as embarrassing as the subject matter was, I needed some perspective.

My grandmother, in her no-nonsense way, assured me that there was nothing wrong with me. She explained that my mother had been the same way. She said that it had all worked out well for my mom because when she finally fell, it was for my father—who was just as head over heels for her. That, she admitted, was the only thing that had frightened my gram. She realized that when my mom finally fell for someone, she would fall hard. If it didn't work out or the other person wasn't as into her, it could do irreparable harm.

My gram's words of wisdom, to this day, have always stayed right below my consciousness, so much so that I didn't push for deep relationships, just friendships. I was afraid, so I kept men at arm's length. Thinking, unrealistically, that that would keep my heart safe. But I found, to my dismay, that your heart overrules your mind; that in the end, what tempts your heart will have you doing whatever to reconcile your brain with the accepted outcome. In actuality, it is the temptation that is so dangerous.

CHAPTER ONE

"*I*ndia!" Kathy yelled, trying to get my attention over the loud music.

I danced my way closer to her so I could hear. I gave her a "What?" look and leaned closer to her.

"The hottest guy I have ever seen hasn't taken his eyes off of you since we've been on the dance floor."

"Yeah, right," I snorted. "You've been trying to hook me up since second grade."

"Girlfriend, I love you and all that, but if this was my doing, I would have him hooking up with me. This man is gorgeous."

There were seven of us on the dance floor. Five were my closest friends, not including Noah, who was out of the country right now. We were in this small club on Bourbon Street not far from the Royal Sonesta Hotel where we were staying this weekend.

"I'm serious, India!" Kathy screamed in my ear. "Switch places with me. You have to see him."

"You are such a pain in the ass." I shook my head at her but did as she asked. "Okay, which guy?"

"You can't miss him." She rolled her eyes at me. "He's standing at the end of the bar. Even you have to drool over this one."

I looked where she indicated and instantly became dumbstruck. He was over six feet, I thought, with very dark, perfectly styled hair. I couldn't tell the color of his eyes from this distance, but I could make out the aquiline nose, high cheekbones, and the sexy soft cleft in his chin. The sculpted lines of his face were absolutely stunning. He had a dark, dangerous, fallen-angel kind of look in the jeans and button-down black shirt he wore.

Even as I gazed at him, a woman sitting on his left kept trying to get his attention. Instead, he just kept looking at me.

Suddenly, he smiled. That smile stopped me in my tracks. His look became hungry as his gaze traveled from my face down my body. When he got back to my face, his look became arrogant even. I felt my face turn red.

"India!" I jumped at the sound of my name. All my friends were standing on the dance floor laughing at me.

"What?"

"The music ended a few minutes ago," Kathy stated, still laughing.

I wished the floor could have opened up and swallowed me. No wonder the arrogant look from Mr. Dark and Dangerous. "Okay. Okay. Y'all can stop laughing now."

"Can't help it," Kathy said, pulling me off the dance floor and back to our table. "It's the first time I've seen you lose your cool in years."

I threw myself into my chair and ordered another top-shelf margarita when the waitress came by. I'm not a snob. I just wasn't that comfortable around different people. I had my inner circle and my work. Don't get me wrong. I have dated. I liked men. I just had never met anyone I was so interested in to lose my head over. I figured when I did, I would fall hard and pray nothing broke on the way down.

"Hey. Do y'all want to go check out some more clubs?" Lace asked, throwing back a shot of Jose with Brittany.

"Not when things are just about to get interesting," Kathy said, almost under her breath.

A TEMPTATION

I felt a touch at my shoulder and looked up. Mr. Arrogant himself was standing over me. "Would you like to dance?" His voice was sexy, very deep and husky. And his eyes were blue. Very light blue. I had never seen eyes that light blue before.

"Ah." I looked at Kathy across the table, and she enthusiastically nodded her head at me. "All right."

He pulled out my chair and, with his hand on the small of my back, led me to the dance floor. It was a slow song. He pulled me into his arms, close to his body, and whispered in my ear, "Relax. I won't bite. Not this time anyway."

And just like that, my heart melted. I laughed and looked up at him. "My name is India. India Leigh."

"I'm Kellan, India Leigh. Do you live here in New Orleans?"

"No. Across the lake in Slidell. My friends and I, whoever can make it, come over about every other weekend. It breaks the monotony." I shrugged. "How about you?"

"I travel a lot for business. I have to be here in New Orleans a lot, and since my favorite woman lives in Mandeville, I decided to buy a house here."

"I would imagine your favorite woman is thrilled," I said, smiling up at him.

"Yes." His smile was so mischievous. "My aunt is getting up there in age, and I wanted to be nearby as often as I can."

I giggled. Me! I don't giggle. "Well, I hope you like it here."

"I love New Orleans. And right now, I see more to my liking." He smiled down at me, and I felt my face turn red. Again.

"You're blushing! I didn't think anyone still did that." He glanced down at me, looking amazed. "It looks beautiful on you."

All too soon, the dance was over. He led me back to my friends and politely seated me. From behind my chair, he leaned down to whisper in my ear, "Have dinner with me tomorrow night, India. I would like to get to know you."

I turned in my chair and looked into his eyes. "But I don't know you at all. I don't think—"

"How are you going to get to know me?" he interrupted. "Look, if it will make you more…comfortable, your friends can join us. But that would kind of defeat my purpose."

As I kept looking into those gorgeous eyes, I was so tempted. I did not recklessly do things. And for me, this was reckless. I was a go-getter in all aspects of my life except this one. When it came to personal relationships, I was so insecure. But I really wanted this, and as he said, how else would we get to know each other?

"Okay." I smiled at him. "But can we stay kind of close to this area?"

"I am sure I can arrange something," he said with a laugh. He reached into his pocket, taking out his card. "Call me if something comes up. If I don't hear from you, I'll assume we have a date. Is seven all right with you?"

"Yes, that's fine." I gave him my room number at the Sonesta.

He leaned in and kissed me on the cheek. "Until then. Good night, India."

And he was gone. He briefly went to the bar, handed the bartender some money, and without another look, he went out the door.

"Well, that's one guy who can keep his eyes off of you," London remarked snidely.

"You're only being a bitch, London," Kathy said, jumping up from her seat and leaning across the table, getting in London's face, "because you're jealous."

"Jealous of what?"

"Of India! Since we were six years old, you've been this way." Kathy sat back because the waitress was suddenly back at our table with a loaded tray.

"Where did these come from?" Brittany asked sweetly.

"From that hot guy that just left," the waitress replied as she placed the drinks around the table. When she got to me, she handed me a top-shelf margarita and a perfect red rose. "He sent this for you too."

I brought the rose to my nose. This simple act from Kellan meant a lot to me. It made me very happy that I accepted his invitation.

A TEMPTATION

"So," London said, drawing our attention back to her after the waitress left, "do all of y'all feel like Kathy?"

No one said a word. London stood up so fast she knocked her chair over. "I will just leave then. I know when I'm not wanted."

I stood up and went over to London. I put my arm around her shoulders, or I should say I tried to. She threw my arm off her shoulder and turned angrily to me. "You, Little Ms. Princess!" she yelled at me. "He might want you now, but as soon as he gets to know you? Cold. Snobby. Unreachable. He won't be around long. A man like that won't put up with your virgin self."

Everyone at the table jumped up and started yelling at London.

"Hey!" I shouted. "Everyone has had a lot to drink. Let's stop before any more damage is done."

"No, India," Kathy spoke up. "Not this time. You have always made excuses for the way London is. She's not worth it. She. Is. Not. A. Friend. Never has been. She can't see any good in anyone because she is so eaten up with jealousy."

She was right. I usually don't put up with much, but from London, I did. I knew how hard her life had always been. I used that as an excuse to forgive her inexcusable behavior for years. It needed to end.

Kathy sat back down, but she wasn't finished. "I for one am done. I wash my hands of her."

Lace, Brittany, Skylar, and Lexie all sat down also.

"I don't need y'all. Not one little bit. I'm calling Blaine to come and pick me up. Have a nice life." And she stomped out of the club.

I sat back down. "I'm sorry."

"Don't you dare apologize, India. That was all London." Kathy raised her glass. "A toast to us. The six musketeers."

"Seven," I cut in. They looked at me as though I was nuts. "You're forgetting Noah."

"Oh God." Kathy laughed. "We can't forget Noah."

CHAPTER TWO

"Arrgh! Why did I say yes?" I actually growled while staring in the mirror at Kat's reflection.

Kathy laughed. "Would you calm down?" She walked over and put her hands on my shoulders. She looked into the mirror, her eyes meeting mine in the reflection. "Look at you, India. You're beautiful. Everyone knows that except you."

"Yeah. Right." I rolled my eyes at her. "I only brought four dresses, and none of them are right."

Kathy shook her head at me. "You could wear a gunnysack, and you would still be the most beautiful woman in the room. This dress is great." She indicated the dress I had just tried on. "He will think you're sexy as hell."

I stared at my reflection. No, I wasn't ugly. But I wasn't going to fool myself either. As gorgeous as Kellan was, he could have his pick of women. So why me?

This last dress, the one we had settled on—maybe. It was black with off-the-shoulders cap sleeves. It fit like a second skin and showed just enough cleavage to be sexy, but not slutty. I was definitely not overly endowed, but I guess I would look unbalanced if I was.

A TEMPTATION

I had very long light-brown hair with a lot of natural gold highlights through it. I had it french-braided with the end tucked under for tonight. My eyes were large, perhaps too large, and a common green. High cheekbones and a dimple in my left cheek. I looked like a pixie, not an elegant, self-assured, independent woman.

I sat on the hotel bed and put on my black heels. "Well, this is as good as it gets," I mutter. Kathy just shook her head.

At seven sharp, there was a knock on the door—not a minute before, not a minute after. What did that say about the man?

I opened the door and had to bite my lower lip to keep my mouth from gaping. I just thought he was gorgeous last night. This was the embodiment of a *GQ* model! In this bright light, his face was flawless. He wore a designer gray pinstripe suit that made his eyes look an even brighter blue. In fact, he also looked like money. I was comfortable, not filthy rich. I was so out of my league.

"You keep biting that lip, beautiful, and I'm going to get jealous."

I blushed, naturally, at his words. But I did release my bottom lip.

"You look beautiful, India. I like that dress on you."

He made me feel as though he were undressing me with his eyes. I had read that expression countless times, but this was the first time that I experienced it.

Kellan asked if I was ready, saying that we had a seven-thirty reservation at Mr. B's Bistro. That was right down Royal. I was great with that.

"It was good seeing you again, Kathy, right?" he asked my friend.

"Correct. Good to see you too. Y'all have a great time."

"Thanks, Mom," I replied laughingly to her.

We left the Royal Sonesta, heading over to Royal Street. The quarter was crowded this Saturday night. With it being April, the temperature was perfect, not sweltering yet.

"I hope the walk won't be too much for you?"

I laughed and turned my head a little to the right so I could see him as I responded. "Are you serious?" I asked incredulously.

Kellan stopped walking and took my hand. "I did not mean anything rude, India. It is just that you are so…tiny."

"Small, Kellan. An inherited family trait from the women in my family. Not sickly." I started us walking again. "Besides, I like walking, and I love the quarter."

"If you like it here so much, why do you live in Slidell and not New Orleans?"

"Because I also like privacy, and quiet too. This way, I get the best of both worlds."

We fell silent, not an awkward silence, but a companionable one.

When we reached the restaurant, I could see it had been a good idea that Kellan had made reservations. There were quite a few people waiting for a table. Kellan gave his name to the hostess, and she took us right away to ours.

Women, young and old, stared longingly at Kellan as we walked through. But for whatever reason, he was with me.

After we were seated, Kellan gave our drink order to the hostess. She had tried flirting with him, but he had not paid the slightest bit of attention, and she huffed off.

"I must admit that this does my ego good."

"Excuse me?" I asked, confused by his comment.

"The eyes of every man in here are on you, India." He narrowed his eyes at me as he continued. "You either play a good game, or you are the least conceited woman I have ever met."

"Kellan," I said, chuckling as I shook my head at him, "I don't understand the game part, but I would imagine that the men were staring because they were pissed that their women's attention was focused on you."

I opened the menu to focus on something else. I felt comfortable with the man. He was funny, respectful, and interesting.

The waiter came to our table with a bottle of wine. He filled our glasses then took our orders.

"Is gumbo really all you are going to eat?" he asked when the waiter left.

"I'm really not a big nighttime eater." I took a sip of the wine, more to have something to do than because I wanted to drink it.

Kellan took a sip out of his, and keeping his glass in his hand, he leaned back in his chair, looking intently at me.

A TEMPTATION

"I'll be up front with you, India. I am a very sexual man. As a result, I live a varied, ah, sexual lifestyle." He placed his wine glass back on the table. "I want you, India Leigh. I'll give you some time to get to know me, but not an endless amount. I am relentless when I want something, regardless if it being personal or business."

What the fuck? I didn't know if I should be concerned or excited. In a way, what he had said sounded kind of ominous; in another, kind of hot. I didn't have firsthand experience of this sort, so I wasn't clear about his meaning. I picked my wine glass back up, draining half its contents.

"Well," I hesitated, "I really don't know how to respond to that."

Kellan gave me a look that I didn't know how to interpret. Before he could say anything, however, the hostess escorted a man to our table.

"Deric, my man!" Kellan exclaimed and stood up to shake his hand. "India, this is Deric Owen, my best friend and my right-hand man in my company. Deric, this is India Leigh."

I held my hand out to shake hands with Kellan's friend. Instead, Deric raised my hand to his lips and placed a kiss there. I felt my face heating up.

"God," Deric said. "You are adorable." He released my hand and turned back to Kellan. "I hate to interrupt, but the rest of that information that you needed came in."

"India, this is important. Would you excuse me for a minute?"

"Of course. It was nice meeting you, Deric."

"The pleasure was all mine, Ms. Leigh."

I watched as the two men walked away. Deric was only about an inch or two shorter than Kellan. He was also good looking, but didn't hold a candle to Kellan.

The waiter, you would know, returned with our food right then. I asked him to bring me a glass of water then sat back to wait on Kellan.

I hated waiting, but true to his words, Kellan was back very quickly.

"Great. Food's here. I'm starving." Kellan sat down and started in on his lamb chops with gusto. "This is excellent!" he exclaimed. "How is your gumbo?"

"I love Mr. B's food. Besides my grandmother's gumbo, this is my favorite. You should try their bread pudding."

We talked while we ate. The more I heard, the more I liked Kellan. By the time the waiter came back to the table to see if we would like desert, I was totally infatuated. We declined desert, and he paid the bill. I hated to see the night come to an end.

Kellan walked me back to my hotel room and took my hand in front of the door.

"I'll be busy next week, India. I close on my house Monday, and then I have to go out of town for business. But I'll call you the following week, if it's all right with you?"

"Absolutely," I said, smiling up at him. "I'll be gone on a long weekend with my friends next weekend anyway. We have had this beach weekend planned for a long time."

"What beach?" Kellan asked me.

"Pensacola."

"That's close. I hope you have a good time."

"I'm sure we will." I grinned up at him. "Can't help but have a good time when all of us get together."

One minute we were just smiling at each other; the next, his lips were on mine. His tongue licked the seam of my mouth, and I opened to him. Our tongues met and danced. Kellan hardened the kiss, and I felt an excitement that I had never experienced before. My nipples hardened, and I grew wet between my legs.

"God!" he exclaimed when we came up for air. He ran his fingers gently down the side of my face. "How long do you think it will take before you know me well enough?" I laughed. "Until the following week, India."

And just that quickly, he was walking away. I called out to him, and he turned back to me.

"Be careful next week."

He smiled at me, said "I will be" and was gone.

A TEMPTATION

Later, when I was taking my shower, I realized he never asked for my phone number.

The six of us climbed out of Kenzie's SUV at the Hilton, on the gulf side of Pensacola Beach. We had planned this weekend a long time ago—Kathy, Brittany, Skylar, Kenzie, Lace, and I. Noah was the only one missing.

A very tall, muscular man held the door to the hotel as we walked in. The man must work out every day to be built like he was.

"Thank you," I said, smiling at him.

"Anytime." He grinned.

"Ooh. Yummy," Kat said, her eyes following the hunk.

"Behave," I said to her. "What would Lucas say?"

"That I wasn't dead," she smarted off to me. "Besides, you can't have him. You're scoping out Mr. Dark and Dangerous."

I chuckled. "I don't want him, and I told you that Kellan didn't get my phone number. So there won't be any getting to know him."

"He said that he would contact you next week. Unless I'm way off the mark, and I never am," she said with a shit-eating grin, "he will find you."

"Shut up, Kathy. There is no way for him to find me without any information."

"You'll see. I'm always right."

"Smart-ass," I said laughingly.

We got our key cards at the registration desk and went up on the elevator to our rooms. We had three rooms, side by side. Kathy and I shared one as we usually did. Before the six of us entered the rooms, Skylar asked what we were doing first so she knew what to change into.

"Well," I said to the group, "I think everyone should do whatever they want during the day then go as a group wherever we decide to go at night."

"That sounds good to me," Lace said, and everyone agreed.

When Kathy and I got into the room, she asked what I was planning to do.

"I'm going to chill out on the beach. I'm going to lay out and not think about anything."

"I'm with you then," Kathy said, "unless you want to be alone?"

"No, I don't want to be alone. It's just that all I have been thinking about for weeks is lying out on that beautiful white beach. That's all I want to do during the day while we're here."

"That's cool. But would you come with me to the boardwalk? I want to do some shopping."

"Sure. Do you mind waiting until tomorrow?"

"No. That's good."

Kathy and I changed into bathing suits, taking beach towels that we brought with us, and headed out to the beach.

It was amazing out here. I laid out my beach towel and sat down, sipping on a bushwhacker. The glare from the sun off the white-quartz beach had me thankful that I had remembered my sunglasses. The wonderful breeze off the Gulf of Mexico kept the temperature mild.

"Damn, this is good," Kathy said, sipping on her own bushwhacker.

"Yeah. It's like an upscale milkshake," I agreed. "I'm going to walk on the beach and look for shells. Do you want to go?"

"Nah." She shook her head. "I'm going to stay right here and enjoy doing nothing."

I grabbed my tote bag, put on my flip flops, and headed down the beach. About thirty minutes later, I was bent over having found some more shells when a shadow fell across me. Startled, I dropped my tote bag and stood up quickly. I looked up into brown eyes that belonged to a good-looking man. He smiled down at me, but there was something cold, calculating even, in that look.

I had a bad feeling about this man.

"If you're picking up shells, you can't be from around here," he said in a gravelly voice.

"No," I responded, retrieving my tote bag and leaving the shells where they lay, "I'm not from here. If you'll excuse me, I have to get back to my friends."

"I'll walk with you. My name is Steve. What's yours?"

A TEMPTATION

I ignored his question. I didn't want this man knowing my name. "I would rather you didn't. Walk with me, that is. I don't mean to be rude, but my friends and I are here getting away from everything. We just want to hang out with each other."

I turned and hurried back to where Kathy was lying on her beach towel. She raised her sunglasses a bit, giving me a strange look as I lowered myself onto my own beach towel.

"You okay?" she asked me. "You look funny."

I smiled at her. "Funny ha-ha or funny weird?"

"You know damn well what I mean, India Leigh. Did something happen on your walk?"

"No. Well, not really."

"What does *not really* mean?"

"Have you ever met someone, and every nerve ending in your body stood up screaming that he wasn't a nice or good person at all?" I asked her, my body getting that creepy feeling again just from talking about it.

"Yeah, I have a time or two. Why? Is that what's bothering you?"

I nodded. "I've never had that happen before. I don't want to feel that again."

"I'm glad your instincts spoke up. You're always so ready to see the good in everyone that it scares me, thinking it would get you into trouble."

"Not a chance of that happening when that feeling comes over me."

"Good," Kat said, rolling over on her stomach to get some sun on her back.

We were all on the dance floor at Bamboo Willies on the Portofino Boardwalk. We had decided that this was where we would go for dinner tonight because we could party at the same place after. The band was excellent, music was good and loud, and I loved to dance. My friends and I hadn't sat out very often; we danced with guys that asked when not all together.

Kathy and I threw ourselves into our chairs, trying to catch our breath. "I need another drink," Kathy said.

"I'm with you," I said breathlessly.

We each ordered another drink from the waitress and drew deeply from them when they arrived.

"Damn," Kathy huffed. "I think we're out of shape, India. Look at them, still dancing up a storm."

I looked over at the dance floor where Brittany, Skylar, Kenzie, and Lace were still going at it. "Yeah. Maybe we should join a gym? They all have physical jobs. We sit behind a desk every day."

"That's a good idea," Kathy agreed. "I'll look into it for us."

We continued to chill out. A few moments later, the short hairs on the back of my neck stood at attention, and I felt a hand grip my shoulder.

"Hello again," said a deep voice that gave me the creepy-crawlies. It was that creepy guy from the beach.

"Hi," I said, being deliberately short. I gave Kathy a look that I knew she would interpret.

"Let's dance," said the creep. I think he said his name was Steve.

"Ah...thank you for the invitation, but we're sitting out for a while."

His eyes narrowed, and the smile disappeared. "You have danced with all the other guys in here. I want mine."

His hand moved from my shoulder to grip my upper arm, and he yanked me out of my chair. For a second, I was too shocked to react. Just for a second.

I looked at his hand on my arm then up to his face. "Get your hand off of me," I snarled at the asshole.

"Not until I get my dance." He started dragging me toward the dance floor, and all hell broke loose. Kathy started yelling. Our other friends, hearing all the commotion, left the dance floor and circled us. I lost it.

Pulling my arm out of his grasp, I brought both my hands against his chest as hard as I could and pushed. He stumbled back a couple of steps, but unfortunately found his balance.

A TEMPTATION

"Stay the hell away from me!" I screamed at him. "I don't want you near me. I don't even want to be able to see you." I turned and started heading back to our table. I was stopped abruptly by a painful grip, once again on my upper arm, and jerked around.

"You bitch," he bit out. "You don't get to treat me this way."

"Get your fucking hand off of her!" Kathy yelled.

I had enough. I threw my hand back and slapped him with all my might across his sinister face. Everything stopped for a moment.

"You fucking cunt." He drew back his hand, and I just knew I was going to get backhanded. But it never came. I watched as a large hand came down, grabbing the asshole's wrist.

"The lady said no," a booming voice stated.

"Who the fuck are you?" my would-be assailant shouted, turning to face the threat.

"Your worst nightmare if you continue."

As if in slow motion, the creep pulled his wrist out of the other man's hold, drawing back his fist. He never made it. The other guy moved so fast that if I hadn't been standing right there, I wouldn't have seen what happened. One muscled arm blocked the creep's punch; the other arm pulled back, and the fist attached to it clipped him in the jaw. The creep went down like a load of bricks.

I lifted my eyes from the man lying prone on the floor of Bamboo Willies, to the face of the man that rescued me. It was the large, muscular man that held the door open for us at the hotel this morning.

"Thank you," I said, which sounded so lame to me.

He put both his hands on my shoulders, bending down, searching my face. "Are you all right? Did he hurt you?"

"No." I shook my head. "You prevented that. I'm just so embarrassed."

"You don't have anything to be embarrassed about. It's all on that asshole."

As if he heard his name, the creep on the floor groaned. Three men came over, two pulling the guy off the floor, one coming over to me.

"Are you okay?" he asked me.

"Yes. Thanks to…I'm sorry. I don't know your name," I said, turning to my savior.

"It's Zack," the big guy said, grinning at me.

I held out my hand to him. "I'm India." I smiled back at him.

He clasped my hand. "Nice to meet you, India."

I released his hand and turned back to the Bamboo Willie employee. "As I was saying, I'm fine, thanks to Zack. I hate that this had to happen here."

"It's not your fault," the man said to me. "Steve has been warned about starting anymore trouble in here. After tonight, he's barred. He won't have the chance to cause any more shit. We apologize for the trouble he caused you, and if you would let us, we would like for you and your party to accept drinks on the house for the rest of the night."

"You really don't need to do that—" I started to tell him.

"It's the least we can do," he stated firmly.

"Well, in that case, I'm sure my friends would like to stay and enjoy that. As for me, I just want to go hide for a little while."

"I'll go back with you, India," Kathy said to me.

"I'm fine, Kat. Stay and have fun."

"I'm going back with you," she insisted.

"I don't want to ruin the rest of your night," I implored her.

"I can't hang. Okay. We really need to join that gym."

I laughed with my best friend. "I'm with you there. Okay, let's get a cab."

"I'm going back to the hotel now. We're staying at the same one, so I would be happy to give you both a ride."

Kathy and I looked at each other. We didn't know Zack, but with his protecting me tonight, I trusted him. "Thank you, Zack. We would love a ride."

The next day, Kathy and I spent the day at the Portofino Boardwalk. We shopped; I spent a lot at Envie, The International Boutique, and Islanders Coastal Outfitter. We had lunch at the Boardwalk Café. It was a wonderful day.

A TEMPTATION

My friends decided to go out to Flounders for dinner and fun. I really did not want to go out tonight. Last night was enough excitement to last me a lifetime. It took me a while to convince my friends to go ahead without me.

After they left, I walked along the beach for a long time. This was more my speed. I liked going out with my friends, and I loved to dance. But I liked this best.

I decided to go have a drink when I went back into the hotel. When I walked into the Pensacola Beach Bar, I saw Zack sitting at the bar.

"Mind if I join you?" I asked him.

He grinned at me. "Please do."

"I'm glad I ran into you. The least I can do is buy you a drink."

"Not necessary," he said.

"Maybe not to you, but I insist."

"Since you twisted my arm," he said, chuckling.

I ordered another drink for Zack and a Grey Goose and cranberry for me. The good-looking bartender smiled and flirted with me. I noticed Zack frowning at him. Taking the hint, the bartender went down to the other end of the bar.

"Where are your friends?" Zack asked me.

"They went out to Flounders."

He frowned down at me. "It's not safe for you to separate from your friends, India."

"I would agree with you if I were going anywhere. I really didn't want to go back out tonight after what happened last night. I went walking on the beach and decided to come and have a drink before going back up to my room."

"That's not safe to do alone either, India. You really need to stick with your group."

"I understand what you're saying, Zack. But I like to be alone at times. And I refuse to live in fear."

He looked as if he wanted to say more, but he shook his head and went back to drinking his drink. After a few moments, I finished my drink and stood up. "It was good seeing you again, Zack."

He quickly finished his drink. "I'll walk you to your room, if you don't mind."

I rolled my eyes because he really hadn't asked. It was a statement.

We got on the elevator, and Zack pressed the button to his floor then looked to me for my floor number. "I'm on the same floor. Quite a few coincidences where you are concerned, Zack," I said, looking at him shrewdly. "By the way, that's not a southern accent I hear. Where are you from?"

"New York." He grinned at me. "Very much not southern."

"We're from right outside New Orleans. We came for the weekend. Are you on vacation?"

"No. I had to be here a few days for my job. I'm flying back tomorrow. How about you guys?"

"We're going back tomorrow also." The elevator pinged, telling us we were on our floor. We walked off and down the hall. "After brunch. Everyone wants to go to Hemingway's for brunch."

I stopped outside the door to my room. Zack waited until I unlocked and opened the door. "It was very nice meeting you, India. Be careful going back home."

"It was nice meeting you too, Zack. Thanks again for everything."

He nodded and made a little shooing motion with one of his hands. I rolled my eyes at him again, walked into my room, and didn't hear him walk off until I threw the bolt lock.

The next day, my friends and I had a great time during brunch at Hemingway's. I told them that I didn't want to drink anything but coffee, for them to indulge all they liked. I would drive us back home. They all took me up on it, and I drove all the way back to Louisiana. The only sound in the SUV was the music I played. All my friends had passed out on me.

CHAPTER THREE

The second Monday after my date with Kellan, Kathy called me around two in the afternoon. She asked if she could come over after work. That took me by surprise. She never asked if she could come over; she just showed up.

At five thirty, there was a knock on my door. I rushed to the door thinking it would be my friend, but it was a flower delivery. I signed for it, took the box, and closed the door. After taking the flowers into the kitchen, another knock sounded before I could read the card. This time it was Kat.

"I have been worried all afternoon, Kat. Since when do you call to see if you can come over? What's going on?"

"I knew I recognized his name on the card he gave you, but it didn't compute then." Kathy didn't even stop while she talked. She just marched right on in and kept going to the kitchen at the back of my house. "I wish I would have put it together then. I am so sorry, India." And with that, she threw what she had in her hand on the kitchen table.

"Have you gone insane, Kat?" I asked her, very concerned. "What the hell are you talking about?"

"Just read it," she interrupted, pointing at what she had placed on the table.

I picked it up and saw that it was the *Times-Picayune*. It was yesterday's paper, and it was on the society section. It was about a benefit dinner, attended by the elite of the elite, at the Marriott Hotel on Canal Street. I still didn't understand where this was going until I turned the page. There was a photograph of a smiling Kellan with a stunning woman, a woman Kat and I had known for years and couldn't stand. Kellan was gorgeous in his tux.

Under the photo, the caption read "Kellan Coventry, CEO of Coventry Technologies, and Alexis Hunt, daughter of New Orleans own Judge Douglas M. Hunt," and so on and so on. As I examined the photo, I thought that Alexis looked like she was more in Kellan's league.

I placed the paper back on the table and looked at my friend. She was pacing back and forth across the kitchen. "Kat, there's no need for you to be upset." I went to her and physically stopped her pacing, bringing her over to the kitchen table. "Sit," I told her, pointing to one of the chairs.

I went to the fridge and grabbed two beers. I handed one to her and sat down. "I told you, Kat. He didn't ask for my phone number. But even if he had, he can see whoever he wants. However many he wants. I don't have any claim on him."

"But if I would have realized who he was, I would have never talked you into going out with him. He's a player, India." She took a long sip from her beer. "And there are stories—"

"So?" I stopped her. "He was honest with me, Kat. He told me about his…about what he wanted." I just didn't tell her that I didn't have the slightest idea what he had meant.

Her eyes just about popped out of her head at my statement. My best friend was looking at me as though she had never seen me before. I tipped my beer back, chugging about half of it. "What?" I almost yelled at her.

"Who are you, and what have you done with my friend?"

I couldn't help but chuckle. "Come on, Kat. I'm not stupid. I haven't had sex with anyone because I haven't found anyone I felt totally comfortable with. Just because I want to wait doesn't mean I have any illusions about our world or the people that inhabit it."

"Well…okay. But I don't want you to get hurt because you think someone is good. And he's a pervert."

I laughed. "Pervert?"

"Laugh all you want, India, but I told you, there are stories."

I held up my hand. "I don't want to hear any stories. We both know what bullshit people can come up with."

"Yeah. You're right." She pointed at the florist box. "Who are the flowers from?"

"Oh. I don't know. With all the…excitement"—I shrugged—"I forgot about them."

"Well, open them now. I'm nosy."

I opened the box. Inside were a dozen long-stemmed red roses. The card said they were from Kellan and that he couldn't wait to see me again.

"How would he get my address?" Before Kathy could say anything, my phone went off. I looked at the screen. It read Coventry Technologies. "Or my phone number?" I looked at Kathy, laying my phone down on the table without answering it.

She snorted. "He probably had you investigated before he trusted his precious bizillionaire ass with you."

"But everything is unlisted because of what I do."

"What part of Coventry Technologies do you not understand, India?"

I didn't like this at all. It made me feel…exposed.

Kathy left about thirty minutes later. I still had a lot of work to do, so I went back to my office.

Kellan called three more times that night. I just let the calls go to voice mail. I was sure it wouldn't take long for his attention to wander elsewhere. It had been nice meeting the man though. I would have liked for it to have gone further, but not if I couldn't trust him.

I finally fell into bed at 4:00 a.m., when I had finished the last of the short stories.

I loved my house and yard. The house sat on five acres at the end of Napoleon Avenue in Bayou Liberty. It was a 3,500-foot Acadian. It sat six feet off the ground due to the bayou that bordered the property. There was a wide staircase that swept up to the wraparound porch.

One acre had been cleared all around the house. It was filled with gardens and flowers. I had the porch loaded down with plants, sitting and hanging from every available surface.

The house itself had five bedrooms and five and a half bathrooms, an extra-large country kitchen, a formal living room, a dining room, a den, and an office.

My parents had bought this place just a few months before the accident that took their lives. Accident? No. Murder by drunk driver. I had only been four years old at that time, so everything had been placed in a trust. There had been life insurance, and monies received from the lawsuit against the drunk driver. My grandparents—my mom's parents, who raised me—would not touch a cent. When I turned eighteen, they turned it over to me. House and money.

It was Saturday, and I was stuck on a point in my second book I was working on. I knew to walk away, get into something else, and it would flow naturally in its own time. So here I was working in my yard, one of my favorite things to do.

I was taking care of some hanging plants under one of the big oak trees in the front yard when this very expensive black Bentley pulled into my driveway. I didn't know anyone who owned one of those.

As I watched, the driver got out of the vehicle then went and opened the back door. I should have known it would be Kellan Coventry.

I stayed where I was. It might have been childish, but hey, I wasn't too happy with him. He was in another designer suit and looking yummy as usual. I was in cutoffs and a very short shirt with no makeup and hair in a ponytail. But that was okay too. I hadn't invited him.

"Hello, India," Kellan said, and he wasn't smiling.

"Hi, Kellan. On your way to see your aunt?" I was very proud of my tone. Couldn't even tell I was pissed off.

A TEMPTATION

"No. I came to find out why you aren't taking my calls."

I put down the watering can, walked over, and stood very close in front of him. "Simple," I stated. "I don't appreciate my privacy being invaded."

His eyebrows lifted, and a confused look came over his face. "What are you talking about?"

"Did you or did you not have me investigated?"

"Yes." He shrugged. "I have to be careful of anyone I don't know."

"I would have told you anything you wanted to know. Instead, you went behind my back for information. Information that is not supposed to be public."

Kellan ran his hands through his hair as if he was getting very frustrated. "Goddamn it, India. I did not do anything against you. I would never let that information get out to anyone else. Some of my work is very sensitive, and I can't take any chances."

"Then you should have given me a choice of whether I wanted to see you or have my life put on display! I didn't know who you were. I just thought you were a regular guy."

He started laughing. The bastard actually started laughing.

"Most women just like the money, India."

I was so pissed at him for laughing, but he kept on grinning.

"Well, I guess I'm not like most women," I snarled at him.

"No. You certainly are not."

Then he had me in his arms, kissing me like I had never been kissed before, his tongue exploring every inch of my mouth as though he couldn't get enough of my taste. My arms wrapped around his neck as if they had a mind of their own. He picked me up, lifting me off my feet, and I found my back pressed against the oak tree. My insides melted. I had never wanted anything as much as I wanted this man.

All too soon, he was setting me back on my feet. We were both breathing heavily. He took a step back and took my hands in his. "Will you have dinner with me at my place?"

"How about you have dinner at mine?" I asked smiling. "You're here already."

CHAPTER FOUR

*K*ellan went to talk to his driver, and I went in to take a shower. I told him when he was finished to come on in and make himself at home.

After my shower, I was pressed for time, so I just slipped on a long sleeveless dress. I left my hair wet and hanging down my back. Still no makeup.

When I got to the kitchen, I found Kellan already there. His jacket was hanging on the back of one of my bar stools. He had his shirtsleeves rolled up and was leaning against one of the kitchen counters.

"I stole one of your Coronas," he said, holding up the beer.

"Well, that will cost you," I teased, opening the refrigerator and pulling things out. "I hope you don't mind leftovers? I made shrimp alfredo last night. I'll just make some garlic bread and a salad to go with it. There's plenty if your driver would like to eat also."

"That sounds great. But Daniel, my driver, went to eat in town."

That sounded good to me. Time alone with Kellan. It didn't get any better that that.

I warmed the alfredo, and Kellan helped me make the salad and garlic bread. It was funny telling Mr. Executive what to do.

A TEMPTATION

We talked while we ate. It was pleasant, and I felt so relaxed with him that before I knew it, I had eaten everything on my plate. Well, I used to not be a big nighttime eater.

After dinner, Kellan insisted that he help me with the dishes. He rinsed, and I loaded the dishwasher. We went on the back porch with glasses of wine. Kellan went and stood at the railing, looking out at the bayou. I looked at Kellan.

"It is beautiful here." He turned and looked at me. "I would think this would inspire a writer."

"It inspires a lot in me." I smiled and looked out over the water. "My stories. My dreams. My hopes. I like to think that this view is what inspired my parents to buy this place. And that in a hundred years, this same view will inspire someone else."

He turned and leaned his hip against the railing. "Do you miss your parents?"

"I don't remember my parents. But I have always missed the idea of parents. My grandparents gave me everything. Love enough for four children, let alone just one. They were great teachers. My grandfather's stories are why I love history and why I became a writer. He's also the reason I like to fish." I laughed, remembering. "And my grandmother? She was the sweetest, most gentle person you could ever meet. She taught me to cook, to sew, and to imagine. I miss them very much, every day."

He walked over and knelt down in front of the chair I was sitting in. He took my glass and set both mine and his on the small table next to my chair.

"How old were you when they died?"

"That wasn't in your report?" I asked sarcastically.

He ignored my sarcasm. "Not how old you were."

I sighed. "I was twenty when my grandfather died, and my gram not a year later. I don't think they could live without each other. They were very lucky to have a love like that."

"And you don't have any other relatives?"

"No. There had just been us."

"Your grandparents did a great job, India." He put his left hand on the armrest of my chair and leaned into me. He placed his right hand around the nape of my neck and pulled me into him. His kiss this time was harder. Commanding. Demanding everything from me.

Abruptly, he stopped and stood up, pulling me up with him. He pulled me against his body, feathering little kisses across my jaw to my neck, down my neck to my left breast. He found my nipple through my dress and bra. He suckled. I gasped. I plunged my hands in his hair. He bit down on my nipple. I moaned.

"Bedroom," he gasped.

"This way." I tried to turn, to lead him to my room, but he was having none of that. With one arm around my back and the other behind my knees, he scooped me up. With my directions, he carried me up the stairs, into my room.

He set me back on my feet in the middle of the room. He began to unbutton my dress, trailing kisses as he went. When he had unbuttoned to my hips, he slipped the dress off my shoulders. He stepped back and looked at me. Thank God for my addiction to Victoria's Secret.

"You are breathtaking," he said in a low, husky vice.

I reached up toward his shirt. "No!" he commanded with a growl. I lowered my arms. Now I was confused.

He went behind me and unhooked my barely-there black lace bra. He pushed the straps down my arms, and it too fell to my feet.

His hands found my breasts. His palms scraped across my nipples. Then he started to pluck at the hardened peaks. I whimpered and had to bite down on my lower lip to keep silent.

"Don't. I like the sounds you make, India," he whispered in my ear. "I have wanted to fuck you since the first moment I saw you."

Then he pinched my nipples hard, and I cried out. My knees went weak. Kellan scooped me back up in his arms, carried me to the bed, and gently laid me down.

I had done a lot of research on sex. I knew he was being very dominant. I also understood about the pleasure/pain thing. I just had never seen myself as being a willing participant. But those pinches had gone from my breasts straight to my sex.

Kellan stood up, and I watched as he began to undress. He was magnificent. He had broad shoulders, sculpted muscular arms, and a chest that was lightly covered with dark hair. His hands went to the waistband of his pants. He undid his belt then unbuttoned and unzipped his pants. He let his pants hit the floor. His black silk boxers followed. My God! Were all men that large? Was this the norm?

I wanted to touch him. I started to sit up when Kellan's voice stopped me.

"Do. Not. Move," he said sternly.

I lay back down. He leaned over me and slowly pulled my thong down and off.

"You don't shave," he stated bluntly, ruffling my pubic hair.

I was so embarrassed. "Uh, I did once. I didn't like the prepubescent look. So I just keep it trimmed." Why was I explaining?

Kellan laughed. "I like it."

He spread my legs apart and climbed up on the bed, kneeling between my thighs. I closed my eyes. I felt unbearably vulnerable—and a little frightened.

"Open your eyes, India," Kellan said softly.

When I did open my eyes, he was staring at my most intimate parts. "I—"

"Shh," he interrupted me. "You are so beautiful. Everywhere."

He leaned over me. Bracing his weight on his arms, one on each side of me, he kissed me with searing passion. Nipping at my lower lip to get me to open, his tongue stormed past my lips to dance with mine.

I melted, so hot for his kisses. For him. I sucked on his tongue, experimenting.

He went wild. The pressure of his mouth bruising now, he glided down my neck, licking and sucking. I moaned. The feelings that he was inundating me with, I could have never imagined.

Then he was at my breast, flicking his tongue over first my right then my left nipple. I arched my back off the bed, crying out. Reaching out, for what I didn't know. He continued down my body, kissing, sucking, and nipping. His tongue played in my navel.

Suddenly, he was kneeling between my thighs. Again. He pushed my legs up, my feet planted flat on the bed. My knees pointed to the ceiling.

"Kellan!" I almost yelled. "I've never done this before. I'm a—"

"I'll make sure you love it, India." He looked into my eyes. He had a wicked smile on his face. "Besides, I will like being your first."

He parted me with his fingers. I sat up abruptly, trying to scoot away from his hands. From him.

"This is to fast!"

"It's too late now, baby," he said huskily. "Come back to me, India."

"Kellan. I—"

"Come back now, India," he snarled.

I reacted to his command. I didn't know what was wrong with me. I would never let anyone tell me what to do. Why did he have this power?

I scooted back down to him, my legs staying together, bent at the knees.

"Good girl. Now lie back.'

I lay back down like he instructed. He parted my knees as far as they could go. "I have to taste you." His hands held my legs open. His mouth descended. He licked between my folds, gently at first. I instinctively tried to close my legs. His hands tightened on my thighs, holding me wide open for him. His tongue rimmed my opening. The feeling was incredible. Then his tongue speared inside me. Licking. Tasting. One of his hands left my thighs, and with two of his fingers, he started massaging my clit in small, tight circles.

"Oh God!" I cried out. My body was coiling as tight as a spring, tension building.

"That's it, India!" Kellan encouraged. One of his fingers entered me, and his tongue touched my clit, fluttering over it. "You are so tight."

I had a death grip on the quilt that covered my bed. He sucked on my clit. Searing pleasure burst through me. My muscles clamped down on his finger. I screamed out his name. He worked me through the first orgasm I had ever had. He kept licking my clit until the rippling in my core and the shaking of my legs quieted.

A TEMPTATION

I looked at him in amazement. He was good at this. He knew just how to make my body respond. Yes. I had made the right decision. Kellan was the perfect man to take my virginity.

"I'm going to have to make you ready to take me, baby," he explained to me. "You are so small and tight."

He leaned over me and kissed me with such passion. He forced his tongue past my lips, and I could taste myself on him. It was so erotic. He sat up and smiled at me.

"I don't want to hurt you. I would rather you feel some discomfort from me getting you ready than pain from my cock. You look beautiful when you come, India. That's the only kind of look I want to see on your face."

Kellan not only had a large cock, but his fingers were long and thick. It took a little time for him to get two fingers inside me. When he had, he thrust gently and shallowly at first. Then he went harder and deeper.

"Fuck!" He jerked his fingers out of me and literally jumped off the bed. He started pacing and running both his hands through his hair over and over.

I sat straight up, putting my back against the headboard of my bed. I grabbed one of the pillows, placing it over me, covering my nudity. I didn't know what had happened to get Kellan so upset.

He stopped pacing and just stared at me. I became very nervous.

"What is it, Kellan? What's wrong?"

"Why didn't you tell me, India?" he accused. "I would never have touched you if I had known."

CHAPTER FIVE

*I*f he would have hit me, he couldn't have hurt me any more. He was talking about my virginity. He must have felt the barrier when he went so deep. Well, screw him.

"I did tell you, Kellan," I spat out at him. I got up and got my robe out of the bathroom. I was not staying naked in front of him any longer. As I pulled on my robe, I almost ran to the kitchen. I poured a glass of wine and went out on my back porch.

As I looked out at the bayou, my tears started to fall. This should have been a wonderful night. A night I would always remember. Well, I would remember it all right, just for a very different reason.

"India?" My whole body tensed when I heard Kellan. I didn't want to do this. I just wanted him to go. "I'm sorry, India. This is my fault. I thought you were talking about oral sex when you said you had never done it before."

"You interrupted me every time I tried to explain more, Kellan. But don't worry. I won't hold you to tonight. You can go with a clear conscience."

"India." He shook his head. "You're right. I went over our conversation. I was wrong, and I handled it all wrong. I wouldn't hurt you for the world, certainly not on purpose. The way you look. How your body responded to me, I would have never thought you were a virgin."

He must have seen me tense up that time.

"I don't mean that in a bad way, India. I mean, you're twenty-four years old! You're beautiful. I would have thought—"

I couldn't listen to any more of this. I cut him off. "Kellan. I'm a virgin because I chose to be, not for any other reason. I've had all types of propositions since I was fifteen. From marriage proposals to just wanting to fuck me. I don't need anything from you, and I didn't ask you for anything."

I took a deep breath before I continued. "I have been waiting for someone I not only liked but respected and felt comfortable with before I had sex. Not because I wanted to be in love and wait until I'm married. I never thought my first time would be with the only person I ever had sex with."

"My lifestyle, India, is not one that I would bring someone like you into. I'm not a man that someone like you should be involved with. It's my fault that things have gone as far as they have."

That was it! I had enough. I had been nice, but he just kept pissing me off. I turned from the railing and faced him. I knew he could see how angry I was. "Okay, Kellan. I thought you were a smart man, but apparently, I was mistaken. What? Did you think I was a slut and that was all right for your lifestyle?"

"No! I—" he started, but I cut him off again.

"Do not interrupt me again, Kellan. I will finish what I have to say." I think I shocked him. Whatever. At least he shut up.

"I wasn't going to see you again because of your investigation into my life. But you so prettily changed my mind. You came after me, Kellan, not the other way around." I couldn't stop there. Oh no. Not me. I wanted to hurt him like he had hurt me.

"Besides," I said as I smiled—and it wasn't a nice one, "I could meet someone tomorrow that I want to sleep with. So tomorrow night, I could lose my virginity."

"The hell you will!" he yelled at me.

He grabbed me by my upper arms and hauled me into his body. His lips took mine in a brutal kiss. Gone was my considerate lover of thirty minutes ago. I struggled against him, but that only made him excited. I felt his erection pressing hard against my stomach.

He picked me up and headed back to my bedroom. He bit my lower lip, demanding that I open to him. When I did, his tongue exploded into my mouth. Taking everything. Demanding everything. I pounded on his chest with both my fists. It had no effect. He somehow landed both of us on my bed, him on top of me. Finally, I bit his lower lip—so hard I drew blood.

He sat up on the side of the bed. He scrubbed a hand over his face and ran his tongue over his bleeding lip. "I have just handled everything wrong with you, India. I saw red when I pictured you with someone else." He sighed. "I had no right to, but I did."

Kellan turned and looked at me. I was sitting, once again, up against the headboard of my bed, tears pouring down my face.

"Oh, baby, no." He cupped my face in his hands, his thumbs wiping my tears away. "Please don't cry."

He touched his forehead to mine and took a deep breath. He moved away just enough to look into my eyes. "I have never reacted to a woman the way I react to you. It's scary. I should stay away from you. But from the way I responded about you with someone else, I know it won't happen. I want you so much I can't see straight."

He rubbed the back of his fingers gently on my cheek. "Would you be willing to start this night over?" he asked softly. "If you agree, we can be together and see where this takes us. I'll try not to be such a dick. I could introduce you into what I like in sex, not my lifestyle. But from the onset, I have to be in control. That can never be questioned."

Okay. He was really into the whole submissive/dominant thing. I had researched S&M. What I didn't feel comfortable with, I could say no to, right? Did I like Kellan enough to try this? Did I want him enough? Yes.

"I want you as much as you say you want me, Kellan. I don't have any experience, as you know, so I'll make no promises that I will agree to everything. If I feel too uncomfortable, I will say no."

He took his fingers from my cheek and placed one of my hands between both of his. "I will never try to force you to do anything you don't want to do. That I promise."

For the first time, I reached out to Kellan, and he let me touch him. I ran my fingers over his face, as if I was blind. I touched his brows. His nose. His lips. His gorgeous cheekbones. Then I cupped both sides of his face in my hands and gently pulled his face the short distance to mine. I kissed him tenderly. I lifted my head and looked into his amazing eyes. Then nodding to myself, I kissed him with everything I had.

Kellan took over at that point, knowing it was all right. His tongue demanded entrance and received it. After careful exploration there, he left my lips, heading down my neck. Using his tongue, he traced along the throbbing vein down the side then suckled at a spot below my ear.

My stomach quivered. His hands found my breasts, kneading them. He untied the sash to my robe, opened it, pushed it down my shoulders, then pulled it from my body. Then he was cupping my naked breast. His mouth found first my right nipple, next the left. He suckled. His tongue rubbing around and on them.

I moaned, the sensual sensations overtaking me. My back arched, pushing my breasts harder into his hungry mouth. My sex throbbed, dripping with my juices.

His hands and mouth left my breast. He pulled me by my legs until I was once again lying down. He spread my thighs apart, and once again knelt between them. I raised my knees, planting my feet flat on the bed.

He smiled at me. His face flushed with lust, the fingers of his right hand running over my sex. "You are so wet for me," he purred.

He took his time inserting two of his fingers. His head came down. He fluttered his tongue over my clit. He added a third finger. I felt uncomfortable until he sucked my clit into his mouth. Another orgasm exploded out of me, shattering me, so much more intensely than the first.

Before my muscles stopped contracting in my core, he removed his pants and rose above me. He produced a condom—from where, I didn't have a clue. I watched in fascination as he sheathed his magnificent cock. He balanced his weight on one arm and took himself in his right hand. He guided his shaft to my entrance, and slowly, gently, he entered me, barely getting inside. He removed his hand and balanced his weight on both his arms. He looked up into my eyes.

"This is one pain that can't be prevented, India. I can't change that," he whispered to me. I nodded. "But I think it would be better to just hurry and get through it rather than drawing it out."

I didn't know what he meant. But all of a sudden, I was afraid—of the unknown and all that.

He thrust with all his strength, pounding through the thin barrier inside me. I yelped. He went deeper. I was trying to get away. Away from the sharp pain and the uncomfortable fullness in my pussy. He grabbed my upper arms and stopped me.

"It's okay. I've got you, India." He spoke softly, calmly to me. "Just be still, and you will adjust to my size. We will just lie like this until then." I listened to him. He was the one with the experience.

"I promise you will never experience any pain with vanilla sex again."

"Vanilla sex?" I questioned him, confused.

He laughed. "We'll talk about that at another time."

Fine with me, I thought. I had enough to occupy my mind at the moment, like what I was starting to feel inside. I wiggled my hips experimentally. *Oh! That felt interesting.* So I thrust my hips into Kellan's pelvis. I groaned.

Kellan, taking the hint, slowly pulled out some then gently pushed back in. I groaned again.

"No more pain?" he asked me. I thrust my hips again in answer.

He chuckled. This time, he pulled almost completely out of me then thrust back in a little harder. I wrapped my legs around his hips instinctively. Kellan nodded and told me to keep my eyes on his. His thrusts became harder and deeper. Every time he thrust back in, his pelvis rubbed over my clitoris. Suddenly, I was meeting him thrust for thrust.

Taking my cue, Kellan reached his hands under my ass, lifting my hips off the bed. Once again, he knelt between my thighs. He started pounding into me, turning his hips as he went. I gasped when his cock hit this one special spot inside me.

He stopped and pulled out of me. I whimpered. He stood up at the side of the bed. Carefully, he moved me diagonally across the bed. He pulled my body down until my ass was sitting right at the edge of the bed. He placed a pillow under my ass and wrapped my legs around his hips. He gathered some of my juices with two of his fingers and started massaging my clit in small circles. He thrust back in. Harder. Deeper. Over and over that delicious spot.

"Come for me, India. Now!" As if his words pulled it from me, I fell. I came apart in a million pieces. I screamed from the searing ecstasy.

Kellan thrust deep a few more times. With the last thrust, he roared and stayed very deep as he came. He was beautiful in his orgasm.

As long as I lived, I would never forget this night. Or this man.

He withdrew and went into the master bath. When he came back, the condom was gone, and he had a washcloth. He came to me and washed very tenderly between my legs. With everything we had done, this seemed the most intimate.

"Can I stay with you tonight? I'd like to spend the day together tomorrow."

"I would like that," I said, trying to hide a yawn.

I barely heard Kellan talking to his driver on his cell. I was exhausted. I must have fallen asleep because the next thing I knew, Kellan was pulling me into his arms.

"Good night, baby. You were wonderful," I thought I heard him whisper.

CHAPTER SIX

I woke up the next morning with my head on Kellan's chest and his arms wrapped around me. I gazed up at him. He looked younger, relaxed in sleep. I eased out of bed. Kellan grunted and turned on his side. I stood still a moment until I was sure he was still asleep. I found my robe on the floor, putting it on as I crossed my room to the dresser. Taking out a pair of pajamas and a thong as quietly as I could, I took one more look at my sleeping beauty. Smiling contentedly to myself, I left the room.

I went down to the kitchen and put the coffee on then went into the downstairs guest bath to take a shower. Twenty minutes later found me on my back porch with my first cup of coffee. I leaned on the railing, watching the first colors of dawn rise over the bayou.

I thought about everything that had happened last night. It had been wonderful, then bad, and then wonderful again. No. Better than wonderful. I had never imagined it could be like that. I also suspected it was because it had happened with Kellan. He could break my heart, I knew, but I had to take the chance.

I was so deep in thought I didn't hear Kellan when he came out the back door. I jumped when his arm came around my waist.

"Sorry. I didn't mean to frighten you."

A TEMPTATION

"It's all right." I turned and looked up at him. "You just startled me. I didn't hear you come outside. Would you like me to make you breakfast?"

"No, thank you. This is all I need," he said, holding up a coffee cup.

He leaned into me and kissed me. With his empty hand, he wrapped my long hair around it. I melted against him. He pulled on my hair to tilt my head to the right angle for him. He deepened the kiss. When Kellan ended the kiss, we were both breathless.

"Are you sore, baby?" he whispered in my ear.

I felt my face turn red. I lowered my head, trying to hide the blush.

He pulled on my hair again so I had to look up. His eyes searched my face. "Don't hide from me, India," he said sternly.

I tried to untangle myself from his hold, but that only made him tighten his grip. "I'm embarrassed, Kellan. I'm new to these feelings…and discussions." I sighed. "To answer your question, yeah. I'm sore. But in a good way."

"Good." He let go of my hair and ran his fingers lightly up and down my cheek. "We'll give your little cunt a rest today. I'm going to take a shower, and then I would like to take you to my house for brunch. Come with me?"

"I'd like that."

Kellan went to take a shower in the same guest room that I had so I could have my bathroom to get ready. Thirty-five minutes later, we were in the back of Kellan's Maybach on the way to New Orleans.

Kellan received a few business calls on the way there. He sounded so different. Even the way he held himself was different. I guess that's what made him so good at his business. Everything was kept separate. Personal Kellan. CEO Kellan. But then, I really didn't know either man. He was all over the page. I never knew what was coming next, nor where it would land me.

I gazed out of the window and realized we were on St. Charles Avenue, in the garden district. Such a wonderful street—so full of history. The storybook mansions always spoke to me of a glorious romantic time gone by.

Kellan's driver, Daniel, drove up to one of the mansions. Daniel opened my door, but Kellan was still on his phone. He motioned for me to go on.

Just walking under the portico of this amazing house made you think of all the history. I had been to a lot of functions in quite a few of these mansions. This one I had never been in. If I remembered correctly, the previous owner had been an elderly recluse. It had been in his family for generations. Apparently, his line had come to an end.

The house itself was magnificent from the foyer and main hall to the glimpses I got of the other rooms. It was filled with priceless antiques. I wondered if Kellan had purchased the antiques along with the house or if he collected them.

Kellan's housekeeper, Mrs. Carter, showed me into the parlor. She was a nice, cheerful woman. She asked if I would care for anything. I told her I would kill for a cup of coffee.

"Well, we can't have you committing murder now, can we?" She laughed.

Ten minutes later, Kellan still hadn't showed, but I had a pot of coffee, and cream and sugar, sitting in front of me. The china was exquisite.

I took my cup of coffee and walked around the room. There were all sorts of knickknacks from around the world. On the mantle were pictures of Kellan at different events. Numerous different women also.

"India?" Kellan called out from the foyer.

"I'm in the parlor, Kellan."

"I apologize." He walked over to me. "An emergency has come up in New York. I have to leave immediately."

"It's not a problem, Kellan." I walked over to the coffee table and placed my cup back on the tray. "I understand."

"It's not okay," he responded, running the fingers of both his hands through his hair. That was his tell. All was not well in Kellan land. "I don't know how long I'll have to be away, but I will keep in touch."

I walked over and stood in front of him. I placed my hands on his chest. "If I can help, Kellan, please tell me?" I had a sneaky suspicion this problem didn't have anything to do with his business.

"I appreciate the thought," he sighed. "I will fix it as quickly as I can and get back here."

I stood on tiptoes and kissed his cheek. "I have to be gone for a couple of weeks. I have some book signings to do. Be careful. I hope everything turns out all right for you."

"If I had more time, I would make it so you would know I have been inside you. You would feel me there the whole time you're away. Me and only me. There will be no one else sharing your body. Do you understand?"

I looked at him. What was he suggesting? I pulled away from him and went over to the couch and picked up my purse.

"Daniel will take you home, India. I've already let him know."

"Don't be silly! You have enough on your plate right now. I can see myself home." I had made it to the threshold of the parlor when I was roughly grabbed by my upper arm. I was hauled around and faced with an angry Kellan.

"Daniel. Will. See. You. Home."

I yanked my arm out of his grasp. I was angry now too. "I agreed to give you control in bed, Kellan. That's all! I run my own life, not anyone else." I shook my head. "Your mood swings are starting to get on my nerves."

I turned to continue out of the room. The next thing I knew, I was over Kellan's shoulder. I pounded on his back. "Put me down, Kellan!"

"Oh, I will." And he did. He put me down in the backseat of his Maybach.

"Where are your book signings, India?" I stared straight ahead and didn't answer him. "Who goes on them with you?"

"Daniel, if you're taking me home, please do so now."

"Okay. Play this way, India. I'll talk to you when I can." He banged on the hood of the car twice, and then he was gone.

As Daniel drove back to Slidell, my head was spinning. The man had me on a roller coaster. At times I wanted his attention. At others, I just wanted to hit him. He kept me more than at arm's length, yet he was trying to control everything about me.

The glass panel in the car between the back and the driver, lowered. "Ms. Leigh, Mr. Coventry says he has been trying your cell, but it keeps going to voice mail."

"I turned it off, Daniel, because I don't want to talk to him. I'm sorry he's putting you in the middle."

He chuckled. "Yes? You heard her? Just a minute. Ms. Leigh, he says if you don't get on the phone, you won't like what he does."

"Oh God!" I took Daniel's cell from him. "Kellan, I don't want to talk to you. But I've learned to expect the unexpected where you're concerned. So what is it that you want?"

"I want to know where your book signings are going to be," he asked. I remained silent.

"I'm not asking now, India," he snarled into the phone.

"Okay, Kellan. Tell me why you are going to New York." Only silence answered me. "Yeah. Just what I thought. You can't have it both ways, Kellan." And I hung up.

I reached over the seat and handed Daniel back his phone.

"You are giving him a run for his money, Ms. Leigh." Daniel was downright laughing now. "I have never seen him this way."

"You mean he gives all his other women freedom to move around?" I could hear the touch of jealousy in my voice, so there wasn't any doubt that Daniel would be able to hear it too.

"What other...Oh! You mean the ones that hang out with him and Mr. Owens? Those are nothing like this, Ms. Leigh. They don't visit at his home, and he doesn't care what they're doing."

"I'm not doing anything, Daniel. But my life is my own. He wants to bulldoze into my life yet I know nothing of his. Of him! Except that he's thirty-one and owns his own business." I took a deep breath. "Sorry. I shouldn't be talking to you about this."

He looked at me in the rearview mirror. "Most people only see the money when they look at him, not the man."

"I don't care about his money, Daniel. I make my own. I didn't even know who he was until my best friend told me. And that was after I went out with him. I...I went out with him because I genuinely liked him." I looked out the car window.

A TEMPTATION

"When he's not going all caveman on me, he's great. He's funny, considerate, and gorgeous." I turned back and looked into the mirror at him. "But I get sick on roller coasters, Daniel."

"Just give it a little time, Ms. Leigh. I think you've thrown him a curveball, and he doesn't know how to handle it."

"I'm not any good at baseball, Daniel."

He chuckled. "I think you'll be good for him."

"Yeah?" I snorted. "But will he be good for me?"

CHAPTER SEVEN

At six the next morning, Kathy was driving me to the New Orleans International Airport and bitching at me the whole way there.

"I told you about him. And what do you do? Do you listen? No! You jump in with both feet. You are going to end up getting hurt."

"Right now," I said rubbing my temples, "I'm just going crazy. And you're adding to that, Kathy Pichon!"

"Sorry," she sighed. "I'm just worried about you." She bit on her lower lip. "But you know, India? I never heard of him reacting like this. Quite the opposite, as a matter of fact. I have never heard of him having a steady, ah, girlfriend, for lack of a better word. The female he's with most often in New Orleans is Alexis Hunt. But I've heard it's just at social functions. Not dating."

"But Alexis Hunt of all people."

"Yeah," Kathy snorted, "our favorite person. Have you heard from him today?"

"No. And that's a good thing. I had twenty-six messages between my cell and home phone. I'm not going to have time to breathe on this trip. I don't want to deal with Kellan right now."

A TEMPTATION

I gave Kathy my itinerary and told her I would see her in two weeks. I made it to the hotel in Seattle at 10:00 p.m. local time. My first day, and I was already tired. Come to think of it, I was always tired lately. I hadn't been sleeping very well. I kept having nightmares. I always had bad dreams when I was under a lot of stress. Whoever said sex was a stress reliever was not having it with Kellan Coventry. That's if one time could be considered having sex with him.

When I checked in at the front desk, I was informed that my room had been upgraded to a suite. I don't know why, but at the time, nothing clicked. I'll blame it on jet lag.

I went up to my suite. The bellboy unlocked the door and let me in ahead of him. There was a large living room, which was filled with flowers. There were also two bedrooms, both with attached baths.

I took the card from the nearest arrangement. It was from my editor. The others? They were all from Kellan. I rolled my eyes. Now I understood the change in accommodations. I stopped the bellboy before he put my bags in one of the bedrooms, and called the front desk. I explained that I needed a room, just what had been booked for me before Mr. Coventry changed it, and I would appreciate it if they could do it quickly. Within minutes, they called back, saying that they did not have two adjoining rooms.

"I do not need two rooms," I said, totally frustrated and quickly running out of patience.

"But what about your bodyguard, ma'am?"

"I don't have a bodyguard!"

"Just a minute, ma'am."

"No!" I screamed into the phone. "I want one room. Now! Or I find another hotel."

"But our owner, Ms. Leigh—"

"Who is the owner?" I paused. "No. Never mind, let me guess. Kellan Coventry?" There was only silence on the other end of the line.

"Look. Would you just call me a cab please? I'll be down in a few minutes."

I asked the bellboy to please take my bags back down to the lobby. I grabbed the flower arrangement that was from my editor and left. When I reached the lobby, the hotel manager was waiting for me.

"I've been asked to detain you, Ms. Leigh."

"You and what army?" I spoke very softly. Everyone who knew me also knew that if I spoke this way, I was at my limit and was going to cause some grief.

"I'll take it from here, Destin. Thank you."

I didn't have to turn around to know whom that voice belonged to. "In five seconds, I am going to cause the worst scene either of you have ever seen." I stared at the man in front of me and ignored the one behind me. "So, Destin, I would suggest you get out of my way."

"We will be in my suite, Destin," the voice behind me said.

"I'm warning you, Mr. Coventry." I was shaking now. I was so mad. "Do. Not. Touch. Me."

I went through Destin but didn't make it much past that. Once again, I found myself over Kellan's shoulder. The flower arrangement fell out of my hands, the vase shattering on the lobby floor. Fuck this! He asked for it. I screamed bloody murder.

"It's all right, folks," my kidnapper was saying. "My wife has had a little too much to drink."

"I am not his wife!" I yelled.

No one got on the elevator with us. I could be going to my death, and not one person would have interfered.

"That's why you need security, India." What? Could he read my mind now?

As soon as the elevator doors closed, he placed me back on my feet.

"If I need security, Kellan, I will take care of it. I've been running my life for quite a while now. I don't need you managing it for me."

"I can't be worrying about you for the two weeks you'll be gone, India."

"Who asked you to?" I looked at him, baffled. "You don't have to worry about me for two seconds, Kellan. I am not your concern."

"I don't know what you are to me, India." He leaned his back against the elevator wall. "All I know is that I have never felt this way before, and I'm not going to let you drive me crazy worrying about your safety."

"Kellan! Do you hear yourself?"

"Yeah." He dragged both his hands roughly through his hair. "I know. Crazy, right? I feel like a caveman, beating on my chest with my head screaming 'mine!'"

I didn't know what to think, much less what to say. He wasn't asking for anything, just trying to take care of me—for his peace of mind. But why? We were nothing to each other. We had sex. Once.

We got off the elevator and went down to Kellan's suite. Surprise, surprise. It was the same suite I had been booked into. He unlocked and opened the door, waiting for me to go in. I rolled my eyes and walked past him. He followed me in, closing the door behind him.

"Tim will be here in a few hours. He works for me, India. He's trustworthy and very good at what he does."

I went and sat on the couch in the living room. Why say anything? He was only going to do what he wanted anyway. I would ditch the guy and Kellan's bullshit after he went back to New York.

"He will go wherever you go."

"Kellan." I sighed. "I have fifteen signings and a lecture."

"In two weeks? You're going to make yourself sick with that schedule," he hissed.

"And yours is any less strenuous?"

"That's different." He walked over and sat on the coffee table in front of me.

"How so? Because you're a man? Never mind." I shook my head. "Not that I owe you an explanation, but this is my first book. I'm going to do all I can to take it as far as I can."

"I admire you for that, India, but it's not safe for you to travel alone."

"Kellan," I continued in a whisper, "you won't always be around. This?" I waved my hand in the air. "Us? Whatever you're thinking, feeling, could all be over tomorrow. What then? Will you not worry then? Or is it out of sight and all that?"

"I. Don't. Know. I don't have any answers to something I don't understand. For now, you are just going to have to put up with my concern."

"This isn't your world, your empire, Kellan. You don't get to insert yourself wherever you want, for however long or short you want, in my life. I can't handle this."

There was a knock at the door. Naturally, Kellan went to answer it. It was the poor bellboy, bringing my luggage back for the second time.

"Which room, India?" Kellan asked me.

"It doesn't matter," I said sullenly.

Kellan directed him to the room on the right. While he tipped the bellboy, I went into the bedroom. I opened the closet to put my bags in and hang up my suits and dresses. Kellan had clothes hanging up in there.

I took out a pair of pajamas and underwear and went into the bathroom. I turned on the shower then went back for my makeup case.

I heard Kellan at the door and a woman's voice. I couldn't tell what was being said, only that the woman didn't sound happy. *Join the club,* I thought.

I also wondered why it was that I wasn't jealous of these women. I guess it was because I wasn't under any illusions. He wasn't mine. I wasn't going to waste any time on empty emotions.

I grabbed my shampoo, conditioner, and body wash from my makeup case and placed them in the shower. I got undressed and climbed in under the warm water. *Ah, heaven.*

I washed my hair, put conditioner in, and then lathered up a wash cloth. The cloth was suddenly taken out of my hands. I gasped and tried to turn around but was prevented.

"What do you think you're doing?"

"I would think that's obvious."

"No! I'm not someone you get to just screw around with, Kellan."

He was so close to me, I felt his body tense. "Don't say another word, India." He sounded pissed.

A TEMPTATION

Two large sudsy hands came around me. Even though he was mad, starting at my neck, he gently and lovingly, it felt like, washed me. They lingered at my breast. At first softly. Then rougher. His fingers plucked at my nipples until I was squirming. Biting my lip to keep myself from crying out, again I tried to turn around. Once again, I was prevented.

His hands traveled and washed down my ribs, over my belly, my hips, then between my legs. They washed the creases of my thighs, between my folds, and over my clit. I moaned. He was killing me. I melted. I wiggled my hips, trying to tell him I needed him.

His hand landed hard on my ass. I yelped and tried to move away from him.

"Be still, India," he hissed into my ear.

I got it. This was going to be my punishment. He would show his displeasure sexually.

He walked me down to the end of the shower. He placed my hands on the shower wall, my palms flat against the tile.

"Don't move."

I didn't know where he was going with this. I started to get a little nervous. I was way out of my depth here. "Kellan, I—"

"Don't make me tell you to keep silent again, India."

He lathered up his hands once more and, starting at my neck again, washed tenderly down my back to my hips. He then washed from my ankles up. At my bottom, he lingered. He washed both cheeks tenderly at first. Then rougher. His hand came down hard on my ass again. I gasped and dropped my hands from the wall, trying to turn around.

Kellan grabbed both my wrists and placed my hands back on the wall. "Every time you disobey, baby, it will just add more licks. I was only going to give you six, now it's ten. It's up to you if the number keeps rising."

I leaned my forehead against the shower wall until his hand connected with my ass again. That was harder than before. My head came up, and I gulped in a lungful of air. Again and again, his hand came down. My buttocks were stinging, but what bothered me more was how aroused I was becoming. Was I a masochist?

After the tenth pop, Kellan turned off the water. He led me out of the shower and dried my body with a warm, plush towel. He led me out of the bathroom to the bed. He had me get on the bed and lie on my stomach. I did as I was I was told. I was nervous, but I had told him I would give him total control in this area. Besides, I needed him. Right now.

He climbed onto the bed after me. He brought me up on my hands and knees. He spread my legs and knelt in between them. With his hand between my shoulder blades, he made me lower my head to the bed. This very submissive position left me with my ass lifted into the air. I was unsure about this. I didn't know what was going on in his mind. I knew he wouldn't physically hurt me, but that was about all I knew.

I decided to let him do whatever he was going to do. Maybe he just had to burn himself out on my body and that would be the end of this. He hadn't kissed me and only touched me enough to get me all hot and bothered. So I knew that he was taking his anger out on me sexually. But was he angry because I wouldn't listen to him? Or because he felt something for me that he didn't want to feel?

Kellan got something out of the bedside table. I felt the head of his penis nudge the opening of my slit. There was lubrication on the condom. Okay. No foreplay. I squeezed my eyes shut and mentally braced myself. I promised myself that I would not make a sound.

He grabbed a hold of my hips and pushed the crown of his cock into me. His hands tightened. In one brutal push, he seated himself all the way in. I gasped. He was so long and thick. There was a delicious burn from the thickness, also a bite of pain where his penis was hitting the end of me. He pulled almost all of the way out then pounded back inside me.

He leaned his chest over my back. "Are you going to keep Tim with you on this trip, India?"

I didn't say a word. He went back to maniacally thrusting in and out. I had to bite my lower lip to keep from crying out. He leaned back over me once again and asked the same question. I still refused to answer.

A TEMPTATION

He brought his right arm around my hips, his fingers finding my clit. He started massaging in small, tight circles. Thrusting hard, but not brutally this time, he found that special spot in my core. My muscles started to clamp down. I was going to come.

He stilled. "Are you going to do as I say, India?" he whispered in my ear.

"Kellan," I gasped. Was he going to torture me by repeatedly bringing me to the edge but never letting me fall over? "Stop this! I agreed to give you control in bed. Not over my life."

"That's not enough with you. So we have to revise."

He started to move again, his hand and penis driving me crazy, my body reaching toward an orgasm that he wouldn't let me have. My muscles started to clamp down on his cock again. He stopped. I was sweating now. My arms and legs were shaking.

"Are you going to do as I say, India?"

"I…you are not going to bully me, Kellan!"

He started to move again. He gently pinched my clit between his thumb and forefinger. That was enough.

"Yes!" I yelled.

"Yes what, India?"

Tears were falling down my face. I couldn't take this anymore. "Yes, I'll do as you say!"

"Whatever and whenever? For your well-being and safety?"

"Yes, damn you!"

He pulled out of me and gently turned me over on my back. He spread my legs and once again placed himself between my thighs. Leaning over me, he kissed me tenderly, gently pushing my sweat-soaked hair off my face and wiping my tears away with his thumbs. "Thank you," he said softly.

He entered me again, but very differently this time. His mouth found one of my nipples, suckling gently, his tongue lathing. With every stroke, his pelvis rubbed against my clit. My muscles started to spasm again. This time, Kellan didn't stop. He thrust harder and brought his teeth down on my nipple.

The orgasm exploded through me, my whole body shaking. I screamed. The pleasure was so intense.

Kellan thrust hard once more. Stilling, deep inside me, he shouted as he came.

He kissed me again and slowly pulled out. He went into the bathroom, returning with a warm wash cloth. He tenderly cleaned between my thighs.

As he started to turn away, I caught his hand. "Who were you angry with, Kellan? Me or you?"

He sighed and ran the back of his fingers down my cheek. "Both," he answered me.

CHAPTER EIGHT

I was soaking in a hot bubble bath in Kellan's suite. It had been a long day—a great day, but long, and I was happily exhausted.

There had been a massive turnout at the signing. It had been held at the Barnes & Noble in downtown Seattle on Pine Street. It had been thrilling to see all the people wanting to buy my book and meet me. There had been so many that the signing had run three hours overtime.

Tomorrow, I was lecturing at the University of Washington, here in Seattle. The literature professor was a friend of mine. Tanner Richardson. We had been friends since we met at LSU, where Kathy, Tanner, and I attended. I had called to let him know I was going to be here, hoping that I would get a chance to see him. He asked if I would consider being a guest speaker and that I could do a signing there afterward. I told him I would be delighted to, so it had been arranged. I couldn't wait to see Tanner. It had been a long time, and I had missed him.

It had also been a long night last night. As I soaked, I thought about everything that had gone down with Kellan last night. After his dominance of me—that was all that it could be called—he turned into the lover of my dreams. He explored every inch of my body with his hands, his lips, his tongue, and his teeth. He gave me three screaming orgasms. Literally.

And for the first time, Kellan let me have free rein with him. It was my first time exploring a male body. I closed my eyes and leaned my head back on the lip of the tub, remembering Kellan laid out on his back with me straddling him. I kissed his lips tenderly, licking the seam so he would open to me. I explored his mouth with my tongue, sucked on his tongue. He groaned, and that encouraged and excited me. I bit his earlobe gently, then kissed and nibbled my way down his neck, nipping along his collarbone while kneading the muscles of his arms with my hands. I played with his small, flat nipples, flicking them with my tongue then suckling him.

He groaned louder and grabbed my behind with both his hands. His fingers flexing tighter and tighter. I ran my tongue down his six-pack and flat belly, taking his engorged penis in my hands, running them up and down, reverently cupping his balls. I had read about giving oral sex to a man, and Kellan had made me feel sexy and wanton while he tasted me. I wanted to make him feel the same way, and I wanted his taste in my mouth.

I held him at the root of his cock, wrapping one of my hands around him. Scooting down his legs, I lowered my head to him and ran my tongue around his plum-colored crown. I took him into my mouth, sucking him in, pulling him to the back of my throat. I loved the taste of him. Hollowing my cheeks, I sucked him harder. Kellan's back arched off the mattress. He grabbed my hair, taking control. He thrust into my mouth, fucking it.

"I'm going to come!" he shouted, trying to pull me off him.

Wrapping my arms around his thighs, I didn't let him. I wanted all of him, all of this. I sucked his cock as hard as I could. Kellan arched again. Roaring my name, he came, hot down my throat. I swallowed and lapped him up with my tongue until I had every drop. I felt powerful having made him lose control.

Kellan lay back on the bed, his breathing ragged. He pulled me up his body by my arms, holding me to him, my head under his chin.

A TEMPTATION

"Have you done that before?" he asked me after he caught his breath. I shook my head against his chest. All my bravado having evaporated, I was now extremely self-conscious.

"Good," he said, rubbing his hands up and down my back. "I'm breaking all my rules where you're concerned."

What was that supposed to mean? Not wanting to ruin this moment, I put it aside to think about later.

There was a knock on the door. Kellan gently placed me on the bed and got up. Quickly pulling on his pants, he went out of the room to answer the door. Feeling happy and sated, I snuggled deeper into the bed. I fell asleep peacefully before Kellan made it back to bed.

He kissed me awake at three in the morning. Tenderly, he made love to me. Not fucking. We made love. My feelings changed for him in that moment. We stayed up after that. Kellan was flying back to New York at six. I wanted to go and see him off, but he said no. He wanted me to relax before I had to be at the university at ten that morning.

He introduced me to Tim. I liked him immediately. When Kellan went to take a shower, I ordered coffee from room service.

Later, we were standing at the door, and Kellan was telling me that Tim would be driving me to the locations that were near. We would be flying in one of his company's planes to all the other cities. I couldn't say anything to that. I had agreed to his terms.

He cupped my face in one of his hands, rubbing his thumb back and forth across my lips. "I will see you as soon as I can. Listen to Tim, India, and be careful. Please?"

He actually asked me to do something, not commanded. This was a new Kellan that I was seeing. He pulled me to him, both of his hands on the sides of my face, and kissed me hard. Then he was gone.

I was in trouble. My feelings for Kellan? I fell. Fell hard just like I knew I would. Fell hard for this wonderful, beautiful man that didn't know why he was reacting to me the way he was.

I sighed heavily and climbed out of the tub and dried off. While I was pulling on my sleep pants and tank top, there was a knock at the door. Tim had gone downstairs to get something to eat since I wasn't hungry. So I hurried to answer it.

I opened the door to see a stunning woman standing there. She was tall with straight blonde hair that hung right above her shoulders. She was wearing a very provocative, designer red dress. It showed a lot of her overly large breasts.

"Who are you?" she demanded very condescendingly.

"You knock on my door and demand I tell you who I am? I don't think so!" I went to shut the door in her face, and she stopped it with both her hands, pressing against it.

"This is Kellan Coventry's suite! Where is he?"

"If Kellan didn't give you his itinerary, I would assume he didn't want you to know."

"You bitch!" she screamed. She made a lunge for me, and I just knew she was going for my hair. My hair hung down to my waist. There was no way I was letting this bitch—whoever she was—touch it or me. I punched her.

She fell on the floor, part of her in the hall, the other across the doorway. She put her hands up to her nose. It was bleeding quite profusely. "You broke my nose!" she yelled, crying now.

"Good," I said bluntly.

My cell went off. I went to the coffee table and picked it up. Of course it was Kellan. "Hey," I said, sighing into the phone.

"What is that god-awful noise?"

"Well, I think it's a friend of yours. Tall blonde female. Does that ring any bells?"

"Yes," he said softly. "Why is she making that noise?"

"I kind of broke her nose," I responded, wincing.

"You what?"

"I punched her, Kellan."

"Okaaay. Where's Tim?"

"He went downstairs for dinner. I wasn't hungry, so I stayed up here and took a bath."

"Are you all right?" he asked, sounding very concerned. "What did she do to you?"

A TEMPTATION

I replayed what had taken place, and to my amazement, he started laughing. That pissed me off. "This isn't funny, Kellan."

"No. No, it isn't." He was still chuckling. *Arrogant asshole.* "It's just...You amaze me, India."

I heard someone yell my name. I looked up. Whoa! I hadn't noticed the crowd gathering out in the hall. Tim came pushing his way into the room.

"Are you all right?" he asked me, taking me by my arm.

"I'm—" I tried to answer Tim. "Okay," I said into my phone. I handed my cell to Tim. "He wants to talk to you."

Tim winced. I didn't have to tell him who it was. "Sorry," I mouthed to him.

"Yes...Okay...I will."

I watched Tim walk over to the blonde. I snickered. She wasn't going to be able to save that dress.

He knelt on the floor beside the woman and held my cell phone to her ear.

"Oh, Kellan," I heard her cry into the phone. "She's crazy! She—"

I was betting Kellan had interrupted her. I would love to be able to hear both sides of this conversation.

This man that I didn't know came through the door, walking up to me. "Ms. Leigh," he said, holding his hand out to me. "I'm Toby. The night manager." I shook his hand. "We are very sorry about this. Believe me, no one will be bothering you again." I thanked him, wondering how the hell Kellan had talked to him. He hadn't had the time!

Tim was back with my cell. "Are you sure you are all right, India?" Kellan asked me when I got back on the phone with him.

"Yes. She didn't touch me, Kellan. She tried to. I stopped her."

"That you did," he said, chuckling. "But that wasn't what I was talking about. Caprielle—that's her name, I'm sorry that you even had to see her."

"It's not your fault, Kellan. It's hers."

"Do you have any questions for me?"

"About her?" I shook my head even though he couldn't see me. "No."

"You are like no other woman I have ever known."

I went over and sat on the couch, pulling my legs under me. "Not so, Kellan," I sighed. "I heard you at the door last night, not what was being said—because I was in the bedroom. But I heard all the noise she was making. Then when she showed up here today and acted like she did, I figured you had ended it with her before I came into the picture. Anything before me is none of my business."

"You figured all that out just from how she acted?" He was silent for a minute. "You're correct on all of it. I told her—on the phone just now—if she came around me, I would have her arrested for stalking. If she came around you, I would do something a lot worse."

Wow! I didn't know what to say. I didn't believe that Kellan explained himself to anyone. The fact that he had to me made my heart feel lighter. About the threat made to Caprielle? Well, I didn't want to think about that.

"So besides the bitch, how was your day, baby?"

CHAPTER NINE

Tim and I arrived at the university at nine thirty the next morning. Tanner was waiting outside Washington Hall for us. I climbed out of the darkly tinted SUV when Tim held open my door. Tanner hugged me tightly, lifting me off my feet.

"It's so good to see you, India," he said, setting me back on my feet.

"Please don't manhandle Ms. Leigh."

Tanner looked at me, puzzled. I shook my head. "Tanner, this is Tim. I'm sorry, Tim. I don't know your last name?"

"Dalton. Tim Dalton." He held his hand out to Tanner.

"Tanner Richardson." He shook Tim's hand.

"I am not to allow anyone to touch Ms. Leigh," Tim said stoically.

"I'm sure that doesn't apply to being greeted by my friend, Tim," I responded.

"I was told, and I quote"—he held up two fingers on both hands, making the sign for quotations—"'No one is to touch her, Tim. Any way, shape, or form. No female and definitely no male. I don't care who they are.' End of quote."

"Well, don't worry about Tanner. He's a very good friend. I will straighten out Kellan."

"What is going on, India?" Tanner asked me, looking totally confused.

Before I could answer, Tim cut in. "I am Ms. Leigh's security guard. I will do just as Mr. Coventry instructed me to do. Sorry, Ms. Leigh."

"Fine, Tim." I was getting pissed off again. What was Kellan thinking? "I will just be the one who touches or hugs or"—I waved my hands around, getting really worked up—"whatever to Tanner. That way, neither you nor Kellan can take exception."

"Oh, I think he'll take exception, Ms. Leigh. In fact, I would bet on it."

"Wait. Coventry?" Tanner asked, looking as if he was getting ready to freak out. "Kellan Coventry?"

"I'll explain later," I sighed. "We need to go in. It's almost time."

Washington Hall was packed. There was even a lot of faculty in attendance. Tanner had given me the subject of the lecture he wanted me to give. It was on the process—before, during, and after—of publishing a book. It had gone well. I was thankful that my publishing experience was not only exciting but funny as hell. The students asked a lot of great questions. It was hard to believe they were only four or less years younger than me. I felt so much older, and I didn't believe I ever sounded that young.

The publishing company had sent three hundred books. We ran out. They took the information from the people who still wanted one. If they paid for it here, they were guaranteed an autographed copy. I was so glad I didn't have to handle that end.

We were finally able to leave around five that afternoon. Not having the time to take a break all day, except for the bathroom, I was starving. Tanner asked me to have dinner with him, and I readily agreed.

Tim said he would drive us and bring Tanner back to his car afterward. Deciding to carefully pick my battles with Kellan, I agreed as long as Tanner was all right with it. Tanner just went along with the flow.

Tanner and I sat in the backseat of the SUV. I took out my cell and saw that Kellan had called quite a few times during the lecture and signing. I returned his call. I was thrilled to hear his voice when he answered. Realizing I missed him brought back to mind how deep I was falling.

"Hey," I breathed into the phone. I wanted to tell him all about the lecture and signing, tell him how well it had turned out. And I wanted to hear all about his day, learn more about him.

"I don't appreciate another man's hands on you, India," he snarled into the phone.

Okay. *This* Kellan again. So much for the pleasant conversation I had wanted. I sighed heavily. "He didn't have his hands on me, Kellan. He gave me a hug."

"Just a hug doesn't lift you off your feet!"

"Kellan, Tanner is a very good friend of mine. I haven't seen him in three years. I am not going to have you telling me how my friends are supposed to act toward me now or vice versa."

"Don't make me leave New York again, India," he growled.

He actually growled! Unbelievable! "I didn't make you leave New York, Kellan. That's all on you. I don't want to talk to you when you're like this."

"How am I supposed to be, India, when I'm stuck here just able to think about you?"

My heart melted. "Everything is all right, Kellan," I said gently. "We just left the university and are going out to dinner."

"Who's we, India?" he asked in that deceptively soft voice, that voice that said he was getting very pissed off.

I shook my head. This was going to be a fight. "Me, my friend Tanner, and Tim."

"No, India! Absolutely not! You are not going out to dinner with another man!" He was shouting. I had to hold the phone away from my ear.

"Listen to me, Kellan Coventry, and listen well. I am going to dinner with my friend. I am not going on a date. I am not going to fuck him." I stole a glance at Tanner. His eyes wide, his face flushed, he looked as though he wanted to put in his two cents. I shook my head at him and held up a finger.

"You cannot tell me I can't spend time with a friend. Besides, I know you didn't run off to New York on business, Kellan. Do you want to tell me about her?" This was just a hunch, but I had learned a long time ago to always listen to my gut.

Kellan didn't make a sound. "You see, Kellan? You want to dictate my life, but you don't want me to even know what's going on with you. You don't tell me anything about you or your life. I agreed to your terms, and I'm abiding by them. But you don't get to interfere with my friends."

"India," Kellan sighed into the phone. "I told you. I'm confused."

"So? Be confused, Kellan! But you can't have this both ways. I'm hanging up now. And I'm turning off my phone. Don't call Tim to speak to me because I won't talk to you." I hung up and turned off my phone. Tears were burning behind my eyes. Bullshit! I wasn't going to let him make me cry. I never used to cry—before Kellan, that is.

Tanner took my hand in his. I looked at him, and he started to say something. I shook my head, reminding him of Tim's presence.

"Tanner, I want a good cheeseburger. Will you tell Tim where to go?"

While Tanner gave directions, I looked out the window, not seeing anything. What was I going to do? My heart was becoming attached more and more. It was saying to take what I could get. My mind on, the other hand, was saying to walk away before I lost it and everything else.

The arguments caused from Kellan's moods and sense of ownership were making me dizzy. I remembered reading once that in good relationships, there were fights, that feelings that strong had to come out in all ways. If you loved so deeply, so too would you feel everything that deeply with that person.

But Kellan didn't love me. He didn't know what he thought about me, much less what he felt.

The SUV had stopped, and Tanner was standing at my door; he had apparently opened it for me. I had been so lost in thought that I had not noticed anything. I got out, and we went in to the restaurant. I was happy to see it was a very casual place. Tanner and I were seated at one table while Tim was seated by himself at another, not close enough to be able to overhear us.

The waitress came over and took our orders. As soon as she left, Tanner concentrated on me.

"Now tell me what's going on, India?"

"This might sound nuts, Tanner. But I don't know."

"But Kellan Coventry?"

"I know. I didn't know anything about Kellan when I met him. Hell, I don't know anything about him now." I shrugged and shook my head. "What I mean is, I didn't know who he was. I had never heard of Kellan Coventry. I didn't know until after I went out with him."

"India, he's known to have women in all the major cities that he does business in. Because of all his business dealings in the area, he's here a lot. There are stories of sexual behavior that isn't mainstream. BDSM relationships are fine and dandy. As long as they are safe and consensual, it's not anyone's business." He shrugged. "But I know you. That's not who you are. I'm not trying to upset you with this, India. I just don't want to see you hurt. What is he to you?"

Whoa! So that's the lifestyle Kellan had been talking about.

"India?"

"Oh right. Sorry. He's nothing and…everything."

"Has he told you you're the only one in his life?"

The waitress came and placed our orders in front of us. I took a long drink of my Diet Coke.

"No. Look, I know this is weird. You don't have to tell me. I stayed away from him, but he pursued. He's possessive and demanding with me, but he won't let me know the least little thing about him or his life. I don't know if he's seeing other women or sleeping with other women. If I found out he's sleeping with others, that would make it easy. I can't do that. I won't do that."

I took a bite of my cheeseburger. It was good. But my appetite had suddenly disappeared.

Tanner reached across the table and placed one of his hands on top of one of mine. "You shouldn't have to be going through this, India. You, more than any woman I know, deserve to be treated like a queen, to be loved totally for the person you are, not subjected to someone's moods and whims."

I shuddered. "I don't want to talk about this anymore, Tanner. Tell me what's been happening in your life. I want to know every juicy detail," I said, wiggling my eyebrows.

It was good to hear Tanner talk about his work and personal life. He had been living and working in Seattle for three years now. We had met at LSU. He was there having gone back to get his doctorate while I was there working on my master's. We had had a lot in common and became fast friends.

He was from Baton Rouge. He would come home with me on some weekends and join my friends and me in whatever we had going on. We liked the same books, the same food, and the same music. He also loved New Orleans. We would have been good together. Tanner had wanted it, but I had only felt friendship toward him. My life would have been so much simpler and uncomplicated if I had felt more.

Until I met Kellan, I thought Tanner and Noah were the most gorgeous guys around. Tanner's blond hair and tanned bronze skin made him look as though he belonged on a California beach. He had blue eyes also. But none of that came near Kellan's dark, dangerous good looks.

I told Tanner about the creative-writing class I taught, that I had some interesting budding talents in there. We both laughed when we discussed some of our students' literary subjects. I raved to him about all the other artists who also volunteered their time teaching classes and how good it felt to try to make a difference. And that we were planning to offer classes to kids next year.

We discussed my book and the one I was currently working on. It was so nice to once again have someone to talk with about the things that were important to me.

All too soon, it was time to call it a night. Tim and I brought Tanner back to his car, and I got out to give him a hug good-bye.

"It was so good to see you, India. I want you to promise to call me if you need me." He pulled away in order to look me in the eye.

A TEMPTATION

"I'm worried about this Coventry thing. His lifestyle is not anything you need to be around. Please be careful."

I promised him I would on both counts and that I wanted him to try to come for a visit. Then I kissed him on the cheek and climbed back in the SUV.

CHAPTER TEN

When Tim and I got back to the suite, I headed straight to the shower. I stayed standing under the hot water for a long time after I finished washing. I pulled on my pajamas and went out to tell Tim that I was going to bed.

Tim said that Kellan had called him and asked if I could turn my phone back on. I responded by saying I was sorry. I had forgotten that I had it off and would turn it back on right away. Before crawling into bed I turned it on and placed it on the nightstand. I was exhausted. Maybe, just maybe I would have a nightmare-free night.

Thirty minutes later, my phone woke me. I checked the screen and saw it was Kellan. I answered it cautiously, not knowing how he was going to react.

"Hi, baby," he said quietly. Oh. He was being cautious too.

"Hi to you too. Is everything going all right for you?"

"As well as can be expected." He was silent for a moment, so quiet that I didn't know if he was still on the line.

"Kellan? Are you still there?"

"Yeah. I'm here, baby. I'm sorry about today, India. I was wrong. I have lunch, even dinner with friends. It means nothing but that. I had no right to react like that." He was silent again. I could imagine him running his fingers through his hair. "I don't know how I am supposed to act. I am so out of my element here."

"You!" I had to laugh. "Kellan. You go off doing God knows what, and I really don't question it because it really isn't any of my business. But when you start demanding that I act in a certain way, tell you what, where, and how? Then I am going to demand the same." I sigh into the phone.

"I...I like you a lot, Kellan. But you aren't the only one confused here. I need to know what you want from me. You are going to have to start talking."

"I agree," he said quietly. "The thought of you with someone else, or of you hurt, it tears me up. I really love that I am the only man who has touched you. And that I am the only man you have touched. I have never felt this way before, India. I don't know if I can do this, but I can't let you go either. I don't want you sullied by my lifestyle, so I have been keeping you and it separate. I will not tell you all the details of why I conduct my personal life the way I do, only that I have to live this way, and I will not have you involved in it."

What could have happened in his life that he, as strong as he was, had to have heavens-knows-what in order to get by?

"Kellan, I've researched the whole dom./sub. thing. I believe that with two consenting adults, what they do behind closed doors is nobody's business."

"There's different degrees to that lifestyle, baby. Degrees that I will make sure you do not experience. But those...things, they're what I need."

I scrub a hand over my face. What a conversation to be having! "I don't know what to tell you, Kellan. There are some things I can and can't live with. If we were just dating, none of it would matter. But we aren't just dating. We are sleeping together. You implied, at first, that you just wanted sex with me. Now you are acting like that isn't enough. Somehow, you are going to have to figure out what this, us, is to you. I'm not a masochist, Kellan. I'm not demanding promises of marriage, but I can't keep heading toward having my heart torn to pieces."

"I get it," he sighed into the phone. "How about we get together when you get back and revise our relationship?"

"You sound like you're preparing a contract," I said, chuckling. "Will you be finished with whatever you are doing in New York by then?"

"Most definitely. It will be rectified by the beginning of next week."

"I'm glad to hear it—for your sake, Kellan."

"You sound tired, baby. Go and get some sleep. I will talk to you tomorrow." He hesitated. "India? I hope you miss me."

I didn't respond to that. "Good night, Kellan," I whispered. "Sweet dreams."

After I hung up with Kellan, I lay there for hours trying to get back to sleep, but I had too much on my mind. I finally got up and went into the living room. Grabbing my laptop by the door, I went and sat on the floor by the coffee table. I turned on the TV—volume low so I wouldn't disturb Tim—and worked on my second book.

I worked until four in the morning, until I was so exhausted I couldn't see straight. I went to bed and must have fallen asleep as soon as I lay down.

I saw Kellan. He was in a room with a bed as big as three king-size beds put together. He wasn't alone in there. There were men and women involved in a lot of different sexual acts scattered all over the room—S&M at its finest, or worst, depending on your point of view.

I watched Kellan get on that giant bed. He was gloriously naked. Two women joined him, just as unclothed. Kellan lay down. One of the women knelt right over his face. She was the blonde from last night. The other woman was Alexis Hunt. She settled right between Kellan's legs and took his cock in her mouth.

Then Deric was there. He knelt behind the blonde woman, Caprielle, Kellan had said her name was. He made her bend her upper body lower. With her ass in the air, Deric thrust roughly into the woman's anus cavity. As soon as Kellan heard the woman's short cry, he grabbed Alexis by the hair and pulled her off him.

Kellan and Deric were so aggressive with these women. There was no respect there at all. No compassion. No *anything*. This was ugly sex. Nothing good that I could see. Why would any woman want this? And what was so wrong to make a man treat women in such a way?

Deric wrapped his arms around Caprielle's waist, taking both of them down on the bed. He was lying on the bottom, she on top, her back to his front. He was still inside her. He put his legs around hers and spread her wide.

Kellan knelt in between both of their legs. He rammed into Caprielle's pussy. He pulled out until just his crown remained sheathed. He and Deric set a rhythm, Kellan thrusting into her from the front, Deric from the back. Soon Caprielle was screaming out her orgasm. Kellan pulled out. He was still hard. Deric kept pounding in and out of her ass.

Kellan knelt on the bed and viciously grabbed Alexis by the hair. He brought her face down to his penis. He fucked her mouth, not mindful of how deep he was going or how rough he was.

But maybe that was the thing. Maybe this was not just about dominance, but these women liked pain. Not the small bite of pain that I learned increased my pleasure. This was more. This was intense. This was insane.

All of a sudden, Kellan yanked Alexis off him. He stood beside the bed and pulled her to the edge. He made her get on her hands and knees and spread her legs apart. He roughly shoved two fingers into her pussy, quickly pulling them out and rubbing her own cream over her anus. He pulled the cheeks of her backside apart, telling her that this was for his pleasure only. She would have none.

Kellan slammed into her ass. Alexis screamed and brought one of her hands between her legs trying to get off. He told her he would beat the shit out of her if she didn't put her hand back down by her side. She complied and started to cry.

I looked at Kellan then. There was emotion showing on his face now. It was rage.

I came up off the bed with a scream. I put my face in my hands and cried. I cried for that Kellan from my dreams, and for those women. What could have happened to them, the men and women alike, to make them want this?

Tim burst through my door. He looked all around my room and in the bathroom. When he was satisfied that there wasn't an intruder, he came over to me, placing a hand on my shoulder.

"What's wrong, Ms. Leigh?" he asked me softly, as if he was afraid to spook me.

"Bad dream." I swiped my hands under my eyes. "I'm sorry I disturbed you, Tim."

"You didn't. If you don't mind me saying so, you don't look so good."

"I'm fine, Tim. I just haven't been getting enough sleep. Been having these damn dreams for a few weeks now. I'm going to go take a shower."

"Okay. Can I get you anything?"

"You could call for some coffee."

He nodded and turned to go to the door. "And, Tim," I said as he turned back to me, "would you please call me India?"

He smiled then. The first smile I had ever seen from him. He nodded again and went out the door.

I got out of bed and went and jumped in the shower. I had been soaking wet with sweat when that dream woke me up. It felt great under the water, but I didn't waste any time in the shower. I was so tired, and Tim and I had to leave for the airport in just a couple of hours.

I quickly dressed, put my hair in a simple ponytail, and applied my makeup. Walking out of the bedroom, I smelled the coffee. Thank God. Getting a cup, I sat down on the couch with it.

My cell went off, and I looked around for it. I remembered that it was on the nightstand by the bed. Tim came out of his room saying he would get my phone for me, telling me to just sit there and relax.

I looked at the screen and saw that it was Kellan.

"Hey," I breathed into the phone.

"Morning, baby," he said huskily. "Do you miss me yet?"

I started laughing. "Yeah. I probably shouldn't admit it to you, but yes, Kellan, I miss you."

"I only had a minute, India. I have to go to a meeting, but I wanted to hear your voice."

A TEMPTATION

"I like hearing from you," I whispered.

"Good. I will call you tonight in San Diego, baby. Take care."

"You too, Kellan."

After I clicked off, I reminded myself to call Kathy tonight. I wanted to tell her about seeing Tanner.

CHAPTER ELEVEN

*I*t was Tuesday; four more days, and this trip was over. I couldn't wait to get home. And I was sure Tim would be happy about that. His babysitting job would be over.

We had come to know each other quite well in the time that we had been forced together. He turned out to be a very nice man. Tim was twenty-six and had been working for Kellan for four years. He had a lot of respect for him.

Tim explained that the security team stayed with Kellan wherever he went, that there were always threats because of all his money. Also, because of the sensitive material of his business, there were guards at his warehouses and offices. Always.

I chuckled and said they must be awfully busy having to guard all of Kellan's women. Fishing for information much? Tim said that this was the only time they had ever guarded another person besides Kellan and his aunt. Whoa! Maybe this was a good sign.

I was sitting at the table in the suite that Tim and I were in this time. No, my publishers didn't supply suites. Kellan had changed all my reservations. Apparently, Mr. Coventry could obtain any information he wanted. I had not supplied him with my itinerary, but he knew just where I had to be. It was creepy.

A TEMPTATION

I was sipping my cup of coffee when Tim came out of his room. He got himself a cup and sat down across from me.

"India, you don't look so good."

"Thanks, Tim. I love you too."

He blushed. "I didn't mean it that way! I mean ill. You look like you're sick."

"I told you. I haven't been sleeping well. I'll be fine."

"I don't know." He looked at me closely. "You're really pale. I think I should take you to the doctor."

"Oh, come on, Tim." I was getting aggravated. "I only have four more days of this, and then I can go home and get plenty of rest." I stood up, grabbed my purse and laptop, and started for the door.

"Come on, Tim!" I called over my shoulder. "It's time to go." I had my hand on the doorknob. All at once, I got very dizzy. The floor looked as if it was coming to meet me. It was getting closer and closer. My vision was blurring. It was starting to go in and out. Then there was just darkness.

I opened my eyes to a strange room. *Hospital,* I thought. *I'm in a hospital room.* What in the hell was I doing here? Taking a slower look around, I saw that there were IVs in my left hand, a blood pressure cuff that was tightening around my right arm, and a heart monitor. What the hell had happened? I didn't remember anything. I pressed the call button. I wanted some answers.

It seemed as though just a minute passed before the door opened. In walked not only a nurse, but a doctor. And Kellan. The last person was whom I looked at.

"Kellan." I had to clear my throat. It was so dry. "What's going on?"

He came over to the bed and took my left hand in his. He leaned over the rail and tenderly placed a kiss on my lips. "You passed out, India. Two days ago. Do you remember?"

Ohhh. That strange feeling I had when Tim and I were going out the door for the book signing. "I remember feeling strange. That's all." I looked around the room again. "Kellan, where's Tim? I owe him an apology. He wanted to take me to the doctor. He said I didn't look good, and I just blew him off."

"He's out in the hall, baby. He'll be happy to see you're awake. You scared him out of a few years. India. This is Dr. Howard. I called my physician in Seattle to see if he knew a competent one here in LA. He contacted a good friend of his." He gestured to the man in question. "Hence, Dr. Howard."

"You are not just tired, Ms. Leigh. You are suffering from exhaustion. You're anemic, your blood pressure is way too low, and you're underweight."

"Could I have some water please?" I asked Kellan.

Then I turned to the good doctor. "I have always been in great health doctor. I haven't been sleeping well at all. Because I was so tired, when I tried to eat, it would make me sick. I have known about the low blood pressure, but it has never caused a problem."

I thanked Kellan for the water he handed me. I moved the straw to the side and chugged it down straight from the Styrofoam cup.

"Well, I want you to stay here for at least another five days. I'm putting you on a diet high in iron, vitamins with iron, and a mild sleeping pill. Everything that is going on with you could eventually put a strain on your heart."

"I can't stay here for another five days!"

"Hush now," Kellan said.

No! I didn't want to stay in here. "Dr. Howard, I appreciate your time and concern. But I want to go home. I'm in a strange city, and my doctor—that I've had for my whole twenty-four years—is there."

"India. You need to do as the doctor says." Kellan refilled my water and handed the cup to me once again.

"I will, Kellan, except for the 'staying here' part. My doctor at home has always treated me for this. When I'm under stress, it comes out in bad dreams, and I get very little sleep because of them. Please. I just want to go home, Kellan."

He ran his fingers slowly up and down the side of my face. "Calm down, baby. Let the doctor and me talk. I'll send Tim in until I get back."

They went out, and a few minutes later, Tim came in. I apologized profusely. He said he was just relieved I was okay.

A TEMPTATION

When Kellan came back in, he said that even though the doctor wasn't happy about it, he would release me—so long as Kellan made sure I followed his instructions. Kellan also had a stipulation. And that was that I stayed at his house so he and his staff could take care of me. He could also guarantee that I was doing as I was told. I didn't exactly feel comfortable with that, but what choice did I have? I wanted to get back to Louisiana.

Kellan called his pilot and told him to ready the plane. He then asked Tim if he would mind coming to New Orleans. He wanted Tim with me whenever he had to leave his house. I tried to object, but Kellan gave me a look so stern that I just shut my mouth.

"Oh my God!" I practically screamed. Kellan and Tim both rushed over to my bed.

"No," I said, shaking my head at their looks of concern. "I'm all right. But the rest of my book signings aren't!" The look that passed between the men said "Yes, she's crazy."

"I've spoken to your editor, India. Several times, in fact. Everything has been taken care of."

"Several times?" I swallowed.

"Yes. When I explained what had happened, she demanded my number so she could check on you."

I started chuckling. Then that progressed to downright laughing. The looks that Kellan and Tim were giving me made me laugh harder. "Hey. If she can demand something of Kellan Coventry, and you listened to her? I need her with me."

His expression hardened. "If I hadn't been so worried about you, it wouldn't have gone over so well, India. It won't happen again."

"Well," I said, grinning up at him mischievously, "you can't blame a girl for trying." Kellan actually smiled at that. I reached for his hand, and he entwined our fingers. "Thank you, Kellan. For everything."

With the fingers of his other hand, he pushed my hair back from my face. "Anytime, baby. Now let me help you get dressed, then I'll go take care of the bill."

"Nice try, Mr. Coventry. I can dress myself, and I have great health insurance. If you will hand me my purse, I'll get you my card."

Tim handed me my purse. After Kellan left with my insurance card, he looked at me and smiled.

"What?" I questioned him.

"I have never seen him act this way with a woman."

"How does he usually act?" I asked curiously.

"I don't know if I can explain it." He shrugged. "Not like…this. He usually could…I guess you could say, care less."

When Tim left the room, I went into the bathroom and washed up. God, I needed a shower. But I couldn't get dressed, much less take a shower, with this IV still in my hand. I had unhooked everything else. I would wait until we got to Kellan's to take a shower. I didn't want to be here any longer than I had to.

As I lay back down to wait, I thought about what Tim had said. I shook my head. I didn't know what to think about the way Kellan was acting. My heart was hoping that it meant his feelings for me mirrored my own for him. But I wouldn't tell Kellan what I felt for him—not until I knew for sure I was more than just a good lay.

While I waited, I called Kathy to let her know what had happened, and also that I would be staying at Kellan's for two weeks. And if she would continue taking care of my plants until I got back home. She said of course she would, then she demanded Kellan's address. I said I didn't know the address, but I would let her know which house on St. Charles was his.

Right after I hung up with Kathy, my cell went off. I looked at the screen. "Noah!" I said excitedly into the phone.

"Hi, Kitten. How are you?"

Noah had called me Kitten since we were eight years old. His older brother had been teasing me and wouldn't let up. Being my catty self, I had swiped my nails down his arm. His brother said I clawed like a kitten, and a nickname had been born.

"Pissed off is how I'm doing. You been gone over a month, and this is the first I've heard from you."

"Sorry, Kitten. I've just been really busy."

"With business or women, Noah Bure?"

"Ah. You know me too well." He laughed.

"Well?" I demanded.

A TEMPTATION

"To be honest? Both."

I laughed then. "Same old Noah."

"Yeah, yeah. Nothing ever changes."

"When are you coming home? I really miss you and need to talk to you. It's not anything I can discuss over the phone."

"I don't know yet. Everything's really fucked up here."

"I hope it's not too much longer. You usually don't have to stay this long."

"Thing's usually aren't this fucked up."

I heard some noise in the background. "I've got to run, Kitten. I'll call you again when I can. Love you."

"I love you too, Noah. Bye."

I looked up after pressing end. Kellan was standing in the open doorway. If looks could kill, the dark one coming from him would have had me dead right where I lay. "Who's Noah, India?" There was his dangerous voice again.

"My best friend. Well, my best guy friend," I corrected.

"Another male friend?" he snarled.

Damn. He could piss me off faster than anyone else I knew. "I have a lot of male friends, Kellan," I remarked snidely. "If I would have wanted to be with any of them, I wouldn't have been a virgin when we met, now would I? You're really going to have to get over this...attitude of yours."

He looked at me with that dark look for another moment. Then just that quickly, I saw the tension leave his body. His eyes turned back to that brilliant blue. No more sparks shooting from them. I swear the man had to suffer from a multipersonality disorder.

"You're right. You're right," he said, throwing up his hands. "I'll try."

Kellan said everything was set. He had filled my prescription downstairs in the hospital pharmacy and had a copy of my medical file for my physician. He had Dr. Howard's orders also. In writing. All we had to wait on was the nurse with the wheelchair.

When the nurse finally arrived, I was so ready to leave. When she saw Kellan, she stopped in her tracks. She gasped, and her eyes widened. She was very pretty. Not stunning like the blonde or Alexis, but really attractive.

Kellan cursed and came over to the bed, ready to move me to the chair. "Wait. The IV," I said, holding up the offending hand.

"Oh, I'll take care of that," said the dazzled nurse.

Unfortunately, she was so busy trying to flirt with Kellan that she wasn't holding down the needle when she ripped off one side of the tape. It jarred the needle so bad I was afraid that it had come out my arm by the pointy end. I gasped. *Shit, that hurt.*

"Get away from her!" Kellan shouted and pushed the nurse out of the way. He picked up my hand and looked at the needle. "Trust me, baby?" he asked, glancing down at me.

I nodded. Kellan placed his thumb firmly on the needle. He ripped the tape off on the other side and removed the needle from my hand, holding a cotton ball to the area for few moments.

"All good?"

I smiled up at him. "Thank you."

He put a Band-Aide on my hand and slipped my hand through my shirt and up my shoulder. Scooping me up from the bed, he gently placed me in the wheelchair.

"I could have walked, Kellan."

"You're not to be on your feet for two weeks, India. Now hush and be good."

Feeling like a child, I snapped my mouth shut. Kellan went behind the chair, backing it out into the hallway.

"I'll get that for you, sir," the nurse simpered and batted her eyelashes at him.

"No you will not," Kellan barked at her.

I snickered. Kellan bent down and whispered in my ear, "I told you to behave, India."

"I am. I am," I said, holding up my hands. "I haven't said a word."

Kellan laughed and wheeled me out.

CHAPTER TWELVE

The next day, I slowly came awake. I had to pee. Badly. Climbing out of the large, high bed, I stood shakily on my feet. Damn! I felt drunk. Stumbling my way to two doors before I found the bathroom, I prayed I didn't face-plant on the floor. Everything was big in here, from the room itself to the tub in the bathroom. Big and beautiful.

I made it to the toilet and practically fell onto the seat. What the hell was wrong with me? When I was finished, I looked longingly at the huge shower. There was no way I could take one like this. Stumbling my way back to bed, I saw my cell on the nightstand. I grabbed it and climbed back up on the bed. Lying back on the pillows, I was panting. *This is so not good.* I checked the time on my phone. Two in the freaking afternoon!

Retracing my steps, so to speak, in my mind back to yesterday, I tried to put some perspective on why I felt like this. Kellan had carried me from the chair to the Mercedes he had waiting outside the hospital.

When we arrived at the airport, he carried me out of the car to a wheelchair that a man had waiting for us. After placing me gently in the chair, Kellan straightened and shook the man's hand. And, of course, he pushed my chair himself.

We didn't have to go through the regular channels of security, not with Kellan being who he was. They came to us, passed a wand over us, then led us outside to the tarmac where Kellan's company plane waited.

His company planes were small jets. The seats were plush and as comfortable as recliners. They sat with four grouped together, with two facing the other two. He placed me in one of the two farthest from the aisle. Kellan sat next to me, and Tim sat across from Kellan.

Thirty minutes later, we were in the air. When we had the pilots okay to undo the seatbelts, the stewardess came rolling a cart. Kellan had lowered our tables, and she placed covered dishes on all three of them. She placed a Diet Coke along with a glass of ice by mine, and beers by the guys. Then she uncovered the dishes. Cheeseburgers and fries!

"How did you know?" I asked Kellan, surprised. He just looked at me, raising his brows.

"Yeah, yeah. Stupid question. Tim works for you." They both chuckled.

It was around five in the afternoon when we had finished eating. I could only eat about a quarter of the burger and fries. I guess that was because I hadn't eaten that much in two days.

Kellan stood after the dishes had been cleared and tables raised, fishing in his pockets. He pulled out a prescription bottle, opened it, and handed me a pill. He said it was what the doctor had ordered for sleep.

I swallowed the pill and lay my head on Kellan's shoulder when he returned to his seat. He raised the two armrests that separated us and pulled me onto his lap. The last thing I remembered was curling into him.

I was only wearing my thong, and a T-shirt that had to be Kellan's. I had no idea where my clothes were, so there was no way I was leaving this room.

Sitting up, I pressed the button that was for Kellan on my phone. "Hey, baby," he answered in that husky, sexy voice.

A TEMPTATION

"Kellan, where are you?" I asked timidly.

"I'm downstairs, baby." His voice grew serious.

"Could you come here please?" And the call ended. I looked at my cell. *Huh?*

Kellan came through the door not a minute later. "What's wrong?"

"Umm, nothing." I shook my head. "Everything. I'm sorry I bothered you, but I didn't know where I was. I couldn't find my clothes, so I couldn't leave the room. And even if I could have, I wouldn't have been able to get down the stairs." I paused to take a breath.

"I'm not taking any more of those pills, Kellan. I feel drunk. Even though I slept until two in the afternoon. Two in the afternoon, Kellan! From five yesterday afternoon! And I don't remember anything from last night!"

"Calm down, India." He sat on the bed next to me. "First, you needed the sleep." He picked up my hand, rubbing his thumb across the knuckles. "Second, your clothes are in my closet. The only thing you don't remember is getting home. I wouldn't have let anything happen to you."

"I didn't think you would have, Kellan. That's not the point. The point is, I don't like feeling this—" I waved my hand around. "This...vulnerable. And," I complained (I never had been a good patient), "I need a shower, but I can't stand up that long."

Kellan threw back his head and laughed. I had never heard him laugh like this. He looked so young and carefree. I would have appreciated it if it hadn't pissed me off so much. I narrowed my eyes and glared at him. "Sorry, baby. I was just waiting for your lower lip to poke out in a cute little pout."

He ran a finger over said lip. I bit it. Not very hard. He chuckled and shook his head. "I'll be right back," he said and rose from the bed.

I watched him walk into the bathroom. I heard the water start running. About five minutes later, it stopped, and Kellan came back out. "Come here, you." He crooked his finger at me.

I scooted down the side of the bed where Kellan stood. He bent down and pulled the T-shirt from my body, followed by my thong, and scooped me up in his arms. "Your bath awaits, madam." I giggled. I loved this Kellan.

He lowered me into the tub. *Ah, warm water.* He had my shampoo, conditioner, and body wash sitting on the ledge of the tub. He washed and conditioned my hair. *Hmm. This is heaven.* I realized that here I was, naked, with Kellan bathing me, and I wasn't embarrassed or self-conscious at all. It just felt…right.

He poured some of my body wash onto a cloth and tenderly, but effectively, washed me from neck down. I started laughing when he got to my feet. "Hey!" I exclaimed, trying to pull my foot out of his grip. "That tickles!"

"You shouldn't have told me that, baby," he said, wiggling his eyebrows, trying to look sinister.

Kellan let the water out of the tub. He told me to stand and hold on to his shoulders so he could dry me off. Then he sat me on the counter by the sink. Taking my body oil and rubbing it between his hands, he massaged it all over into my skin. I moaned.

"Whenever I smell jasmine now, it reminds me of you," he whispered in my ear.

He dressed me in a pair of my pajamas. "Thank you, Kellan," I said softly.

"Believe me, baby, it was my pleasure." He placed a chaste kiss on my forehead, ran my pick through my long hair, and stood back. "You'll do, I guess."

"Hey!" I slapped him on the shoulder.

He laughed. Scooping me off the counter and back into his arms, he bent his head and nuzzled his nose with mine.

I clasped his face in my hands. "You're a good man, Mr. Coventry."

He gave me a puzzling look. "Only when I'm with you."

Kellan carried me downstairs and into the kitchen. He sat me down on top of the granite island. It was a great kitchen. It was huge like everything else in this house, but the kitchen had a cozy, homey feel to it.

"Beth, this is Ms. Leigh. We have to get her healthy again. So we need to fatten her up. I know if anyone can do it, you can."

A TEMPTATION

Kellan was leaning back against the island. He was standing next to me with his hand on my thigh.

Beth looked to be in her forties. She was short and round with a very kind, pretty face. She went to the refrigerator and pulled out a tray, placing it on the island close to us. "Will this do until dinner? Or would you like me to prepare something for you now, Ms. Leigh?"

The tray was artfully arranged with meats, cheeses, crackers, and fruit. "Please call me India, Beth." I took a grape from the tray and fed it to Kellan. "I won't need dinner after eating some of this." I smiled at her. "I really don't want to put any of you out with me staying here."

"Heavens, child! There's no trouble at all. It will be nice having a woman to cook for, for a change. Now eat up."

That's interesting. Does that mean Kellan doesn't have women over? Beth laughed at us as we playfully fed each other from the tray.

Kellan and I asked questions about each other. Our favorite color, song, movie, and artist. Our favorite things to do. The books we liked to read. Places we had been to and others that we still wanted to go to.

He had me laughing about predicaments he and Deric had found themselves in when they were in college. And I regaled him with tales of the terrible trio—Kathy, Noah, and I.

The effects of the sleeping pill had finally worn off. I felt good, better than I had in weeks. Kellan tried to feed me another strawberry. I turned my head to the side and put up one hand. "No more please," I pleaded. "I'm stuffed."

I hopped down from the island. "Hey. Watch it now," Kellan said sternly. "You have to take it very easy for the next two weeks. Remember?"

"Yes, captain." I saluted him. "I remember."

I asked him where the nearest bathroom was so I could wash my hands. He led me down a hall off the kitchen to a powder room. I used the restroom and washed my hands. I was walking back toward the kitchen when I heard Deric's voice.

"I didn't know she was here, Kellan. You never bring women to your house. This is one of the nights we usually meet. When Alexis called me right after my plane landed and asked if I could pick her up, I didn't see a problem." He shrugged. "Besides, India was going to be brought in eventually, so what's the deal?"

"India is never being brought in," Kellan snarled at his friend. "She's mine. I haven't seen you, Deric. Everything has changed." He was silent a moment. "Why would you bring one of the women into my home?" Kellan ran both his hands through his hair, staring at Deric.

"It was only going to be for a minute, Kellan. I didn't think that would matter. But I don't understand. What do you mean that everything has changed?"

They had their backs to me, and Beth was no longer in the kitchen. They had no way of knowing that I was there.

"This part of my life does not touch India. Not one word. Not one deed."

"How's that going to work, Kellan? This is a great deal of all our lives. If you're still going to see India, how can it not touch her?"

"She's mine, Deric. And only mine."

"I get it." Deric narrowed his eyes. "Have you told her about this part of your life?"

"I've implied about a part of my life that I will not let her be a part of. Nothing beyond that."

Alexis walked into the kitchen from the other side. "What are you doing here?" she barked, looking at me as though I were a piece of trash.

Kellan and Deric jerked around. They both wore an "oh shit" look on their faces when they saw me.

"Baby," Kellan said as he walked over to me, "let's get you back to bed."

"I don't need to be back in bed, Kellan. I told you I feel fine."

"Dr. Howard said—"

"He said I couldn't do anything, Kellan." I interrupted him. But I didn't give a shit. I didn't like what I had heard, and I liked even

A TEMPTATION

less the vibes that were running in this room. "Not that I had to stay physically in bed for the next two weeks."

Alexis's eyes grew wide, and her mouth dropped open.

"Boy, everything has changed," Deric muttered.

"Only where India is concerned," Kellan stated flatly.

He picked me back up in his arms, carried me over, and sat me back on the island. He stood beside me once again and entwined our hands together. That really pissed Alexis off.

I felt very conspicuous sitting there in my silk pajamas with no makeup and my hair in a ponytail while they were dressed to the nines. But there was no way in hell that I was leaving this room.

"What's going on, Kellan?" Alexis demanded.

"Do you demand or question me, Alexis?"

The look that came over Kellan's face when he said this scared me. This was the dark Kellan. Gone was the man who took such gentle care of me, who tenderly made love to me. In his place was a stranger, from the cold expression on his face to the rage I felt rumbling through his body.

"I asked you a question, Alexis!" I jumped. Kellan's voice cracked like a whip.

"No. But she—" Alexis started.

"Is none of your concern!"

"But I'm—"

"Not another word, Alexis, or you will regret it."

Alexis shut up then. A looked passed between her and Kellan, which had Alexis lowering her head, gaze cast down on the floor. But strangely, a small smile played on her lips. This was so not good.

"I want you out of here, baby. None of this shit touches you."

I found myself back up in Kellan's arms. Circling my arms around his neck, I buried my face in his shoulder.

"Don't move, Alexis," Kellan snarled at her as he carried me out of the kitchen.

I was shaking all over by the time Kellan laid me back on his bed. He took my face in his hands. "It's all right, baby. I promise."

I looked into his eyes. My Kellan was back. "I don't understand any of this."

"I know, baby. Let me deal with this, and then we'll talk. Okay?"

"What are you going to do?" I asked, only a touch above a whisper.

"I asked you a question, India." Kellan's voice hardened.

Oh hell no! "Don't talk to me like you did to Alexis. I'm not her. I'm not anything like her."

"Thank God for that!" came rushing out of his mouth.

His hands left my face and raked through his hair. "Baby, I really need to take care of this before I can talk to you. Okay?"

I nodded my head. He came to me and placed a gentle kiss on my lips.

CHAPTER THIRTEEN

I looked at the alarm clock on the bedside table—an hour and thirty minutes. That's how long Kellan had been gone. What was wrong with me? Sitting in the middle of Kellan's bed, I had my knees pulled up under my chin and my arms wrapped around my legs, and I was rocking back and forth. I was trying to hold myself together so I didn't scream. If I had any self-respect left, I would go home and leave Kellan and all this crap behind.

That was just it. I was losing my self-respect where Kellan was concerned. I had fallen in love with him, and that topped everything. But whatever was going on between Kellan and Alexis—oh yeah, and Deric, I wanted no part of.

I couldn't talk to another guy without Kellan going ballistic, yet he could have this whole other…*thing* with Alexis? And what about all the other women in the other cities? What was going down with Kellan, Deric, and Alexis? It wasn't good or healthy in any way I could see. I couldn't cut it.

Getting out of bed, I threw on a pair of jeans and a T-shirt, slipped on sandals, grabbed my purse and laptop—he could throw away the rest of my belongings as far as I was concerned—and left the room.

I found Tim in the kitchen eating dinner. He looked up at me when I came in and frowned. "Should you be up? You look awfully pale again."

"I'm fine, Tim." I shrugged. "Physically, anyway. Would you please drive me home?"

Tim put down his fork and started shaking his head. "No. No way, India. Are you trying to get me killed? Mr. Coventry said you were to stay here for the two weeks to recover."

"Okay," I said, pulling out my cell phone to call Kathy.

"Kat." Thank God she answered. "Hey. Sorry to bother you, but could you pick me up from Kellan's and take me home?" Tears started falling down my face. My emotions had stayed bottled up as long as they were going to.

"India! What the hell is wrong! Did that son of a bitch hurt you?"

"I can't explain it now, Kat, but I have to get out of here." I sniffled into the phone.

"I'll be there in a few. I'm already in New Orleans. I had dinner with some friends."

"Thanks, Kat. I'll be waiting for you outside."

"India? I can't let you do this," Tim said, getting up from the bar stool he had been sitting on. "You need someone with you until you're well again."

I swiped my hands across my face. It did no good. The tears kept falling. "I'm sorry it's come to this, Tim. You've been great, and I appreciate everything, but don't try to stop me. I'm an adult. You're not my father nor my brother. And believe me, you've never met anyone like my best friend. She will chew you up, spit you out, then stomp all over you and laugh while she does it. The stink she would raise if you didn't let me leave would bring all of the city down on your head."

"You're upset. Just wait for Mr. Coventry, India. He'll make everything right." He walked over to me and placed a hand on my shoulder. "I hate seeing you like this. It isn't like you. What can I do?"

I shook my head. "You can't do anything, Tim, and I've waited for Kellan long enough. He has to fight his demons his way, I suppose, but he'll have to do it without me."

A TEMPTATION

I placed my hand over his on my shoulder. "It was nice meeting you, Tim. Take care."

I retrieved my laptop from the kitchen island where I had placed it when I had called Kathy. The doorbell rang before I made it out of the kitchen. I hurried to the front door. I wanted to be long gone before Kellan got back.

I opened the front door before Mrs. Carter, Kellan's housekeeper, could. When I saw my friend's worried face, I fell apart. I was sobbing so hard it was a wonder I didn't break anything.

Kathy grabbed me. "What has that asshole done to you?"

"Ms. Leigh, you should be back in bed. You're going to make yourself sick again."

"It's all right, Mrs. Carter. I'll take care of her." Tim bent down and picked me up in his arms. "It will be all right, India. Hush now. She's right. You will make yourself sick."

"Until I find out what's going on here, I don't want any of you near her," Kathy spat out.

"I'm going with you guys. She has been really sick and shouldn't be alone."

"And why should I trust you?"

"I have been with her the last two weeks, lady. Just the two of us. Do you think if I was going to hurt her, I would wait until we got back here?"

"I don't know what you're capable of, bud! I don't know you. Period. Except for the fact that you work for the asshole who got her like this."

"My job is to protect her. It didn't stipulate what I wasn't to protect her from. I don't care who I work for."

"Tim, I don't want to cause problems for you. You should stay here."

"I'm not letting you go home alone, India. You let me worry about me. Okay?" Tim laid me down in the backseat of Kathy's car. He placed my head in his lap. He kept running his hand over my hair. It was soothing. If nothing else, I had made another good friend.

On the way to Slidell, Kathy demanded to know what was going on. I told her she had to wait until we got to my house. There was no way I was talking about this in front of Tim. He didn't need to hear about this shit with Kellan. The man was his boss. And I would die of embarrassment talking about it in front of him.

The movement of the car, and all my tears, put me to sleep. That was all right by me. I wished I could sleep for a week right then—anything just so I wouldn't have to think about Kellan.

The closing of a car door brought me awake. Tim helped me out of the car and started to pick me up again. I said it was unnecessary, that I could walk now that my hysterics were over.

After unlocking my front door, I walked straight back to the kitchen. I started the coffeemaker, grabbed three mugs and spoons, and placed them along with cream and sugar on the kitchen table. I was happy to be home.

Tim and Kathy came in while I poured coffee into the mugs. I took mine out on the back porch. Staring out at my beloved bayou, I was reminded that this was where I truly belonged. I never felt alone here. I felt my family here.

I won't regret loving Kellan. I might have even understood whatever he was going to tell me, but he never should have left me to go do whatever in God's name they did together. It gave me too much time to think about how Kellan had been with Alexis. Too much time for my imagination to go off with a hundred different scenarios.

I heard the back door open and close. This would be hard. I hated telling Kellan's secrets. But I needed to talk about this. It was killing me.

"How you is girlfriend?"

I smiled. Kathy always talked like that when she was trying to lighten things up.

I spilled everything—from the first time Kellan had said he wanted me through what had happened last night. Kathy's eyes were as wide as saucers. I believed that was the first time I had ever seen my best friend shocked.

"So all the stories are true?"

I shrugged. How the hell would I know? I heard the ringtone on my cell. "That would be Kellan," I said quietly to her. "He would call as soon as he knew I was gone. What time is it Kat?"

A TEMPTATION

"A quarter to eleven."

"Almost six hours," I murmured.

"What?"

"Almost six hours since he went to deal with Alexis. I wouldn't treat someone I despised so callously."

"He's a bastard, India. He's not worthy of you. I'm so sorry you are going through this. I could kick myself for talking you into going out with him."

My cell kept going off.

"I wouldn't change it. And I can't really tell you that were finished."

"India!" She looked at me as if I had lost my mind. "After all this, you can still say that?"

"Hey. I'm not saying that I'm going to put up with being treated like this. And if he's fucking other women, I'm history. But I love him, Kat. I love the man he is when he's with me. There are so many sides to Kellan. Some I like, some…not so much. The man I'm talking about? He's gentle and kind. Caring and tender. Possessive and demanding."

I turned and looked at her sternly. "I don't want any of this turning into another story about him."

"I won't say anything to anyone. But I have a lot I'm going to say to him."

Tim came out on the porch holding up his phone. "I tried to tell him that he should give you some time, India, but I don't think he's going to listen."

I sighed. "No. You're right. He won't listen."

I wrapped my arms around my waist. I was cold deep inside. So cold. "He'll be here in about forty-five minutes. It would probably be better for you two if you left."

"No way!" they exclaimed in sync.

I gave a small smile. "Okay then. Who wants more coffee? It's going to be a long night."

CHAPTER FIFTEEN

The next morning, I had an appointment with Dr. Hayden. Waking up later than I should have, I took a fast shower and slipped on jeans and a T-shirt. I practically ran down into the kitchen. Tim was at the table eating breakfast. I stopped short when a woman I didn't know poured him a cup of coffee.

"Hi, Ms. Leigh. I'm Bridgette. Mr. Coventry sent me here to be your cook and housekeeper."

"Hello, Bridgette. But I think there is some mistake."

"Oh, no ma'am. Mr. Coventry said I was to take care of you now. Well, me and Tim."

Shit! Tim had told me last night that Kellan wanted him to stay as my personal protection and driver. I didn't fuss about it because I had been afraid Kellan would have fired Tim because he had stood against him. But this? This was too much.

"I've always taken care of my own house, Bridgette. And the cooking. Kellan doesn't have the authority to hire people for me. I'm sorry."

The little maid looked so downcast that I told her to hang on a second and asked Tim to come with me. We went into my office, and I asked him if he knew Bridgette. He explained that she was also

A TEMPTATION

from New York, that he had known her for about two years, and she was a great person. He also said that Kellan had spoken to her last week about coming down here and working for me.

We went back into the kitchen and joined Bridgette once again. I made it clear to both of them—while I found a travel mug and poured some much needed coffee into it—that we would see how this worked out. But they were to get in touch with Kellan and tell him I would be taking care of their salaries from now on.

Tim got right on his cell and called Kellan. Walking out, not wanting to hear the conversation between the men, I went into the living room to collect my purse and laptop. Before I started to turn to go back to the kitchen, Tim was there, saying that Kellan wanted to talk to me. I shook my head, telling him I had nothing to say and that we needed to leave as I was going to be late. Tim got back on the phone relaying while I went to retrieve my travel mug and tell Bridgette that we shouldn't be too long. Tim stopped me again, saying Kellan wanted to know what the doctor had to say after the appointment.

Trying to keep my temper in check, I said I wasn't trying to be rude, but Kellan need not concern himself with anything going on with me. I winced when Tim held his phone away from his ear. I could plainly hear how loud and angry Kellan was. Oh well. I didn't need to worry about his anger anymore.

I went outside, walking toward my Mustang. Tim stopped me and led me over to a Cadillac SUV with darkly tinted windows.

Ten minutes later, we were pulling up to Dr. Hayden's office. I signed in at the reception window and had barely sat down when I was called back. Tim stopped me and handed me some papers he pulled out of his back pocket. They were Dr. Howard's report and findings.

After the nurse took my vitals, I was shown into the small exam room. I read over all the posters on the wall, just to have something to do, and had picked up a brochure when Dr. Hayden walked in.

"Hi, my girl. What brings you in?"

I smiled at the elderly doctor. He looked all crooked as usual, from his white coat to his glasses and stethoscope.

I explained what had happened in California and told him the reason for it. I gave him the papers and waited while he went over them. He looked at me when he had finished, saying the anemia was very slight, and the iron supplement and diet was the right way to go. However, he did want to monitor with a blood test every six months.

He said absolutely not to the sleeping pills that had been prescribed, explaining to me that it was Valium he always put me on—a very low dose, in fact. Dr. Hayden went on to say that I had lost weight, and while I would probably never be a large person, I was becoming too scrawny. I needed to address whatever was causing the stress.

It was on the tip of my tongue to tell him the problem no longer existed, when we heard the commotion.

"Sir, you cannot be back here."

That was Dr. Hayden's nurse's voice. I had a bad feeling I knew whom she was talking to. Sure enough, Kellan came barging through the door. The nurse was behind him, and Tim was behind her. How had Kellan made it here so fast? I swear the man was bipolar! I put my face in my hands and willed everyone to disappear.

"Doctor, I'm sorry," Dr. Hayden's nurse explained. "We couldn't stop him. Should I call the authorities?"

"It's all right, Lisa. I'll take it from here." The nurse turned. "And Lisa?" She stopped. "Don't call anyone." The nurse shot Kellan one last dirty look then went out the door.

"Now, young man," Dr. Hayden said as he turned to Kellan, "I would imagine you would be with India."

I removed my hands from my face. No such luck. They were still there.

"Hello, doctor," Kellan said, holding his hand out. They introduced themselves.

"So what can I do for you, Mr. Coventry?"

"I want to know the state of Ms. Leigh's health." It was a demand, not a question.

"Now I can't give you that information unless India says I can."

Kellan gave me a very angry look, which dared me to say the doctor couldn't tell him. I indicated with my hand that he could

A TEMPTATION

tell Kellan. I just wanted him to hurry so Kellan would leave. I was beyond embarrassed.

While the doctor spoke to him, I looked at Kellan. It wasn't fair. He was still as gorgeous as ever. And except for being angry, he didn't seem the worse for wear with our breakup.

"So does she need to take it easy like Dr. Howard said?"

"She needs to take it slower, and she needs to put on some weight. But most of all, she needs to deal with the stress, which I gather would be you."

"It's all right, Dr. Hayden. That isn't an issue any longer," I said.

"No?" Dr. Hayden smiled at me. "You could have fooled me."

"It really isn't," I stressed. "We aren't going to see each other anymore."

"No, India," Kellan said angrily to me. "You said sex. No sex because of the"—he waved his hand around—"other thing. It does not mean that I stop caring or taking care of things."

He was so arrogant. *How dare he throw out my sex life publicly?* My anger exploded.

"The hell you will!" I hopped off the exam table. "You made your decision, Kellan. You can't have half measures. My life is just that. My. Life. It doesn't concern you." I poked him in the chest with my finger.

"I made myself clear last night. But as usual, you want to call all of the shots. Well, you're not. Not with me."

He narrowed his eyes at me. "You want to make a bet, India?"

"No," I told him. I walked over to the chair where I had laid my purse and laptop. Picking them up, I asked Dr. Hayden if he was finished. He stated that I had to come back in two weeks for the first blood test and so he could check my weight. I thanked him then turned to Kellan.

"No, I don't want to make a bet, Kellan. You made your choice. It's done. I'm done."

"Not by a long shot, baby."

Arrgh! I gritted my teeth, shook my head, turned on my heel, and walked out of the room. I paid my copayment, got my prescription and my next appointment time, then went outside and waited by the car for Tim.

Kellan and Tim came out a few moments later. They stood to the side, talking. Well, Kellan was talking; Tim was just shaking his head.

Tim came over and opened my door for me then went around to the driver's side. I went to close the door, but Kellan grabbed the side of it, preventing me. He stood as close to me as he could get with the car seat in his way. He ran his fingers lightly down my face.

"We are not over, India. We will never be over. You're mine." He gazed intensely into my eyes. "It will just be a little different for right now until I can figure things out."

"No, Kellan." I pulled away from him, out of his reach. "My life is my own. You live your life the way you see fit. I have no place there. I don't want a place there. You know that. So this is futile. Let it go."

"I will never let you go, India. You can fight all you like, but it's wasted effort. It will all work out." He backed up and closed the door of the SUV. I didn't look back at him. He could think whatever he wanted. I was going to be doing whatever I wished. Kellan was no longer an issue as far as I was concerned. His lifestyle, which he was still leading, saw to that. He couldn't have it both ways no matter what he thought. He needed to get that through his head as soon as possible. Besides, I couldn't take seeing and hearing about his other life.

"You know, Tim," I spoke to him on our way back home, "because Kellan has to be ruthless in his business dealings and has to govern all those people and responsibilities with an iron fist, and he also has to be the same way with those…extracurricular activities? Well, I think he feels that if he takes that same stand with everything, it will fall where and how he wants it. Because people are so blindsided by all his wealth, and usually that's the only thing they want from him, they cave to his conditions.

"But that won't work with me. Not the attitude. Not the bullying. I had only wanted Kellan. Not his prestige. I've never been impressed by it. Definitely not his money. Just him. All the different

A TEMPTATION

sides of him, save one. That's what I had wanted. A normal relationship between a man and a woman."

"I don't think he knows what that is, India. And I believe the feelings that he feels for you—feelings that he has never felt before—scare him. It's like if he puts you in a box, and he can control that box, then it, you, can't hurt him. And can't leave him." He looked at me from the rearview mirror. "Look. You and I both know nothing can survive like that."

I really didn't know what to make of Kellan's reasoning. How could he think that by just cutting out the sex part of our relationship, but he continued to carry on his life as he always had, there was still an us?

After we arrived home, Tim, Bridgette, and I discussed how we would carry on together. They both told me that Kellan said in no uncertain terms were their salaries to be paid by me. That because he was the one that wanted the peace of mind they gave him by being here and taking care of me, it was his responsibility. Also, that way they would still have their benefits covered by Coventry Industries.

I relented. I wasn't going to fight this issue anymore. It would be a waste of breath. But if they or Kellan thought that because of it, they would report my comings and goings, the deal was off. And they would have to return to Kellan. They agreed to my terms.

I said I would get debit cards for them to cover the expenses for the SUV, and for Bridgette to make purchases for the house. If they needed anything else, to let me know. Also, they didn't have to wear their Coventry uniforms unless they wanted to, that I was really laid-back.

It would take some getting used to, having these two people so close in my life. I already thought the world of Tim. Hopefully, I would feel the same way about Bridgette.

As for Kellan, I wasn't going to think about that anymore. No matter what he said, I was not having a relationship on those terms. Anything that could have been between us was over. My head and heart couldn't take Kellan's choices.

CHAPTER SIXTEEN

Two weeks later, on a Saturday night, Bridgette and I were cooking. We were having a big crawfish boil tomorrow. Bridgette didn't know how to cook Cajun food, and I didn't bake, so we made a good team. I had been cooking gumbo all day and night, my grandmother's recipe. Bridgette was baking cakes, pies, and cookies. We had also made a lot of different salads.

Tim had cut and weed-whacked the yard yesterday. He had taken over the yard work, saying he didn't have enough to do. My enterprise of one was not up to Coventry Industries. I had one condition to this venture. It was that I paid him what I usually paid the landscaping company. He tried to argue, but I was adamant. In the end, I was the winner of this small debate. But hey! You have to celebrate the little victories. Sometimes they are all you get.

Tim was also going to pick up the two hundred pounds of live crawfish early tomorrow morning. We had already set up the four large cookers outside. Four large ice chests were out there, waiting for all the beer and soft drinks. The tables were set up and ready to go.

Bridgette and Tim had given me some grief when I said they would be out there with my friends, as friends. They did not seem to think that was appropriate since they worked for me.

A TEMPTATION

I explained that my friends and I had friends that had all sorts of jobs. They didn't come from money, nor did they have a lot of it. This would be quite different from Kellan's social class, and they would be very welcome. Besides, this was their home now. They had more right to be there than my other friends.

Bridgette had burst out crying. I didn't know what to do, so I just said that I felt she and Tim had become like family to me, and to please stop crying or she would make me cry. Tim had gone out the door saying he definitely couldn't take both of us blubbering. That turned her tears to laughter.

We had things to celebrate tomorrow. Wednesday, I had received a clean bill of health from Dr. Hayden. I had gained a pound, and my blood pressure was up a little. I just had to go for the blood test every six months. It was all good.

With Bridgette and Tim here, I had very little to do at home. As a result, I had finished my second book, months ahead of schedule. In return, that would make my third book I was starting now ahead of schedule also.

I had not seen or heard from Kellan since he had stormed into Dr. Hayden's office. It was for the best. If only my heart would listen. Everything had been easier before I had known him. That saying "knowledge is power"? In this instant, I would say bull. I would go with "ignorance is bliss." What I hadn't known, I couldn't miss.

When the gumbo was finished, Tim put the two large pots into the extra refrigerator in the utility room. I took myself off to bed.

After taking a long shower, I climbed into bed and cried myself to sleep. It's what always happened when I thought about Kellan. I dreamed about Kellan that night for the first time in two weeks.

I was naked, laid out in the middle of his huge bed. Kellan was standing beside the bed. He leaned down and took my mouth in a searing kiss. God, I had missed this. I went to wrap my arms around his neck, but he grabbed my wrists and pinned them down above my head. When he ended the kiss, he released my wrists. I wanted to touch him. I started to reach out to him, but my arms were still pinned. I pulled, but it was no use. I twisted my neck to see what was pinning my arms and found that they were cuffed to the headboard of his bed.

"Kellan?"

"Hush, baby," he whispered. "You're okay. I've got you."

He ran his fingers lightly down my body, over my breasts and down my belly and hips. He did not go near my sex but went down both my legs at one time. Stopping at my ankles, he gripped them in his hands and spread my legs wide. The next thing I knew, my left ankle was cuffed to one side of the footboard. Before he could cuff the right, I pulled my leg out of his grasp.

"No!" I yelled. "I don't like this, Kellan. Let me go. Now."

He caught my right leg again and cuffed that ankle. "You're not calling the shots this time."

I couldn't move. I yanked and pulled both my arms and legs.

"Be still, India. You're going to hurt yourself."

"I'll be still when you release me. I'm not one of your subs, Kellan. You can't treat me like this."

"I don't treat my subs like this, baby. This is all about pleasure. Your pleasure. But I will throw in some lessons."

I was panicking. "Lessons? What are you talking about?"

He came back to the head of the bed and opened the drawer in the nightstand, taking out a couple of boxes and placing them next to me on the bed. "I am going to study and learn your body so well that no one else will ever satisfy you." He ran his hands up the inside of my thighs, close to my sex.

"Fine, Kellan. Whatever you say. Just please release me. You can do this without me being restrained."

"No, baby, I can't. This lesson—" His fingers dipped in between my folds, fluttering over my clit. Then one finger rimmed my opening, and I gasped. "The lesson for you will be to start placing your trust in me."

Kellan removed his hands from my body and slowly removed his clothes. He was fully erect, his body so hard and defined he took my breath away.

He knelt between my thighs. "You are so pink and pretty," he purred.

A TEMPTATION

I had never felt so vulnerable in my life.

Turning, he fiddled with something down by the footboard. When he turned back to me, he pushed my legs up to my bottom. My feet planted flat on the bed, my knees pointing to the ceiling.

I grew wet between my thighs. Even with all this apprehension, I was so aroused. I wanted this man as I wanted my next breath.

Kellan leaned down and quickly placed a kiss on my mound. When he straightened back up, he opened one of the boxes he had placed on the bed. It was a bottle of some sort of oil. He dabbed some onto one of his palms then rubbed his hands together.

He inserted two fingers inside of me and explored. Warmth exploded inside me wherever his fingers touched. What was that oil?

He gently scraped his fingers up and down my front vaginal wall. A moan escaped me, and my legs fell farther apart shamelessly. I twisted and wiggled, my body coiling tight. I needed…He inserted a third finger and tickled against that same wall. I detonated, breaking apart into a million pieces. My climax was so strong I was afraid I would never return to my body. I screamed Kellan's name.

"Shh, baby," he soothed me.

Kellan experimented with that oil all over my body. He brought me in so many ways I couldn't think. When he finally entered me with that magnificent cock, I was so sensitized that I climaxed before he was fully inside me. My sex rippled around his penis, the muscles tightly gripping him and sucking him in deeper.

"Oh sweet Jesus!" Kellan shouted as he came inside me.

Jerking instantly awake, I sat straight up in bed. My hands were searching for Kellan. I looked around. This was my bedroom. Kellan wasn't here. It had been a dream. Just another dream.

I got out of bed and went into the bathroom, splashing my face with cold water. Looking at my reflection in the mirror above the sink, I could see that my eyes looked haunted. My mind knew that I had made the right decision with Kellan. My heart and body, however, wanted and missed him.

Knowing there was no way I would be able to go back to sleep, I went down to the kitchen and put the coffee on. I would get an early start on the crawfish boil.

By one in the afternoon, my house and yard were filled with friends and neighbors. There were at least fifty people, laughing, talking, eating, drinking, and having a great time. There was even a comical volleyball game taking place on one side of the yard.

I had gone back into the kitchen to get more Styrofoam plates when the doorbell rang.

There was a serious card game going on in the dining room. Passing by on my way to answer the door, I saw Tim starting to rise from one of the dining room chairs. I waved him back down. Normally, Tim would have argued the point; that he didn't attested to how serious the game was.

When I opened the front door, I found William, Kathy's older brother, on the other side. I hadn't seen him since Christmas dinner at their parents' house.

"Will!" I exclaimed, hugging him. "I'm so happy you could make it. I don't get to see you nearly enough."

William pulled back and took a long look at me. I was wearing black jean shorts and a red-and-black halter top with smart black sandals that I purchased last week, just to wear with this outfit.

"You're just as beautiful as ever, kid."

I chuckled. "You're only six years older than Kathy, Will. When are you going to stop calling me kid?"

"Never." he laughed. "India, this is Devyn Troyer. He's a friend of mine from New York."

I hadn't noticed the man with Will until that moment. He had been standing at one corner of the porch, looking out over the yard and bayou that could be seen from there.

The man in question turned when he heard his name. As he walked toward us, I noticed the same predatory walk that Kellan had.

I looked up at him as he approached. Okay. I am such a superficial bitch. I hadn't known that about myself until this moment. This man was gorgeous. He could give Kellan a run for his money.

"I hope you don't mind that I tagged along with William?" he asked once he stopped in front of me.

"Not at all, Mr. Troyer. Any friend of Wills is welcome."

A TEMPTATION

I held my hand out to him. As he clasped my hand, I noticed his darkly tanned skin. I had already noted his wavy chestnut hair. His eyes were a rich dark brown, and they were framed by long, thick eyelashes.

The look in those eyes held interest as his gaze took me in. It was a more calculated look than Kellan's.

I had to stop this—stop thinking about Kellan and comparing other men to him. It was ridiculous.

"It's Devyn." He released my hand. "My name is Devyn."

"Okay, Devyn. Y'all come in."

They followed me in. I introduced Devyn to others as we made our way to the back. I saw Tim do a double take as we passed the dining room. Hmm. I didn't have a clue what that was about. I showed Will and Devyn out the back door, told them to have a good time, then I went back to mingle.

I went over to Kathy when I spotted her. "Your brother's here. And he's brought a friend."

"Female?" she asked, her eyes sparkling with interest.

"Nope. A guy. A friend of his from New York. Devyn Troyer?"

"Yeah. I've only met him once. Years ago. They went to Harvard together." We walked over to one of the ice chests so Kathy could grab another beer. "Is he still hot?" she asked, wiggling her eyebrows.

"Oh yeah," I said, laughing at her expression. "That he is."

Tim came up to us and put a cell phone in my hand. If I had been paying attention, I would have seen it wasn't mine and wouldn't have spoken into it.

"Stay away from Devyn Troyer, India," Kellan growled at me through the phone before I even finished saying hello.

I walked away so no one could overhear this conversation. "I don't want to talk to you, Kellan. Go back to whatever or whoever you're doing."

"I'm serious, India. This isn't about me being jealous."

Kathy and Tim walked over to me. I gave Tim a very dirty look. He held his hands up, palms out, telling me he had nothing to do with this.

"I don't care what it's about, Kellan. I'm not having this conversation with you again."

"Goddamn it, India!" he yelled so loud I held the phone away from my ear. "I've been in New York for almost three weeks, stuck in meetings. But I swear, if you don't stay away from him, I'll be back down there so fast—"

I tossed the phone back to Tim. There was no way I was getting into a screaming match with Kellan while I had all these people here. I walked back over to the ice chest, grabbed a Corona, and drank half of it before coming up for air. Damn, he could piss me off faster and worse than anyone I had ever known.

"Sorry, India," Tim said as he walked up to me. "He called, and I asked him if there was anything I needed to know about Devyn Troyer besides them being business rivals. He asked why and you know the rest." He shrugged his big shoulders.

"Of all the days for him to call." I shook my head. "It's like he has radar that tells him just when he can piss me off the most."

"India, he calls every day to make sure you're all right." Tim said. "I never said anything to you because I didn't want to upset you."

"I understand." I started to turn away but thought of something. "Why would you ask Kellan if there was more going on between him and Devyn than being business rivals?"

"Because he hates the man, India. Absolutely despises him. I have never known him to react like that to another person, nor has anyone else that works for him."

I nodded. "Thanks, Tim."

I turned and walked right into someone's chest. Strong hands wrapped around my waist and steadied me. I raised my eyes. *Oh great!* Devyn. He had to have heard that conversation.

"Are you all right?" Devyn asked me.

"Yes. Just clumsy." I stepped back from him. "I'm sorry you overheard that. It was very rude of me."

"You have nothing to apologize for. I am very aware of Kellan Coventry's opinion of me. Not something I lose any sleep over."

Devyn shifted his gaze to Tim. "Don't you work for Coventry?" he asked him.

"And for Ms. Leigh," Tim stated.

"Well, isn't that interesting. I've never known Kellan to share well."

Devyn's attention shifted back to me. There was a strange intense look in his eyes. "If I may be so rude, are you involved with Coventry, India?"

I cocked my head to the side. What was his deal? "No, I'm not. But I won't listen to anything derogatory about him."

Devyn chuckled. "The last thing I want to do with you is talk about Kellan Coventry."

Tim started toward Devyn, not at all happy with his suggestive comment. I turned and placed my hand on Tim's chest to keep him from going any closer to Devyn.

"You watch your mouth," Tim growled.

"This is none of your concern. Run along now. I want a private word with your employer." He moved his hand in a shooing motion.

Tim's eyes narrowed dangerously.

"It's all right, Tim. Go on. I would like a word with Mr. Troyer also."

"Okay," Tim said reluctantly. "But I won't be far." As he said the last, he gave Devyn an ominous look. He walked only yards away, turned, crossed his arms over his chest, and didn't take his eyes off of Devyn.

"How dare you?" I turned on Devyn. "What gives you the right to talk to him that way."

"He was in my way. Besides, he is just an employee."

"He is not just an employee, you arrogant ass." This man might look good, but that was about the only thing good about him. I didn't like him. "Tim Dalton is a friend. But even if he was just my employee, you still wouldn't have the right to treat him with such disrespect."

He narrowed his eyes at me. "I don't put up with disrespect from women, India. You would do well to remember that."

My eyes widened. "Was that a threat, Mr. Troyer?"

"Not at all, Ms. Leigh," he said snidely. "Stating a fact." With that, he turned and walked off.

"Are you all right, India?" Tim asked as he walked back over to me.

"Yeah," I sighed. "I hate to admit it, but this is one time I agree with Kellan. There is something seriously wrong with that man. Do I have a sign on my back advertising for weird men or what?"

Tim chuckled and put his arm around my shoulders. "Come on. I'll buy you a beer, you strange lady you."

CHAPTER SEVENTEEN

The last person had left last night at eight. I was exhausted. After Tim, Bridgette, and I put the food that was left up, I declared that everything else could wait until tomorrow. I took a long, hot shower, fell into bed, and was asleep before my head hit the pillow. Dream-free.

The next morning, I woke up at five thirty and felt great. It's a wonder what a little sleep would do. I got out of bed, pulling old shorts and a T-shirt out of my dresser, washed my face, brushed my teeth, and got dressed. I was the only one awake. I made coffee and took a cup out with me on the back porch. What a mess.

Before long, I heard Bridgette puttering around in the kitchen. A few minutes later, I heard Tim. Bridgette giggled then sighed. Curious, I walked over and peered into the glass on the back door. Tim was standing behind Bridgette. They were facing the stove and ovens, which put them sideways to my gaze. Bridgette's head rested back against Tim. He was kissing down her neck, and as I watched, he started caressing her breast.

Okay! I tiptoed away from the door and went back to my spot by the railing. A voyeur I'm not. Tim and Bridgette? Wow. I waited about ten minutes, making a lot of noise, before going back into the kitchen.

"Good morning," Tim said. "I didn't know you were awake already."

I would have loved to have teased him. But as red as Tim's face was, I didn't want to embarrass him further.

"Just came in for another cup of coffee before I start tackling the backyard."

"I'll come out and help," Tim said.

I motioned to the kitchen table. "Have your breakfast first." I went into the walk-in pantry, brought out a large box of trash bags, refilled my coffee and then headed back out.

Tim and I finished in the yard at around one that afternoon. I was hot and sweaty and wanted a shower. Before I headed inside, I turned to Tim, who was getting ready to take all the garbage bags to the street for pickup.

"I have a formal dinner to go to Wednesday night. Since you have to attend with me, I was wondering if you would like to bring Bridgette. I have two extra tickets." Tim's eyes grew wide as he stared at me.

"You do have something to wear?" I went on pretending not to notice his discomfort. "I mean, with all Kellan's formal engagements, I would assume you did."

"A-a tux," he stuttered. "I have a tux. But why are you suggesting the Bridgette thing?"

"Come on, Tim. The house isn't that big." I chuckled as I watched his face turn beet red.

Later that afternoon, Bridgette came into my office all excited. Tim had told her about the dinner, and she was honored that I had thought about her. She also hoped that their relationship would not cause a problem. I said not at all. She giggled and hugged me then said she was off to find a dress.

I wished Noah was back so he could go with me. Wait! Will. I'll call Will, and maybe he wouldn't have a date. I knew his parents wouldn't let him get out of going since he was in town.

A TEMPTATION

I called his cell, and he picked up after the first ring. "India! Is anything wrong?" I rarely called him, but it had not occurred to me that he would think there was a problem.

"No. No, there is nothing wrong. I was just wondering if you were going to the arts benefit dinner Wednesday night."

"You gave me a scare, kid."

I winced. "Sorry."

"Unfortunately, I have to attend Wednesday night. Why?"

"Well, I don't want to date anyone right now. I thought if you didn't have a date…would it be too much to ask if we went together?"

"That's the best offer I've had in a long time. I'm not with anyone at the moment. I'm tired of them all wanting commitments. I'm not ready, nor do I want a forever kind of thing right now."

We talked a little longer about the pitfalls of dating then made our plans for Wednesday night. I felt better when I ended the call. Now I wouldn't feel like a sore thumb.

Wednesday night came in the blink of an eye. I had taken Bridgette with me that morning. We had our hair, nails, and toenails done. When we got back late that afternoon, I soaked in the bathtub, the water liberally sprinkled with my jasmine bath oil. I shaved my legs while I was in there and vaguely wondered why I was going through all this trouble.

My dress was hanging in a garment bag from the top of my closet door. I walked to the bed and slid on my red lace thong. I couldn't wear a bra with this dress. Taking the dress out of the garment bag, I once again thought what a beautiful gown it was. It was, without a doubt, the most sensual piece of clothing I had ever owned.

I had purchased it with Kellan in mind, intending to ask him to the event. But that was before. *Oh well.* I shrugged. As much as this gown cost, I was wearing it.

I hadn't heard from Kellan since his tirade on the phone Sunday. That was a good thing, but surprising.

I stepped into the gorgeous red gown, pulling it up over my breasts. It dragged to the floor, but that would be taken care of by the matching three-inch fuck-me stilettos. I held it off the floor as I walked over to the cheval mirror.

Oh. My. God. Did I really have enough nerve to wear this? I knew others did it all the time, but not me. Then again, I wanted my life to change, did I not? My hair had been piled on top of my head in a riot of curls. So there was nothing to impede all the skin the gown left bare.

There was embroidery with tiny glass beads over the entire gown. It was sleeveless, and in front, it V'd down to right past my belly button. It had a tiny gold buckle that held the two sides together, right between my breasts. I picked up the hand mirror off of my dresser then looked back into the cheval mirror through the hand mirror.

The back hung, draped open to right above my ass. A thin, silk-covered piece of elastic ran from one side to the other. It's main purpose? To keep my boobs from hanging out of the sides of the gown. I turned to the side, eyeing the slit that ran up from my ankle to my upper right thigh.

The doorbell rang. Too late to change now. The only jewelry I wore was a solitaire diamond on a delicate gold chain around my neck, small diamond hoop earrings, and my mother's diamond waterfall ring. Putting on my shoes and grabbing my matching red silk clutch, I walked out of my bedroom. I heard my friend's voices as I descended the stairs, Bridgette sounding so excited, with the subdued voices of William and Tim.

As I neared the bottom of the stairway, Tim looked up, and his mouth dropped open. Will and Bridgette turned to see what the problem was, and they looked stunned.

"Okay. That does it. I'm going to change. Y'all will just have to wait," I said over my shoulder. I heard someone on the stairs behind me. I didn't stop until a hand grabbed my arm. Turning my head, I saw it was Will.

"Don't you dare change, India." I had never seen Will so serious. I was sure he was with business and such, but with me, he had always been playful.

"You are the most beautiful woman I have ever seen." His eyes roamed over me as though he were seeing me for the first time. "I always thought of you as another kid sister. For the first time, I'm very glad you're not."

A TEMPTATION

I felt myself blushing. I gave a small uncomfortable laugh. "Does that mean you will stop calling me kid?"

"Hell yeah," he responded.

"For that, I won't change."

We walked out to the limo, arm in arm, Tim and Bridgette following behind us. The driver opened the door for Will and me then went around to the other side to open the door for Tim and Bridgette. We four sat together on one seat. Across from us were Lucas—Kathy's boyfriend—then Kathy and, unfortunately, Devyn Troyer.

"Statement much?" Kathy asked me with raised brows.

"Most definitely," I answered with a shit-eating grin.

"It's about time!" She rubbed her hands together in wicked glee. "I can't wait to see the green come out on all those bitches."

"You're absolutely stunning, Ms. Leigh," Devyn said huskily.

I shivered. The look in his eyes scared me.

"Are you chilly, India?" Will asked.

I shook my head, trying to clear out the intrusive feeling. "No. I'm fine, Will. Thank you."

Will poured champagne and handed the glasses around. He raised his glass. "To good friends."

Before long, we were in front of the Marriott Hotel on Canal Street. Will exited the limo then extended his hand to me. When I got out, he dropped his hand, placing it on the small of my back.

I put my show face on as the flashbulbs went off. I hated this part. In fact, it was the reason I never went to any of the other causes I championed. The arts, however, I had to attend because I was very involved.

The gala was being held in the massive 27,089-square-foot hotel ballroom. It had been divided with the tables and podium on one end, the band and dance floor on the other. Our party was led to a front table where three other couples were already seated. These couples were the reason there was an arts program. As we reached the table, the three gentlemen already seated, rose. Included in the trio was Mr. Grey Pichon, Kathy and Will's father.

It was very nice through dinner. The food was excellent and the company great. We laughed and caught up with the elder Pichons.

When the last of the dishes were removed, Grey Pichon went up to the podium.

"Good evening," he said into the microphone in his booming voice. "Thank you all for being here tonight and for the continuing support." As the room quieted, and everyone's attention focused on Mr. Pichon, he continued. "We want to take this time to offer our thanks to one of us that not only donates her money but a great deal of her time. Without this outstanding young lady, we would not have the arts classes. Through them, some of our recipients have achieved far-reaching goals with their talents.

"Mrs. Traci Allgood, my co-chair, will join me to give this exceptional young woman a small token of our esteem."

I was sipping wine and listening to Will telling an amusing story about a coworker, so I was only half paying attention to what was being said at the podium.

"India," Kat hissed at me. "I think you should pay attention to what's being said up there."

"What?" I asked.

"So without further ado," Mrs. Allgood was saying, "we give you our own Ms. India Leigh."

I just about spit the wine that was in my mouth all over the table. I swallowed slowly and started shaking my head. Everyone was standing and applauding. William reached a hand down to me and brought me to my feet. "I'm not going up there, Will."

"You have to." He smiled at me and leaned in to whisper, "Just pretend they're all naked."

"Ew. That's just gross," I said, scrunching up my nose. He laughed and gave me a little push. With dread, I went up to the podium.

Mrs. Allgood handed me a beautifully styled plaque, and the applause increased. As I stood in front of the mic, waiting for the applause to die down, I looked out at all the faces. My eyes froze on the one person I dreaded seeing. Kellan.

His look, even at this distance, felt as though it was burning through me. He didn't look happy. Next to him was a stunning blonde woman and, of course, Alexis and Deric. I swiftly removed my gaze. Who Kellan was with was none of my business.

A TEMPTATION

"Thank you for this." I spoke clearly into the mic when the applause ended, and raised the plaque. "This really doesn't belong to me alone. It also belongs to all of the other artists that instruct our recipients. Also to the recipients themselves, whom our chairman has spoken about. Through diligence and hard work, some have become published writers, still others, commissioned artists. Most of all, it belongs to all of you. Who donates all the funds for which everything that we do in and with the arts program would not be possible. So I will accept this for us all."

I walked back down to the table through the sound of thundering applause. Kathy, Will, and the rest of my friends congratulated me with excited hugs. Placing the plaque on the table, I announced to no one, or maybe everyone, that I was going to the bar for a drink.

"India, I'll go," Will spoke up. "Another glass of wine?"

I snorted. "After that? Wine is not going to cut it, Will, and I would really like to step away for a minute. But thanks." Turning quickly, I headed to the bar. I wanted to be alone. Well, as alone as one could be in a room with hundreds of other people. Before I had gotten even halfway to the bar, someone grabbed me roughly by the arm and dragged me out of the ballroom.

"Hey," I squealed as my back was roughly pressed against a wall in the hallway outside the ballroom. I looked up at the face of my would-be aggressor. I rolled my eyes. I should have known.

"What the fuck are you wearing?" Kellan snarled down at me.

I really was at a loss for words. I knew this deranged man didn't really want to talk about my gown. When his hands tightened on my upper arms, I became very angry.

"Get your hands off of me, Mr. Coventry!" I demanded out of gritted teeth.

"No, Ms. Leigh," he snapped back. "I want to know who you're fucking."

"What?" I asked amazed. My God! What was wrong with this man? Why would he ask me something like this? I couldn't take this. As much as I had wanted him, as much as I had wanted to be enough for him so he wouldn't need the others, it was all too much.

"I demand to know India." He shook me as he said this. "I demand you tell me who thinks he can touch what's mine."

"I. Am. Not. Yours!" I yelled. "How dare you treat me like this?"

"You are mine, India. How dare you wear a come-fuck-me dress like a whore!"

I snatched my right arm away from him, and before I knew what I intended to do, I slapped him as hard as I could. My eyes widened at the handprint I left on his face.

Kellan grabbed my arm again and took my lips in a hard, rough, aggressive kiss. He plunged his tongue into my mouth without tenderness, but with anger and dominance.

Tears started filling my eyes. Fuck this! No way am I wasting any more tears on Kellan Coventry. I brought my teeth down on his tongue.

"Son of a bitch!" he yelled as he jerked back, bringing a hand up to his mouth.

I pulled my remaining arm out of his grasp and stumbled away from him.

CHAPTER EIGHTEEN

I returned to my friends with a double Grey Goose and cranberry, downing it before my butt hit the chair. Signaling the waitress, I ordered two double Grey Goose and cranberry. When the waitress was seeing what the others wanted to drink, Kathy leaned across the table.

"India. What is it? What's going on?"

"I can't talk about it right now, Kat."

"You mean you won't." She shook her head. "You're not acting like yourself, and your hands are shaking. What happened?"

"Not what. *Who*. I don't want any more trouble here." I stared her down. "I know you're worried. I swear I will tell you everything when we leave." Kathy put both her hands up, palms facing me in a surrender fashion, and sat back down.

When my drinks arrived, I turned the first one up, downing it in two seconds. Picking up the second glass, I looked up and caught everyone staring at me. "What?" I asked.

Will leaned into me. "Are you all right?"

Looking into his worried eyes, eyes that looked so much like his sister's, I knew I was going to lose it. Not wanting to blubber in front of my friends, and everyone else in the ballroom, I stood up so fast I knocked my chair over.

"I-I'm sorry," I started. "I'll be back."

Will, Kathy, Lucas, Tim, and Bridgette all stood, saying they would come with. "No!" I put my right hand up, took a deep breath, and continued softly. "Please. I won't be long."

I escaped out a side exit from the hallway. I was on the side of the hotel, out of sight from everyone. Leaning my back against the outside wall, not caring about my gown—I hated it now—I closed my eyes, taking several deep breaths.

This was bullshit. Kellan was making me miserable. I wouldn't make the mistake of attending anything else that there was even a possibility he could be there. Being so deep in thought, it took me a while to register that the short hairs on the back of my neck were standing at attention. A prickle of unease shot from my neck down my spine. My eyes shot open, self-preservation at the forefront of my brain. Devyn Troyer stood right before me.

I gasped. "Mr. Troyer. If you don't mind, I would really like to be alone right now."

"Shut your mouth, you whore," he snarled. "You might have everyone else fooled, but not me."

As much as this man frightened me, my temper overruled. "Excuse me?" I yelled at him. "You don't know me, and you damn sure don't get to talk to me like this. Get out of my face, and don't even make the mistake of breathing in my direction."

Pulling at the door I had come out of, my mind must have gone into stupid mode because it couldn't figure out why it refused to open.

"I activated the lock before I closed the door, you stupid whore," he hissed.

What's with these guys calling me whore tonight? I turned to go around the building to get to the front of the hotel. Terrified now, I needed to get to where other people were sure to be. I hadn't made it a foot away before I was roughly stopped by a painful grip on my upper arm. Devyn threw me up against the wall. With the wall behind me and a psycho in my face, it was fight time.

A TEMPTATION

"Let go of me, Devyn." I was shaking so bad I was surprised I could talk. "I don't know who you think you are, but you're in my town, my state, and I know everyone. You'll be in a world of shit if you so much as touch me."

He laughed. It sounded pure evil. "My family's money trumps who you know, bitch."

I hit him, not slapped; I punched him. Right in his smart-ass mouth. "You bitch!" He yelled. His bottom lip was bleeding where his teeth had punctured it.

As if I was a bystander watching a story unfold, I saw him bring his right hand up to his lip. When he brought his hand down, seeing the blood, all reason drained from his face. He backhanded me with that same hand. The blow was so hard I saw stars. Then he brought both his hands up and ripped the whole front of my gown.

Suddenly, he was gone. As if in one of my dreams, I observed a furious Kellan beating the shit out of Devyn Troyer. My back slid slowly down the wall until my butt hit the ground. Arms came around me. A man's jacket was draped over my naked shoulders and breasts.

"No! No one touches her but me." That was Kellan's voice.

"She's in shock." That from Tim. "She needs to go to the hospital."

"I'll have my physician meet us at my house." Then I was in his arms, cradled against his chest.

"We aren't leaving her." That was Kathy. The rest of my friends voiced their agreement.

I don't remember the drive to Kellan's house, don't remember him carrying me up the stairs to his bedroom and placing me on his bed. But I definitely woke up when he went to remove what was left of my gown.

Screaming, I leaped off the other side of the bed and crawled to a corner of his room. I didn't know where I was or who tried to undress me. I curled up into a ball and kept screaming. The door to the room burst open. All of my friends and Kellan's security force poured through.

Kathy immediately was on the floor beside me, pulling me up and into her arms and rocking as though I were a small child.

"Hush now, India," Kathy said gently. "You will make yourself sick."

"What the hell did you do, Coventry?" Will demanded. I had never heard him sound so angry.

At that, I pulled myself out of Kathy's arms and sat up next to her, swiping at the tears on my face that I hadn't realized had fallen. "He didn't do anything, Will. I kind of freaked out. I was confused, thinking it was Devyn."

"It was my fault, India. With what happened tonight, I shouldn't have tried to undress you."

"You did *what?*" Will exploded. "She's our family, you asshole. You don't touch her—"

"Uh, Will," Kathy interrupted her brother, "they are kind of seeing each other. Or were." She shrugged.

"*Were* being the operative word, Kat. He doesn't touch her."

"You're right, Will. No man should touch her right now."

Whoa. Kellan actually agreeing with someone?

"Kathy, will you help her get out of that gown? She can wear this for the time being." He handed Kathy one of his T-shirts, then he and everyone else went out of the room.

Kathy didn't want to, but she left me alone after she helped me undress. I went into Kellan's bathroom and washed my face. I still had a toothbrush here, so I made use of it. Both of those mundane things made me feel more like myself. I walked back into Kellan's bedroom. What had taken place the last time I was here hit me square in the face. I couldn't stay here.

When I got downstairs, I heard voices coming from the kitchen. Following the sounds, I stopped at the threshold when I heard what they were discussing.

"Sorry, Will. I know you think of the man as a friend, but you don't know him. He's dangerous to women. This isn't the first time something like this has happened." I snorted to myself. That was really ironic coming from Kellan.

"Hell. He's nothing to me anymore. Not after what he did to India," Will spat out.

"I had to go to New York a few months ago because of what he did to a…an acquaintance of mine. It took a while for her to heal physically. Mentally? I don't know if she will ever be the same."

"Did she press charges?" Kathy asked.

"No. She was afraid of the publicity. She's from a very well-connected family in New York. She didn't think she could face the embarrassment to her family or the notoriety of what would be revealed about her life."

"Don't you mean her lifestyle, Kellan?" I spoke up. Everyone looked up. They hadn't known I was there. "I don't say that to be rude. What consenting adults do behind closed doors is no one's business. It just makes sense that she wouldn't want her family or the rest of the world knowing.

"Me? I want to forget it ever happened. He can't hurt me any more than he already has. I'm sure he will be sticking to the East Coast from now on."

"You shouldn't be out of bed, India," Tim said, coming up behind me. He looked so concerned, and I was sorry for that.

"Goddamn it, India!" Kellan's outburst had me turning back to him. "What are you doing down here dressed like that?"

I looked down at Kellan's T-shirt that I was wearing. It covered me to the middle of my thighs. I was descent. His words, however, still stung.

"Because I don't have anything else. Duh."

"Sarcasm doesn't become you, baby."

Chastised, I looked up at him, embarrassed. "I'm sorry. You didn't deserve that." I sighed. "Thank you for what you did, but I can't stay here, Kellan."

"You need to see the doctor, baby. He'll be here at any minute. After that, I will take you home."

"I'm fine now, Kellan. I'll see my doctor if I need to."

"Damn it! Quit being so hardheaded." Oh, he was mad now because I didn't just fall in line wherever he wanted to place me. "You need someone to take charge of you. You are not going off half cocked again. That's what landed you in trouble to begin with."

"Oh yeah?" I yelled back. He was the reason that I had put myself in that position. "You're why I had to get out of there by myself. You called me a whore, Kellan. You more than anyone else knows that is so far from the truth."

He put his hands on my shoulders and gazed intensely into my eyes. He looked so exasperated. "I did not call you a whore."

"No. That's right. You just said I looked like one."

My friends got pissed off at that and started objecting. Kellan ignored them as if we were the only ones in the room. "I told you. You're mine, baby. I don't want anyone seeing what is only mine to see."

"There is no us, Kellan. Remember?"

"Semantics, baby," he smirked at me.

"Don't smirk at me, Kellan Coventry." I pulled my shoulders out of his grasp.

"Excuse me," someone said from behind Tim. "The doctor's here."

"Back up to the bedroom, baby."

"I told you that I don't—"

"Now, India," he demanded. His voice dangerously low.

"Argh!" I growled. But I turned on my heel and went back up to Kellan's room.

After the doctor left, saying I was fine, thank you very much, there were demands from my friends to call the police and for me to press charges against Devyn Troyer. Unlike Kellan's friend, there wasn't anything unsavory, past or present, that I was afraid would come to light. But at the end of the day, I didn't want that kind of publicity to run head-to-head with the release of my first book. So I put my foot down and stated in no uncertain terms that I would not be pressing charges.

CHAPTER NINETEEN

True to his word, after getting a clean bill of health, Kellan put me into the back of his car and took me back to Slidell.

"You didn't have to do this, Kellan. I could have gone back with the others."

"Like I would let you go back in that limo dressed only in my T-shirt. Not going to happen." He turned away from the window and faced me. This man that looked out at me from Kellan's gorgeous blue eyes was not the person I was familiar with. His was a tortured soul. Desolate.

"When I saw you with Troyer's hands on you, I wanted to kill him. I probably would have if not for my security detail." He raised his hand and lightly ran his fingers down the left side of my face—that was now bruised and sporting a very fat lip. "I am not going to let anything like this happen again, India. I am not going to let anyone or anything get close enough to even breathe wrong in your direction."

"You can't protect me from everything, Kellan," I whispered.

"I will protect what's mine," he said harshly.

I shook my head and started to open my mouth. He narrowed his eyes at me, and I swallowed what I had been about to say. I didn't want this Kellan pissed at me.

"As long as you're in Slidell, Tim is fine. But—" He put his fingers under my chin, raising my head so he could look deeper into my eyes. He leaned in and rested his forehead against mine. "He goes everywhere with you. And I mean everywhere. No exceptions. You venture out of Slidell, you notify me ahead of time, and you have a detail of three, not including Tim."

"I can't—"

"For once, will you just shut up and listen." He pulled away from me and pointed a finger in front of my face. "You don't have a choice, India. I'm not giving you a choice. Your name is now linked to mine. I'm sorry. It's my fault. I haven't exactly kept it secret how I feel about you."

"Kellan. Listen to yourself." I pushed his hand away from my face. "I'm nothing to you. Besides you screwing me a few times and your caveman attitude towards me, nothing."

He started to open his mouth. "No," I stopped him. "You listen to me now." I waited and watched him argue silently with himself. Then he sat up straighter and nodded at me.

"I have told you that I like you very much. I had wanted to get to know you. But as you already know, I can't. Not with how you're choosing to live. If I let myself get closer to you, the way things are? I'm just asking to get hurt. I'm not going to do that.

"You need to worry about the women you run around with. If, as you say, my name has been linked with yours, it will be quickly forgotten since we're never seen together. In retrospect, Kellan, You don't owe me anything. Nor I you."

"Yeah, well," he said as he chuckled at himself, "I have found that I can't do this. If I have to make a choice between you and the... other? There's no contest. I was afraid I would hurt you if I didn't have the other, and that would destroy me. But look what happened because I wasn't right there to protect you. You're mine. I protect what's mine no matter what I have to do. We have to be together in order for me to do that. I want you with me. In my life. In my bed. In every aspect that is feasibly possible."

Whoa. I'm dumbfounded. I didn't expect this. "Kellan, it's not that simple. This is not how it works. You have been intimate with those other women just five minutes ago. I'm sorry. I don't believe I can get beyond that."

"That's just it, India. I haven't had sex with them. Not since the first time we were together. Not even that day with Alexis at my house. They weren't you, and I didn't want anyone but you."

"That's just semantics, Kellan, and you know it. The act of sex alone doesn't change that fact. Other acts are as intimate. Some even more so."

"Nothing I have done with them, since you, has been even remotely intimate. I have done things with them, I won't lie to you. But nothing sexual."

I didn't even want to know what those acts were. "Kellan," I said, shaking my head, "having a relationship is difficult in itself. One person thinking they have to change themselves or their life in order to keep that relationship, that's a disaster in the making. I'm not asking you to do this, Kellan. I wouldn't. I would be afraid you would wake up one day and hate me because of it."

He lifted one of my hands from my lap. Bringing it up to his lips and turning it over, he placed a kiss tenderly in the center of my palm. I shivered. I could feel that kiss in other intimate places down my body.

"This is my choice, baby. That's a very big difference. I would imagine that if two people were already in a committed relationship and then one tried to change the other, that wouldn't work. I'm coming into this with my eyes wide open.

"You're sweet and innocent. In reality, I should walk away for your own good. But I'm a selfish bastard. I can't do it. I want you, and I want to see where this will take us."

He was stroking his thumb back and forth across my knuckles. God! I wanted him too. Could this work? Was it this simple?

"I'm not saying it will be easy." *What? Could he read my mind now?* "It will be anything but. I'm a hard man, India. I want and demand things my way. I will change my life for you, but you will also have to change your life because of mine. If we work together, I have no doubt we can do this."

"Not that I have a problem with working hard for what I want, but to what degree will I have to change my life?"

"The security for one, India. I have to be out of town for business a lot, and I need to know you're safe. I will make no pretense with you. I will not tolerate disobedience in this. Second, I have found when it comes to you, I am a very jealous and possessive man."

I rolled my eyes. "You don't say," I said dryly.

"Yes, smart-ass. I say. So do well and remember that."

"Hey! If this is your idea of sweet-talking me into this, you have a lot to learn."

"I don't sweet-talk India. I'm trying to tell you my faults." He smiled that panty-melting smile of his. "You'll learn to live with them."

"You think so, huh?" I grinned back at him.

"Yes, I do." He pulled me onto his lap and wrapped his arms around me. In that instant, I felt cherished. Loved.

"By the way," he whispered into my ear, "I didn't screw you. For the first time in my life, I made love to a woman." And with those words, I fell madly in love with Kellan Coventry.

"What do you say, baby? You want to travel this road with me?"

I turned in his lap and tenderly, gently, pressed my lips to his. "Lead on, Macduff," I said.

"You did not just call me a dog?" He laughed. "Oh, Ms. Leigh. Whatever am I going to do with you?"

"I'm sure you can think of something, Mr. Coventry." I smiled shyly at him.

"The possibilities are endless, baby."

My inner alarm clock woke me up before sunrise as usual the next morning. I was lying with my head on Kellan's chest, and he had both his arms wrapped around me. I grinned. I could get used to this.

Very carefully, I eased myself off him and out of his arms. Sitting up, I gazed at his beautiful face. In sleep, he looked so much younger. Peaceful.

A TEMPTATION

After getting dressed in my bathroom so I wouldn't wake him, I made coffee and took a cup with me out to my favorite place. Kellan had been wonderful last night. When we went to bed, he pulled me into his arms, my head pillowed on his chest, and he stroking my hair. It was his way of comforting after everything that happened last night. It felt more intimate than sex. It was perfect.

You would know that I would fall in love with the first man I ever had sex with. And naturally, he had to be an enigma like Kellan Coventry.

Later that morning, I was in my office working. It was seven when Kellan said "knock, knock" at my opened door. He was holding up both hands, each bearing a mug. "Bridgette said you only drink breakfast. I thought I would bring you a cup and see if I could bribe my way in here."

I laughed and motioned him in. "You can bribe me with coffee anytime. Thank you."

Kellan placed the mugs on my desk, pulled a chair over, and sat on the other side.

"You talk in your sleep."

I jerked my eyes up to Kellan's. Oh wow. How embarrassing. I felt the heat in my cheeks. "I know. My grandmother used to tell me that if I did anything wrong, I would tell on myself in my sleep."

"Hey," he said softly, "I didn't mean to embarrass you. Look," he said, changing the subject. "Do you have anything that you can't get out of for a few days?"

I thought that over. "No. Nothing that I can think of."

"I have to be in New York for a meeting Wednesday morning. I cleared the rest of my calendar. I thought we could get away for a few days. Just us. Away from everything. Maybe start over right." He took a sip of his coffee, watching me closely for my reaction.

"Where?" I asked.

Placing his mug back on the desk, he smiled. "It's a surprise."

"Okay." I shrugged. "I'm game.

CHAPTER TWENTY

"Wow." There were no other words. The place was magnificent.

We were in the Caribbean at a private resort. Naturally, we had a suite, a beautiful indoor tropical paradise. But right outside the sliding glass door I was looking out of? Truly God's work of art. Hell! I had been impressed with the flight over on Kellan's private jet. This was absolutely breathtaking.

"Is this yours too?" I asked him over my shoulder.

"Yes." He was just standing in the middle of the suite's living room with his hands in the pocket of his jeans. "Do you like it?"

"Like it? It's magnificent, Kellan."

He chuckled. "Are you hungry?"

"Hell no!" I laughed. Who could think of food with that sand calling my name? "I am going to go buy a bathing suit and hit the beach."

"Everything you need is in the bedroom on your right."

I went into the bedroom, and sure enough, there were bathing suits and lingerie in the dresser. Opening the walk-in closet, there were dresses, shoes, and bags. I turned to go back into the living room and ran smack into Kellan.

A TEMPTATION

"Whoa there." He gripped me by my shoulders to keep me on my feet.

"Who do all the clothes belong to?" My heart was beating so hard I could feel the pulse in my ears. I was so afraid that this might be where Kellan brought all of those, uh, women. If so, I was on the first commercial flight out of there.

He narrowed his eyes at me. I swear the man was a mind reader. "Don't go thinking that way. I have never brought another woman on a trip with me, nor have I purchased clothing for one—besides my aunt that is. Everything is for you."

I pulled out of his grip and glared up at him. "I don't mean to sound like a shrew, and I know your heart was in the right place. But clothes and personal items? That's not your place."

"Everything about and for you, India, is my place."

"No, Kellan. It's not." I put my hands on my hips. "I don't care if you have more money than God. I don't need a keeper. I buy my own shit."

He smiled at me. "I know you don't care about any of this. It's one of the things I love about you." He clasped my face between his hands. "We had this discussion. You're mine. I take care of what's mine."

"But this. It makes me feel like a—"

"Don't even finish that," he interrupted me. "I will spank your ass, India, and not for pleasure."

My eyes widened. "You've got to be joking."

"I told you what was required on your part. I also stressed there would be consequences."

I stepped back. "I'm not into pain and humiliation, Kellan."

"I would never humiliate you, baby, and pain is not something I want to inflict on you. But I will do whatever it takes to have your obedience. That way, I'll know you will heed the important rules that will keep you safe."

I opened my mouth, thought better of it, and promptly closed it once again. This man, the one that was becoming so dear to me, this was what he needed. Total control. I had accepted that, not really knowing what that would entail. I knew he wasn't cruel. To him, this would ensure that he was taking care of me and I was, at all times, safe.

"Okay, okay." I nodded at him. "I'm so not happy about this, but I agreed I would give you peace of mind." I stood up on my tiptoes and placed a brief kiss on his lips. Looking into his beautiful eyes, I smiled. "Thank you," I whispered.

He smiled back at me. "You're quite welcome. Now go change."

I quickly went back into the bedroom and grabbed a beautiful black iridescent, itty-bitty bikini.

Looking into the mirror at my reflection once I had it on, I had to laugh. No way was Kellan going to like this. It would serve him right. I went back into the dresser, pulled out a cover-up, wrapped it around my waist, then went to find Kellan.

We walked hand in hand down to the water's edge. Kellan spread two very large beach towels over the sand. I sank down to my knees on one. The crystal-clear blue-green water was mesmerizing.

"It's amazing," I said, turning to him as he settled down beside me.

"So are you," he responded and kissed the tip of my nose.

I watched as Kellan pulled off his T-shirt. He looked scrumptious bare chested with swim trunks that hung low on his hips. Strong, lean, and tanned. Come to think of it, he was tan all over. No tan lines.

Looking around, I spotted two of Kellan's security team, knowing without a doubt the others weren't that far away. Zack, the big guy from Pensacola Beach, was one of them. I was flabbergasted when I saw that he worked for Kellan.

There were quite a few people on the beach. Most of the women were wearing thong bikinis. Great. Now I wouldn't feel as though I was naked on a public beach. Grinning over at Kellan, I stood, let the cover-up fall, and ran into the water. Laughing out loud when I heard Kellan's curses behind me, I tried to run faster, squealing as I was caught from behind by two strong hands.

Kellan turned me around to face him, his eyes hotly traveling down my body. "India, that suit." He shook his head.

"Hey." I laughed up at him. "All the rest were thongs. I didn't think you would like it if I wore one of those."

"Damn straight I wouldn't. But this isn't much better."

"I didn't buy it," I said, grinning from ear to ear.

"I know, smart-ass."

"Just saying." I chuckled.

"I will make damn sure from now on that I'm very specific about what I want purchased for you."

"I have to tell you, I wouldn't have taken off the cover-up until I saw what the other women weren't wearing."

"Point taken." He leaned down and kissed me. "But you're only to wear it when I'm with you."

Laughing again, I shook my head slowly. "What do I wear when you're not around?"

"Coveralls." He smirked. "I will buy you some."

I cupped some water into my hands and splashed him, then I turned around quickly to try to avoid any retaliation.

"Not so fast, brat." He scooped me up in his arms. "You want to play, baby?" His smile was so wickedly gorgeous as he launched me into the air.

It was Sunday morning, and the first glorious colors of dawn were just streaking across the sky above the Caribbean. I was sitting on the beach with a huge travel mug of coffee, meeting the light of the new day.

I would have loved walking the beach at this time of day, but thought I would make it easier for Kellan's security guys if I sat at the water's edge right outside of our resort suite. Oh, I didn't see the guys this morning. But they were always there. Somewhere.

This was the first dawn that I had been able to greet since we had been here. Kellan had been keeping me extremely busy—not that I was complaining. We went snorkeling, parasailing, and Jet Ski riding. We went sightseeing and shopping. We had romantic dinners and fun picnics. We talked and laughed and enjoyed each other's company.

And sex! Oh heaven, the sex. Even thinking about it made me blush. Kellan was giving me an education, and I reveled in it. He knew just what to do. He played my body like a fine-tuned instrument, knowing exactly which string to strum to bring me, pushing me to the boundaries of my endurance, showing me how a small bite of pain ramped up the pleasure. Of course, I didn't want to think about how he learned all of this. Then again, his past was his past and really was none of my business.

Last night had been all about him. I hugged my knees to my chest, getting goose bumps just thinking about it. I explored every inch of Kellan's body with my hands, lips, tongue, and teeth. He taught me what he liked, and I absolutely loved pleasuring him. Who would have thought that the act of oral sex on a man could make a woman feel so powerful. Licking his rugged cock, sucking it hard, down to the back of my throat. Swallowing all of his essence, taking it into me. Watching him fall apart for me as I did for him.

I sipped my coffee watching the sky lighten. It was so beautiful. Nothing beat watching the dawn come up over my beloved bayou, but seeing it from different locations was indeed wonderful.

"Someone else who likes to watch the sunrise."

That deep voice startled me so badly that I dropped my mug into the sand at my feet. A large tanned hand picked it up and held it out to me. I raised my head as I reached for the mug. He looked like what I imagined a California surfer would look like, shaggy dark blond hair that hung to his shoulders and a golden tan on all his exposed skin.

"I didn't mean to frighten you," surfer dude said, smiling down at me.

"Um—" Regardless of his kind eyes, after the fiasco with Devyn Troyer, I was rather nervous. I stood up quickly, backing up so I could turn swiftly and get back into Kellan's suite.

Surfer guy's hand shot out fast and latched onto my left wrist. The mug hit the ground again. This time, it could stay there. "I really am sorry, miss. Please tell me that you are okay?"

I tried to snatch my wrist out of his grasp. It was no use. His grip was to strong. Hell! Where were those security guys?

"Let go of me," I snarled. I'll be damned if I was going to be treated like this again.

A TEMPTATION

"Get your fucking hands off her!" Kellan growled from behind me. Boy, was he pissed.

Surfer guy let go of my wrist, holding his hands in front of him, palms outward, as Kellan and four of his security team walked up to me. "Hey man, I was only trying to make sure she was all right."

"Step away from Ms. Leigh, sir," one of Kellan's security guys said—Bret, I think his name was, the head of Kellan's security.

Kellan wrapped his hand tightly around my left upper arm. "Let's go, India," he spit out at me.

What? He was mad at me? "Kellan, I—"

"Shut up, India," he said through his gritted teeth.

"Wait a second." I dug my heels in the sand. "You can't be upset at—"

He turned toward me. That phrase that I had read so often in romance novels, "fire flashing from his eyes," now I knew what it meant.

"For all that is holy"—his grip tightened on my arm—"do as you're told and don't say another word."

"Hey!" That was surfer dude running his mouth. "You need to watch how you're treating her, man."

I heard Bret once again talking to surfer guy, but I couldn't make out what was being said because Kellan was just about dragging me back to the suite.

CHAPTER TWENTY-ONE

*K*ellan ushered me into the suite ahead of him through the opened sliding glass door. He closed it with a bang that made me jump. He locked it and then lowered the blinds.

"Obedience, India," he bit out in that dangerously low voice. "What happened to your promise?" He had his back to me, still facing the closed covered doors.

"I didn't go back on my word, Kellan," I said to his back, totally confused.

"Oh no?" He turned and walked over to me. "Then how did that asshole's hands end up on you?"

"Kellan, I was just—"

"Take off your dress, India," he interrupted me.

"Ex-excuse me?" I stuttered, wide eyed. "I don't think—"

"Don't think, India. Do as I say. *Now*. Or I will do it for you."

Okay. This didn't sound like it was going to be fun, but I really didn't want to make him any angrier. I had on a halter sundress. I pulled the tie loose on the neck, sliding the dress down past my hips, and let it puddle on the floor at my feet. Stepping over it, I bent down to pick it up.

"Leave it," Kellan commanded.

A TEMPTATION

Right. I straightened back up, squared my shoulders, and lifted my chin. I was only wearing a thong now, but I'd be damned if I would lower my eyes in shame.

"The thong too, India. And ditch the attitude, or this will go even worse." Now he was scaring me. He went to the bedroom while I was removing my thong. He was back in a second and sat on the edge of the sofa. "Come. Stand in front of me." I slowly walked over to him, stopping about a foot away. He looked up at me then. His eyes cold.

"I am not going to punish you because I want to inflict pain on you." He was talking calmly, but in that soft, dangerous tone. "Neither is it for sexual pleasure. I am going to punish you so you will remember about your safety, first and foremost. And that will save my sanity."

I backed away from him. Was he crazy? "Don't make the mistake of trying to get away from me, India. It will only make your punishment worse."

"Are you crazy?" I was getting angry now. And more than a little bit frightened. I put my hands on my hips and stared right back at him. "I am not a child for you to discipline, Kellan, nor am I one of your women who get off on this. Besides that, I did not break my word to you. I didn't go anywhere. I was sitting by the water right outside the suite, thinking that your security guys were standing back, giving me some privacy."

"You are not a stupid woman, India. Yet you want me to believe that you thought so little of my concern for you, that I would allow that man to put his hands on you before someone intervened? He stood up and got right up in my face. "It killed me what Troyer did to you. Then to see what I saw this morning?" He shook his head slowly. "Only one guard is on duty all of the time. The rest come into play when I notify them. That is, any time I venture out. The same for you now."

I tried to say something, but he cut me off. He held his index finger up in front of my face. "Not another word." He waited until I closed my mouth before he continued. "Believe me, that guard paid a high price for not being where you were. He will be looking for a new job."

I did interrupt then. "Kellan, that's not fair. I didn't know how this worked, but I also do not want to be the cause for someone losing their livelihood."

"Everyone who works for me, India, knows what the consequences are if they're not 100 percent committed to what I want. And as I already stated, you are not a stupid woman. If you didn't think this is how things work, you will remember from now on."

"You cannot truly think to do this, Kellan?" I could not believe this. I had no clue how his mind worked.

"I most definitely do mean this. We have been over this. I told you. I am gone a lot. I need to know you're safe. If I have to beat safety measures into you, I will."

He sat back down on the edge of the sofa and looked up at me. "You agreed to my terms on this relationship. I explained what I needed, and you agreed. Are you going to renege now?"

I stared at him, opening and closing my mouth a few times before I found the power of speech. "I didn't know you meant anything like this. How is this any different than what you do with the others?"

"The others aren't mine, India. You are. I don't care about what they do or don't do, and I wouldn't waste my time worrying about their safety when they aren't with me. They would love this. Not you. But you will remember about your safety because you will not want this to happen again."

What was I supposed to do? I didn't think this was healthy, but on the other hand, he had laid out his terms to me.

"If I can't be sure of you when I'm not with you, India, this is never going to work."

That made my decision for me. I did want to try to have a relationship with him. I walked back over to him. "Come over to my right side, India, and lay across my lap." How humiliating! I did as he instructed, however.

"As I said, I am not doing this for my enjoyment. It is a means to an end. It is important that you understand this." He sounded so

A TEMPTATION

matter-of-fact and impersonal. "Let your hands rest on the floor as much as possible. Do not move them any higher or your punishment will increase. Do you understand?"

I nodded. I mean, what could I say?

"Say it, India!" he commanded.

"I understand."

He wrapped his right leg around both of mine and pressed his left hand between my shoulder blades. That's when I became very frightened. It was just a moment that I heard a swoosh, and fire cracked across my ass. Fuck! That was a belt and it hurt. I started struggling, but Kellan was strong.

"Keep fighting me, India, and this will be worse. As it is, you moved your hands, which I told you not to do for your protection. Your ass can take this, not your hands. I always keep my word, so your strikes will now be harder."

He meant it. Damn, this hurt. But I didn't struggle, and I didn't move my hands. I bit into my bottom lip to keep from crying out. I would not give him the satisfaction. Boy, he was right. I would never forget this. For all my bravado, tears started falling down my face, but I still didn't make a sound.

After what seemed like forever, he stopped. He unwrapped his leg from mine and removed his hand from between my shoulder blades. He went to help me up, but I jumped up too fast.

"No!" I exclaimed, not facing him. "Don't touch me!" I ran into the bedroom, slamming the door. Climbing onto the bed, I pulled the covers over my head and cried myself to sleep.

I was awakened by my burning ass. Kellan was sitting on the side of the bed where I lay. The bedside lamp was on. My abused backside was uncovered, and he was applying some sort of ointment. It wasn't a pleasant feeling, so I tried to move away. Kellan grabbed my hip to keep me where I was.

"Keep still, baby. This will take the pain away."

"Why would you want to do that, Kellan? Isn't this what you wanted?" I asked bitterly.

"I never wanted to hurt you, India," he sighed. He resettled the covers over me and placed the ointment on the table next to the bed. "But tell me this, will you remember the safety measures from now on?"

"I'll try," I said quietly.

"Do more than try, India," his voice hardened. "Next time, ointment or no ointment, you won't be able to sit for a week."

"You're being a bastard, Kellan."

"Be that as it may, baby. I have to know you'll be safe."

Kellan handed me some Excedrin and a glass of orange juice. He leaned down, kissed me tenderly on the forehead, and stated that he had some work to do for his meeting Wednesday. When the bedroom door closed behind Kellan, I went into the bathroom and washed my face. As I looked at my reflection, my eyes caught sight of the full-length mirror behind me. Son of a bitch! My ass was covered in welts! I had to get out of here for a while.

Still naked from when Kellan had me strip, I put on another sundress and a soft pair of silk boy shorts. Putting my hair in a ponytail and grabbing my sunglasses so no one would see my red, swollen eyes, I left the room.

Kellan was working on his laptop in the living room. I felt his eyes follow me as I went and poured myself another travel mug of coffee.

"Are you going somewhere, India?" Kellan asked me. He had a strange look on his face. Was he afraid I was going to leave? If only I was that smart.

"Yes. I want to go walk on the beach, so if you could let my babysitters know, I would appreciate it."

He seemed to exhale a relieved breath. He pulled out his cell phone and punched in a couple of numbers. "They'll be outside waiting for you, baby. Be careful please." I nodded, turned, and went out the door, feeling his eyes on me the entire time.

Bret and three others were waiting for me right outside the sliding glass doors. I walked down to the water, going in to my ankles, turned to the left, and started walking. Two of my babysitters were a few feet in front of me, the other two the same distance behind me.

I saw nothing of the beautiful scenery I was passing because I was so deep in thought. Did it make me a masochist because I still loved Kellan? No, I didn't think so. I didn't like pain, and I definitely didn't want to go through that again. Angry with him? Damn straight.

But what did it say about me that I wasn't running as fast and far away from Kellan Coventry as possible? I know that I had agreed to his terms because he needed control, but that he would take measures to this extreme? I had had no clue. Did I really want to be with a man who needed this much control?

"Excuse me, Ms. Leigh?" Bret's voice startled me. I looked over my shoulder at him. "Mr. Coventry would like to know if you're ready for lunch."

"Would you tell him to go ahead without me, Bret, please? I'm really not hungry."

I took a sip of my coffee. Yuck! We must have been walking longer than I realized. It was cold. Telling the guys, we turned and started back the way we had come. When we got back to the suite, I found that we had been gone over an hour. Kellan was still working on his laptop. So I retrieved mine and went out on the covered patio. Very gingerly, I sat on a plush outdoor chair and went to work on my book.

I wanted to finish the second and third books of the trilogy. I always expressed my honest emotions when I wrote. The one constructive thing about that walk on the beach? I knew what the next series of books would be. They would be our story. Mine and Kellan's. Wherever this story led us. Of course, I would change the names of places and people, and change some things. Kellan, if he ever read them, would know that they were of us. Anyone else could assume whatever they liked. I could care less.

CHAPTER TWENTY-TWO

I was still typing away when Kellan came and stood before me. "Would you please come in and have dinner with me, baby?"

The sun was setting. I had been so wrapped up in my writing goals that I hadn't noticed how much time had passed Looking up at him, I closed my laptop. When he extended his hand to me, I placed mine in his. He squeezed it lightly in relief and pulled me to my feet.

"I thought you would be more comfortable on the sofa," he said softly as we walked inside.

There were candles lit all over the living room of the suite and covered dishes on the coffee table. It was beautiful and romantic. "Thank you, Kellan. It's lovely."

He seated me on the sofa in front of the coffee table. Before he took his place beside me, he looked down at me and gently cupped my face between his hands. "I'm sorry that I don't know the right things to do with you. I just have to do what I think is best."

Looking at this gorgeous man, I wished I knew the deep, dark secrets that there must be to make him the way he was. I wanted to make whatever they were disappear. I had a bad feeling that they would play hell with whatever future we had.

"I won't pretend to understand your reasoning, Kellan, because I don't. But I agreed to your terms. I haven't changed my mind. I still want to see where this, us, will go. With my eyes wide open, let's just take it from here."

He looked deeply into my eyes for a few moments longer. Apparently satisfied with what he saw, he nodded.

Dinner was a wonderful shrimp alfredo, Caesar salad, and fresh baked rolls. Desert was a scrumptious turtle cheesecake. I hadn't realized how hungry I was until I smelled what was before me. I ate almost everything.

"I got this for you the other day, India. I wanted you to remember our time here. I've had more fun than I can ever remember having." He handed me a flat jeweler's box. I opened it to see a delicate silver—no, probably platinum; this was Kellan after all—sand dollar on an intricately cut chain.

"It's perfect, Kellan. I love it." He walked behind me, took the necklace, and fastened it around my neck.

"No. You're perfect, baby." Sometimes the things he said floored me.

I took the sand dollar between the fingers of my right hand as he once again sat beside me. "Thank you," I said sincerely. "But I didn't need anything to remind me of our time here. I could never forget it. I've loved having all this time alone with you."

"Well, what would you like to do tonight?"

"Would you mind staying in? We could watch movies or something." But then I remembered what night it was. "Wait. It's Sunday. *True Blood* comes on."

"True what?"

I laughed at his confused look. "The series, *True Blood*. I read all the books. Loved them. The series doesn't stay true to them, but I got hooked all the same."

"Someone actually wrote a series of books called True Blood?" he asked, arching his brows.

"No, silly." I laughed harder. "The series is called *The Sookie Stackhouse Novels*. Written by Charlaine Harris. 'True blood' is a synthetic blood that was created for the vampires so they wouldn't hurt humans."

He shook his head and looked at me as if he had never seen me before. "I like seeing you like this. Animated. With excitement shining in your eyes."

Kellan reached for the remote and turned the huge flat screen on to HBO. Fifteen minutes later, I was laughing at his expression as he watched the program. "This is soft porn, India." He sounded so shocked.

"Yeah. It's great, isn't it?"

He grinned at me and asked me to tell him all about the series. After I told him as much as I could explain, he looked at me, pretending to be serious. "What a surprise you are. You're a little pervert."

"Hey!" I threw a throw pillow at him. "Who's calling who a pervert?"

He swatted the pillow aside and pulled me gently to him with a hand around the nape of my neck. He lifted me onto his lap, settled me against his chest, and wrapped me up with his strong arms. "I want it to always be like this, India. I want this to work."

I lifted my head from his chest and looked at him. His expression was so haunted, it gutted me. I clasped his face in my hands, staring intently into his eyes. "Everything is all right, Kellan. We're good."

Kellan nodded and pulled me back into his chest.

When *True Blood* was over, he asked if I was ready for bed. When I nodded, he turned off the flat screen and stood with me still in his arms. Wrapping my arms around his neck, I snuggled as close as I could get to him. At that moment, if I could crawl into him, I would have.

Kellan placed me gently on the bed and carefully removed my sundress and boy shorts. Then he stood, methodically undressing. My eyes followed his every move. I would never grow tired of looking at his yummy body.

With only boxer briefs remaining, I couldn't resist sitting up and running my fingers down his happy trail. Keeping eye contact with him, I pulled his boxer briefs slowly down his muscular thighs. Kissing him and running my tongue from his navel down to his magnificent erect shaft, I placed a tender kiss on the top of his crown then ran my tongue across the small slit. He moaned. It was so thrilling to see what I did to him. Wrapping my mouth around him. Loving him with my tongue. Then sucking him in hard back to the back of my throat.

"Enough, baby," Kellan growled, yanking me off him. "I want to be inside you."

I licked my lips, still tasting him. "I want you inside me too," I said, fluttering my eyelashes at him.

He roared with laughter. "Are you flirting with me?"

"Yep. Is it working?"

"God!" He stepped out of his boxer briefs. "I've created a monster." His look sobered. "Your ass is blistered, baby. I don't want to cause you any more pain."

"I'm sure as the resident pervert," I said, grinning up at him, "you know a position that won't smart."

"You're going to be the death of me, woman." He sat on the bed next to me and lay back. "Straddle me, baby," he said hoarsely.

I did as he instructed. My nether lips hit his erection in such a delicious way. My eyes closed, and I moaned, rocking myself against him until I was about to come just from that.

"Can you reach a condom, baby?"

I looked over at the nightstand where the condoms were located and then remembered once again that it was Sunday. "Kellan, you don't have to wear one if you don't want to." I felt my face burning. "I mean, you know I have never been with anyone else, so—"

"No," he interrupted me. "I don't want you to get pregnant. Would you want that?" He bit out.

"No! Of course not," I said emphatically. "It's just that I forgot to tell you that I had my doctor put me on the pill." I lowered my eyes. I was so embarrassed. "From today on, I'm safe. Can't get pregnant."

Kellan gently put a hand under my chin and lifted my face. "I've always wore protection, India. But with us being in a monogamous relationship, I would love nothing more than being skin to skin. If you trust me, I'm clean. I have checkups all the time."

"I trust you, Kellan."

He smiled up at me. "Raise up, baby. I can't wait any longer." I lifted up onto my knees for him. "Hmm. You're so wet." He gripped his cock in his right hand. "Lower yourself slowly onto me."

I lowered myself, slowly taking him inch by inch. Oh, this was heaven. When I had taken him all the way, I whimpered. He was so deep this way. I moved slowly up and down. It was a glorious feeling, Kellan without a condom. Just knowing that I was the only woman he had ever had bare, it was powerful.

"Damn," he moaned.

Leaning into him as I was, my clit was being rubbed just right, every time I moved over him. His large cock was gripped tightly in my pussy, rubbing the front wall, hitting that G-spot. He was deeper than I had ever felt him. My body started tightening, coiling with tension. I was going to lose myself with this orgasm. It was wonderful. It was frightening. I imploded, screaming his name.

He caught me by the waist. Lifting me up then bringing me down. Harder. Faster. The same time he was bringing me down, he was arching his lean hips, slamming into me over and over, over that sensitive nub. I was quickening again. No! I wouldn't survive this one.

Tears started leaking from the corners of my eyes. So much sensation. Such emotion. Suddenly, Kellan slammed into me one last time and stilled, his hot come flooding me deep inside. He roared my name, taking me over the cliff with him.

I collapsed on his chest. I didn't want to face him. The tears kept coming as I realized for the first time that I wouldn't survive if Kellan and I didn't work out. Oh, I would live, but as half a person. He owned me.

"Hey, you." He lifted me, and I was once again straddling him. "What's this?" He gently cupped my face with both hands, his thumbs wiping the tears from my face. "Did I hurt you, baby?"

"N-no," I stuttered and tried to clear my throat. "That was so intense." I lowered my eyes. I didn't want him to see the half-truth.

"Yes, it was." He chuckled. "For me too." He lay me back down on his chest and slowly pulled out of me. He rubbed soothing circles on my back. "Go to sleep, baby. You're exhausted. It's been a long day."

A TEMPTATION

I didn't say anything. I didn't trust myself to. Kellan had the power to destroy me, and I would only have myself to blame if he did, knowing who he was and not knowing what he would end up wanting. But it was too late for me to turn back now.

It was a long time before sleep found me.

Kellan cuffed my wrists from restraints that fell from the ceiling, and my ankles from restraints that were bolted into the floor. I was standing, naked, arms and legs spread. I couldn't move.

I didn't know where I was. As soon as that thought passed through my mind, the room became lighter. There were men and women that I could see now. They were watching me. And I was naked! What was Kellan thinking?

I looked frantically for him. I didn't see him out there anywhere in front of me, and I couldn't turn my head to look behind. The men and women started laughing. I heard a crack, and fire spread down my back. A whip! Kellan was using a whip on me. Instead of shredding my back, though, he shredded my heart and soul. I screamed.

I was still screaming when I was jerked awake by Kellan shaking me by my shoulders. "Christ, India!" he yelled.

I was on my back with Kellan leaning over me. He said something over his shoulder. Oh no. One of the security guys?

Kellan sat up, taking me with him onto his lap. He slowly rocked me. "Hush, baby. It was just a nightmare." He kept whispering words of encouragement against my ear. I felt cherished. Loved. Or was that wishful thinking?

I pulled out of his arms. "I'm so sorry, Kellan."

"You're telling me you're sorry? For having a nightmare?" He looked at me, astonished.

"Uh…no." I stood up. "For disturbing you."

"That's ridiculous, India. I don't give a shit about being woken up," he said sternly. "I only care about you. That you're okay. Do you want to talk about it, baby?"

"No. It's not important," I responded hurriedly. "I'm going to take a bath."

CHAPTER TWENTY-THREE

*I*t was very late when we landed back in New Orleans. Daniel was waiting to drive us back to Kellan's. The security team tailed us the whole way in the black SUV that they had arrived at the airport in.

Kellan took my hand as we got out of the car in front of his house. Daniel was standing beside the front door he held open for us. As we passed him, he smiled at me and gave me a wink. I grinned back at him.

Deric was waiting for Kellan in the foyer. "Sorry to hit you with this as soon as you get in Kellan, but it's urgent." He looked coolly at me. "India." He bobbed his head.

I only acknowledged him with a small nod. Deric didn't like me very much. I had taken his playmate away.

Kellan kissed me tenderly. "I'll be up soon, baby."

When I got up to Kellan's bedroom, I was happy to see our bags were already there. Kellan had purchased a set of luggage so we could bring all the clothes and stuff that we had at the resort. I pulled a clean pair of panties out of one bag and a T-shirt of Kellan's out of another. Grabbing the makeup bag, I went into the bathroom to take a long, hot shower.

A TEMPTATION

Kellan was still absent when I went back into the bedroom. I got my laptop and sat in his bed with my back against the headboard. My butt wasn't that sore anymore, thank goodness.

Before I could even open the laptop, Kellan was coming through the door. One look at his face had me putting it aside and sitting up on the side of his bed. "What is it, Kellan?" I asked nervously. "What's wrong?"

He looked at me. "Nothing," he said, running his hand through his hair. That was his tell. He was worried, and he wasn't telling me the truth.

"It's just that…I'm going to have to work all night, baby." He gave me his wicked grin. "And that is not how I wanted to spend the rest of this night."

"Oh." I stood up. "I understand. I've monopolized your time this last week, Kellan. I'll go on home." I walked over to the bags so I could get something to put on. Before I could open it, Kellan wrapped his arms around me from behind.

"No, baby," he said softly into my ear. "I want to know you're up here in my bed."

I slowly turned in his arms and wound my arms around his neck. "I don't want you having to worry about me when you obviously have a lot going on. It's all right, Kellan. I'll just go and—"

"I said no, India." He glared down at me. "If you don't want me to worry, you'll stay."

I took my arms from around his neck and took a step back. Kellan's arms fell to his side. "What's that supposed to mean? What's going on?"

"Enough, India," he said through gritted teeth. "Just do as you're goddamn told."

"Fuck you, Kellan!" I lashed out and turned to go back to the suitcases.

I was roughly swung around. "If I have to, India, I will lock you in this room."

Looking into his eyes, I saw the same hard, cold look that I had seen Sunday morning. He meant every word.

"I'm not doing this with you," I said in a calm voice when in reality, I was trembling inside. "I'm a grown woman. Not you or anyone else gets to treat me this way."

He didn't say a word. He turned, grabbed my cell phone from the nightstand, and went out the door, closing it behind him.

I ran to the door. He locked it! The son of a bitch locked me in! "Kellan!" I screamed. "Let me out right now! You have no right!" Only silence greeted me. I grabbed the lamp off the nightstand. It was large and heavy, probably expensive. Good. I threw it with all my might against the door. It shattered loudly, but he didn't return.

For a while, I paced back and forth across Kellan's bedroom. I was so pissed. Stupid things ran through my head. *I could break a window and climb out.* That wouldn't work. His security guys would stop me. *I could e-mail Kathy or one of my other friends.* Did I want them to get involved in this? No. I really didn't. I stomped into the bathroom and got the wastebasket, bringing it into the bedroom. I picked up the broken pieces of the lamp and threw them into the basket. I shoved what was left of it, the hardware, in and placed the lampshade on top.

Climbing back onto the bed, I went back to work on my laptop. I didn't have much more before I finished this third book. It was the final story in my trilogy. I was very excited because I wanted to get to work on my new idea for my next books.

It was four in the morning before Kellan came up to bed. He unlocked the door and had the nerve to just walk through into the bathroom, closing the door behind him. Not one look. Not one word. A few moments later, I heard the shower turn on.

That bastard! Getting out of bed, I rummaged through the suitcase for a pair of shorts, a bra, and a shirt. Throwing it all on with a pair of sandals, I took my purse and laptop and went down to the kitchen.

It was too early to bother Daniel or anyone else, so I put on a pot of coffee.

Yes. I loved Kellan, but I couldn't do this. It would kill me not to be with him, but it would make me less of a woman if I continued to let him do this.

A TEMPTATION

I was sitting at the island with a mug of coffee when Kellan came into the kitchen, his beautiful chest bare, wearing only a pair of pajama pants hanging low on his hips. His hair was wet from the shower he just got out of. I would miss this.

After getting himself a mug of coffee, he sat across the island from me. I watched him take a sip from his coffee and slowly swallow. "We've had something come up that's very serious, India." He put his mug down on the granite countertop hard enough for the liquid to slosh over the top.

I sat still and silent. I was too hurt and angry.

"I needed you to stay here until I could look into it." He got up, walking over next to the sink and pulling paper towels off the roll. He returned to his seat and cleaned up the mess he had made. "I'm not used to someone questioning me."

When I finally found my voice, I was proud of how calm and cool I sounded. "I'm not one of your employees, Kellan. Nor one of those other women. We are supposed to be in a relationship. I can't do it like this."

"I know. I was wrong. I told you I would be crazy where your safety is concerned." As if that made how he reacted okay.

"What are you talking about, Kellan?"

"Someone has threatened me."

I felt my heart in my throat. "What? How?" I asked, bringing my hand up to my throat.

"Through e-mail, by mail, and by phone. I have people working on it. On tracing"—he searched for the right words—"something. As good as we are, so is he."

"What is this person saying, Kellan?"

"He's threatening my company. And anyone close to me." He looked at me, his eyes staring intensely into mine. "It's not me I'm worried about."

I got up and refilled our coffee. Now I understood what had set him off.

"Thank you, baby." He gave me a weak smile.

I nodded and sat back down. "You believe these threats?"

"Big corporations and their heads are always getting threats. Most are just crazy bullshit. These are different. These are personal. This person has to know me because he knows so much."

"You said *he*, Kellan." I took a deep breath. "With it being personal, couldn't it be a woman?"

"Anything is possible. But Noel believes it's a man because of the context. And he's the best at what he does."

I lowered my mug that I had started to raise to my lips. "Who's Noel?"

"He's the head of my technical security. He can find anyone or anything. He'll solve this thing."

"Oh." What do you say to that? This Noel person was probably the one that dug up all my personal information. Sometimes Kellan's power and reach—yes, and all his money—overwhelmed me.

"So this is why you pulled that crazy stunt last night?" It was half question, half statement.

"Yes," he said bluntly, seemingly put out.

"Kellan." I rolled my eyes at him. "I am a person. Not a possession."

"I'm not stupid, India," he said, glaring at me. "I know what and who you are very well. I will do whatever it takes to keep you safe."

"You should have talked to me!" I raised my voice. He was so, so aggravating. "If you would have explained things to me, I would have stayed here gladly. You can't go all caveman and lock me away. No matter how I feel about you, I can't and won't put up with it."

"I know." He sighed. "I wouldn't put up with it if it were reversed."

So what? I thought. *Is this over? Us?*

"I am sorry," he whispered. He reached across the island and took one of my hands in his, his thumb softly rubbing back and forth across my knuckles. "I just need to know you're safe. I'm not used to this, er, relationship thing. If you forgive me, I will try my best to talk things through with you."

My heart melted. "That's all I ask, Kellan," I said softly.

"Thank you," he said sincerely, smiling his wonderful smile at me. "So can we discuss security?"

"You've told me what you wanted in regards to that, and I agreed." I looked at him, puzzled.

A TEMPTATION

"We had to revise it. It needs to be increased, India. With this subject, I will try to explain the situations with you. But I need you—" He shook his head. "No. You have to listen and follow what I think is best for your safety. Can you, will you do that?"

"I'll do my best, Kellan." I shrugged. "I have a life. I have things I have to do and things I want to do."

"I understand that, baby, and I will do my best not to interfere with that. I just need you to do things a little differently."

"Explain what you mean," I demanded, narrowing my eyes at him.

"I want a four-man team with you at all times. You have a choice of staying here"—he shrugged—"or they go with you to your house."

"Don't you think you're going a little overboard?"

"No."

Shit. I sighed deeply. "All right, Kellan. I'll agree with this if it makes you happy, but I want to go home. You're going to New York. I don't want to be here when you aren't. Besides, I need my own space."

He nodded. "Nowhere. I mean nowhere without the security detail," he emphasized.

He was so intense. Jeez! "Yes, sir master."

"Better be careful, baby." His voice was so carnal. "I could learn to like that from you."

"I was being sarcastic, Kellan." And I was serious. "Not from me. You'll never get that from me."

He sighed. "I was joking, India. That's not what I want from you." He raised my hand to his lips and kissed my fingers.

"I would feel a lot better if you were coming with me. All I will do is worry until we're together again." He released my hand and reached for his mug once more.

"I can go with you at times if you like, Kellan. But this week, I have a meeting before classes Thursday night."

He took a sip of his coffee. "That reminds me,. I have a dinner to go to Friday night in New York. How do you feel about someone else going with me if you can't be there?"

I cocked my eyebrows. "About as well as you would like it if I had someone else escort me to an event," I responded snidely.

He winced. "That good, huh?"

I nodded. "I could be wrong, but I think having lunch with a friend"—I made air quotes—"or going out with friends without the other is fine. But to escort a person of the opposite sex? That implies more."

"I agree."

"You do?"

"Yes." He smiled broadly at me. "So can you meet me in New York Friday?"

"Why didn't you ask me that in the first place? Like a normal person," I said, exasperated.

"Where's the fun in that?"

"You're such a smart-ass."

CHAPTER TWENTY-FOUR

I was sitting on my back porch Wednesday morning, watching the sunrise over the bayou. I had missed this so much. It was amazing to me how much a part of this place I was, or vice versa. It calmed me.

My escape.

That being said, I was so tense since my return. I couldn't sleep last night because Kellan wasn't in bed next to me. *I am so screwed!* If he hadn't called and left so many text messages, I would probably be a basket case.

I shook my head and went to search out Zach to tell him I would be working in my office. Zack was Bret's second in command. He was in charge of the security detail that had to stay with me.

I had been so used to being alone in my house. Now there were four men, and Bridgette, sharing it with me. My life had changed so much. So fast.

At 10 a.m., I was just finishing the last of my trilogy. I needed to talk to Kathy. We could celebrate this. We had only spoken a few times since the dinner last week, for no more than a couple of minutes each time. I picked up my cell phone and called Kat at work.

"Hey," I said when she picked up.

"The voice is the voice of my best friend," she said. "But that can't be because she fell off the face of the planet!"

"Ha-ha! Kat, look. I just finished my third book. I'm going to send both manuscripts out tomorrow. I thought if you don't have plans, you could come over for dinner tonight. We could celebrate and catch up."

"Sounds good to me. Besides, it will let me make sure the pervert hasn't done you any irreparable harm."

"Kathy," I snarled in warning.

"Okay. I won't say anything bad about the pervert."

"Never mind, Kathy. If this is how you're going to be, I damn sure don't want to talk about Kellan with you."

"I'm sorry, India," she said quietly and seriously. "I'm just really worried about you. I don't want to see you get hurt. I've never seen you this way with a guy. The longer you're with him, the more emotionally tied you're going to become. Then if he acts like all the stories I've heard and walks away?" She left that thought hanging.

"It's already too late, Kat," I whispered.

"Ah, shit." That's my best friend. Such a way with words.

I told her to be at the house after work, that we would talk more at that time. Then I ended the call and went to tell Bridgette about dinner.

Shutting myself back in my office, I started printing out my manuscripts. I called Mallory, my editor, to let her know I was sending her the manuscripts. She was speechless. Both books completed before the second was even due? She had never had that happen before.

I told her the idea about my new series. She assured me that it was sound. The genre was very popular since the sensation of *Fifty Shades* by E. L. James. Cool. I loved the *Fifty Shades* trilogy.

By four that afternoon, I had both manuscripts boxed and ready to go. I went up to take a much needed shower. I put on a pair of leggings and a long shirt. With my wet hair in a ponytail and with bare feet, I went back down to start on my new book until Kathy got here.

A TEMPTATION

I was on a roll, the words pouring out, the story line shaping up. This was personal. Parts of me were flowing into print. I was so embedded that I didn't hear the door.

"Who the fuck are you?"

Uh-oh. That was Kathy yelling. I forgot to tell the security team she was coming over. I saved my work, closed my laptop, and ran to the front door.

"It's okay, Zack." I pushed my way past another one of the guys to where Zack was blocking the doorway, not letting Kathy enter. "This is Kathy Pichon. My best friend. You can let her in whenever she comes over."

Zack reluctantly stepped aside to let Kat inside. The look that was blazing out of her eyes at the guy was rather frightening. I introduced her to Zack and to the other guy, James.

"What the hell is going on, India?"

I sighed. "Kathy, let's go in the kitchen, and I'll tell you all about it while we eat."

I was glad it was after seven. Everyone else had already eaten by this time, so Kathy and I had the kitchen all to ourselves. Over dinner, I told her everything that had taken place since the night of the arts dinner. There were a few things I left out. I wanted Kellan alive after all.

Kathy looked appalled. "And you're okay living like this?"

"It wouldn't be my first choice, Kathy. But if I want to be with Kellan, this is how it has to be right now."

Kathy grabbed the bottle of white wine that we had been drinking with dinner. She refilled our glasses, taking a large sip of hers. "Do you hear yourself when you're telling me how controlling he is?"

"Yes, Kat. I know firsthand how controlling he is. I agreed to some of his terms, not all. He knows there are…things I will not put up with. Not even from him."

"Well, I'm glad you haven't gone completely insane." She put her wine glass down on the kitchen table. Leaning into the table, closer so she could lower her voice and still be heard, she asked, "What about those other women, India?" She waved her hand around. "His dealings with them and, um, all that stuff?"

"Stuff?" I laughed.

"Shut up! You know what I'm talking about, India," she snarled at me.

"Yes. I know." I shivered. I didn't like thinking about that "stuff," as Kathy called it. "Kellan wants us to have a monogamous relationship, Kat. He's not doing any of that anymore. Besides, I thought you knew me better than that. No way would I be able to be with him if he was still involved elsewhere."

"Okay. Okay," she said, raising both her hands. "I'm always behind you. I do have to state for the record, though, I have a bad feeling about this."

"I wish I could say I disagree with you. But in all honesty, I can't." I took a sip of my wine. "It doesn't matter anyway. I love him."

"God! I wish you hadn't said that. Does he know?" I shook my head. "Didn't think so." She pushed her wine glass away. "We need tequila. Not this."

My phone binged. It was a text from Kellan, "Miss you. Can't wait until Friday. Still at business dinner."

I sent him a text back. "I miss you too. Just finished dinner with Kathy. We are about to start drinking tequila."

"That good, huh," he sent back. "She doesn't like me very much."

I typed in, "I could say the same about Deric."

My phone rang. It startled me. "Hello?"

"What do you mean about Deric?" Kellan demanded through the phone.

"Just what I said, Kellan." I rolled my eyes, looking at Kathy. "I thought you said you were at a business dinner?"

"I am."

"Well, I hope you stepped out. I—"

"No. I did not," he interrupted. "I don't give a damn who hears. Tell me why you said that. Has he said anything to you?"

"No! He hasn't said anything to me. It's just the way he acts. And don't snap at me!"

"What do you mean it's the way he acts?" There was that dangerous low tone, right on cue.

A TEMPTATION

"Kellan, can we talk about this later, like when you're not surrounded by at least a hundred people who are listening to your every word?"

"No! I want you to answer me now, India!"

I held the phone away from my ear. Asshole! He was being an asshole! "I'm hanging up now, Kellan."

"You better not hang up on me, India!"

And I ended the call. Kathy's eyes were as wide as saucers. "Ready for that tequila now?" I asked, smiling innocently at her.

My phone kept ringing, and I kept not answering. Finally, I turned it off.

"India!" Kathy exclaimed, looking at me intently. "This is not normal. You have to realize that."

"Yeah. Well, Kellan's not a normal kind of guy. I don't think he knows how to do things except at full throttle. He's not used to anyone not jumping and doing exactly what he says, when he says."

Zack came into the kitchen with his cell phone at his ear. "Ms. Leigh, it's Mr. Coventry. He would like to talk to you." He held his phone away from his ear. Kellan was yelling so loud Kathy and I could hear him.

"Damn!" I just about yelled. I took a couple of deep breaths, in and out, so I could speak calmly. "Sorry, Zack. I didn't mean for you to end up in the middle of this."

"Sir?" Zack asked into the phone. He slowly shook his head, holding out his phone to me.

"Ms. Leigh, Mr. Coventry says if you don't get on the phone, he'll be here in a couple of hours."

I knew that wasn't an idle threat. I took Zack's phone from him, waiting until he was out of earshot before getting on the line.

"Kellan," I said a whole hell of a lot more calmly than I felt. "No. Don't. Say. Anything. Just listen." I waited a moment for him to be silent before I continued. "We talked about this, but you still tried to bulldoze your way over me. You made a statement about Kathy. I didn't yell at you. I made a statement about Deric, and you yelled, demanding me to answer. You embarrassed me by talking to me like that in front of whoever was in that room. If this has to be this hard, it's probably not meant to be."

Tears pricked at the back of my eyes. Man, did that hurt to say. But what could I do? I agreed to hand over control in bed and about safety, not to be treated like a second-class citizen.

"Baby," he breathlessly said into the phone. He sounded tired. I could picture him running his fingers through his hair. "I am pissed, but not at you. I did yell, but I wasn't really yelling at you. I will not have anyone say or do anything to you. Yes. Deric is my friend. My best friend. But not even he gets to treat you with anything but respect. He doesn't have to like you." He paused for a moment. "You make me feel so helpless at times. I'm not used to this feeling, and I don't like it much."

"First of all, Kellan," I said softly, "how am I supposed to know the difference? You need to communicate. I'm a very private person. I don't take embarrassment well. Second, you say you feel helpless? You're not the only one. I feel blindsided."

"I'm sorry, India," he said sincerely. "I didn't mean to embarrass you. I just get crazy where you're concerned."

"That's what I'm talking about, Kellan," I replied, barely above a whisper. "We are supposed to complement each other. Not this."

"I would imagine that it takes quite a while to learn one another in a relationship. Remember, I don't know my way around one of these either. I told you I would try, baby. Not that I would get it right, right off the bat. You gave me your terms, so I will ask you for patience. I believe this, us, is worth it."

"Thank you for your apology," I sighed into the phone. "I think we're worth it also. I will do my best to give you the patience you've asked for."

"Thank you, baby." I heard his smile. "Everything will be fine. You'll see. I'll let you get back to your friend. Good night, baby. I'll talk to you tomorrow."

"Good night, Kellan." As I ended the call, I felt as I always did after an argument with Kellan—as if I had been on a roller coaster.

"I think you're playing with fire, India," Kathy said.

A TEMPTATION

She was right. How many times had I told myself to walk away? It might hurt now, but the longer it continued, I wouldn't only end up hurt, I would end up destroyed. On the other hand, there was this soft voice that insisted if I didn't see where this could lead, I would regret it for the rest of my life.

I was still thinking about Kellan as I pulled my Mustang into a parking spot outside of the arts program building in the warehouse district. Shaking my head as I climbed out of my car, I told myself to put him out of my mind and start concentrating on the meeting about to take place. Besides, it was Thursday evening. I would see Kellan tomorrow in New York.

I let myself inside my assigned room where the other instructors and subs were already there waiting for me.

"Why is it that every time we have a meeting, it's held in my room?" I asked no one in particular.

"Because yours is always so clean and picked up, beautiful," a sexy male voice replied.

I looked up at Blaze's sexy grin. He was the instructor for paintings. He did everything from still life to portraits, watercolors, oils, chalks, and pencils. He was very talented.

"I'm sure you know the cure to make your room the same way, Blaze."

"Naturally. But that would hurt my artistic ability," he said, his grin growing wider.

"You're not right," I said as I chuckled. I leaned back on the front of my desk, facing the room. The other instructors, Heather, Meredith, Becky, and AJ, were seated at one table. The subs, Shannon, Robin, Kristie, Tracy, Justin, and Katelynn, were seated at another.

"This is our quarterly catch-up meeting," I spoke to the group. "It is important that we all know the progress of our recipients. Whoever would like to start, please do."

"Emily's planter design has been picked for lining the streets down the quarter," Heather volunteered. She and Meredith were the instructors in clay and ceramics.

"That's great," I said. "That will give her a lot of recognition."

"James was commissioned to produce a sculpture for outside an office complex downtown."

"AJ, if you will keep us posted on his progress so when the piece is finished and on display, we can all go to admire his work, I would appreciate it. Also, if everyone would fill out the forms on your recipients' achievements, I have to turn those in to the committee."

"Mellissa and Taylor both have showings next month in local galleries," Blaze added. "I believe Taylor's historical reflections will go over big with the tourists."

"I am happy to add that Kelly's novel has been accepted by my publisher for review," I told everyone excitedly. "I have faith that it will be accepted for publication. Also, Audrey's short stories have been picked up for novellas. Everyone should be proud of what we are accomplishing here. I truly thank y'all for everything that is done here, and outside, for our recipients."

"Thankful enough to finally go out with me?" Blaze chirped in hopefully.

"Only if everyone else is going to be there," I said, chuckling.

"Ouch," AJ said to Blaze. "I feel for you, man."

"I thought you liked me, India," Blaze pouted. "Why do you keep shooting me down?"

"I do like you, Blaze. You're funny, sweet, and very talented. I value your friendship and want to keep it that way."

"You're going to give me a complex, beautiful."

"With all of those girls following you around? Quit being so dramatic." I laughed.

"Can't blame me for trying," Blaze added with a wicked grin.

"Okay." I shook my head. "If we can get back on track here, Robin, I will need you to fill in for me starting next week until further notice. I will keep on top of everything for Kelly and Audrey, and you can contact me anytime on my cell."

"Of course. I love being with the class," Robin said. "But if you don't mind my asking, is everything all right with you? It's not like you to be gone for an extended period of time."

"Everything is fine. The guy that I'm seeing has to be in New York most of the time. I need to be there for him for all of his business and personal functions. I can go back and forth for when I am needed here, but I will need you to take the class."

"Oh wow!" Meredith piped in. "We want to hear all about this guy, India."

I felt my face turn red. "There's nothing to tell."

"Yeah. Right. Like you would run off to New York for just any guy," Blaze spit out.

"Yeah, India. Spill. We want to hear about this guy. If you're running off to another state for him, he has to be something," Meredith kept up.

"That's enough. I don't have anything more to say on the subject. Go fill out the paperwork I need, all of you, before the classes start."

I sat behind my desk after all the instructors went off to their own rooms. Not that I would talk about Kellan to anyone other than Kathy and Noah, but there was nothing to say. Neither one of us knew what this was between us. I think Kellan just didn't want anyone coming between us before we had a chance to find out.

Also, there was his whole possessive thing. What's good for the goose is good for the gander. In other words, if I couldn't be around the opposite sex, neither could he. That was the whole reason that I was going to New York. I was not sure if this was a healthy way to go, but then again, what did I know?

CHAPTER TWENTY-FIVE

I had my earbuds on, listening to my favorite songs. "A Thousand Years" by Christina Perri was playing on my iPod as I disembarked from Kellan's private jet. Bret was waiting at the bottom of the steps. He and the three of my security team—Tim having stayed in Slidell—surrounded me as a couple of homeland security checked the plane and luggage, Kellan's power giving us curb service.

We arrived at a very tall apartment building on Madison Avenue. *The Huntley*, I silently read. I knew I looked like a gawking tourist. But hey, I was a gawking tourist. I had only been in New York one other time—that had been for only one day and night when I signed with my publisher.

Bret parked the big dark-windowed SUV in the underground parking garage, and he and Zack got on the elevator with me. Bret punched some numbers on a keypad and inserted a key. Penthouse. How come I wasn't surprised?

The elevator opened up right into a marble-floored foyer. French doors opened into the apartment proper at the end of the foyer. It was huge. Stark. Modern. Very expensive. This was totally different from the mansion on St. Charles. Different ends of the spectrum.

A TEMPTATION

The mansion, while very elegant and expensive, was all Old World charm and comfortable. This place was like walking into a museum of modern art. Maybe this was what he needed in Manhattan to entertain for business and whatever. My taste ran more toward the mansion on St. Charles.

I walked through the expansive formal living room to a wall of glass, opening a part of a glass door that walked out to a wide balcony. It was beautiful out here. Sitting areas with views of the city all around. Sturdy plants in wonderful containers.

My cell phone went off. It was Kellan's ring tone. Yeah. I gave him a ring tone—and giggled every time I heard it. It was the country song, "Gettin' You Home" by Chris Young.

"Hey," I said excitedly into the phone.

"You're here," he answered almost reverently. "Finally."

I laughed. "Yeah. I missed you too."

"I'm sorry, baby. I hate it, but I'll be tied up here until I have to hurry home to change."

"It's okay, Kellan," I assured him. "I can work until it's time to take a shower and get ready. That's the great thing about writing. I can work anywhere."

"Okay then. I can't wait to see you."

I met Kellan's housekeeper, Mrs. Parker, when I walked back into the apartment. "Would you like anything special for lunch, Ms. Leigh?"

"Just coffee for me, Mrs. Parker, please," I replied with a huge smile. "I live on it."

I worked on my new book until 5:00 p.m. then took a long, hot shower in Kellan's master bathroom, using all those wonderful showerheads in the massive black marble space to work all the kinks out of my muscles. Feeling boneless when I finally stepped out, I wrapped a large, fluffy black towel around me and another around my long hair.

Thursday morning, Kellan had called me, asking me not to get upset with him until after he explained. He said that he felt since it was because of his business that I would be going to all the black-tie affairs and cocktail parties, he wanted to provide my wardrobe. I tried to tell him it wasn't necessary, but he went on to say he would feel privileged to do this small thing. It was such a romantic thing to say that it swept any argument of mine aside. So I agreed and said I would never get angry with him if we talked things out.

I opened the double doors to one of Kellan's walk-in closets. This one was filled with all of Kellan's things. Shutting the door, I went to the other one. When I opened the doors, I was shocked. It was full of not only evening and cocktail dresses, but casual dresses, pantsuits, capris, and jeans, shirts, shoes, purses, lingerie, and pajamas. I opened one of the slender velvet-lined drawers. Jewelry. Lots of very expensive jewelry. This was not what I had agreed to.

I went back into the bathroom to get my phone from where I left it on the vanity. Pulling up Kellan's number, I hit send.

"Hey, baby," he answered.

"Kellan," I choked out. "I agreed to evening gowns and cocktail dresses. Not…not this!"

"I know, baby," he sighed. "But when I talked to the personal shopper, she made me realize that this way, you wouldn't have to pack anything going back and forth. It would be a lot more convenient for you."

"It's way too much, Kellan," I told him, exasperated. "I feel like a…a kept woman."

He snorted. "A kept woman, India? Really? You sound like a romance novel."

"I'm a writer, Kellan," I snarled back at him.

"Please don't be upset, baby. I really was only thinking of you."

"What am I going to do with you?"

He chuckled. "I can think of a few things, baby."

I heard someone say something to him on his end. "I'll let you get back to work, Kellan. I'll see you when you get home."

"Sounds great, baby."

I went back to the walk-in closet that held my new wardrobe and chose a black silk evening gown. It was sleeveless with metallic silver threads running all through it. Very low in the front and back. Simple and elegant, but also sexy. I paired it with silver stilettos, an evening bag, a thin platinum and emerald choker, bracelet, and earrings, and sexy black lace lingerie and silk stockings.

A TEMPTATION

I blow-dried my hair, piling it on top of my head with a few curls hanging down the sides and back. I applied my makeup and got dressed. I was putting on the last shoe when Kellan walked into the room. I rose from the side of the bed where I had sat to put on my shoes. Kellan just stared at me for what seemed like an endless moment.

"My God, you're exquisite." He gasped.

I blushed and smiled shyly. "You're not so bad yourself," I returned.

In a heartbeat, he was across the room, pulling me into his arms. His lips found mine, the kiss hard and hungry. I wrapped my arms around his neck, and he pulled me tighter into his body. I felt his penis harden against me.

He lifted his head, his breathing harsh. "If I don't stop, we won't be going to that damn dinner."

Thirty minutes later, Kellan led me out of the elevator and into the lobby; it was all white marble. Stark modern beauty like Kellan's apartment. Bret and Zack were right on our heels. The doorman held the door for us, tipping his hat. Bret saw us into the limo that was waiting, then he and Zack got into the SUV that was right behind it.

The dinner was at the Sherry-Netherland on Fifth Avenue. It was a luxury hotel overlooking Central Park. The limo opened. Kellan exited then reached back into the car for me. I placed my hand in his and stepped out beside him, into utter chaos. There were at least a hundred photographers. In New Orleans, there had only been a few from *The Times-Picayune* and a couple of social magazines. This? I wanted to jump back into the limo.

As if he sensed my discomfort, Kellan wrapped his arm around my waist and pulled me into his side. "Don't worry, baby," he whispered in my ear. "I won't let anyone get too close." He placed a chaste kiss on my lips.

Flashbulbs went off ferociously. I smiled up at Kellan and gave him a slight nod. He kept a possessive arm around me as we walked into the entrance of the Sherry-Netherland.

I had never seen anything quite like the Sherry-Netherland. I had read that the lobby had been patterned after the Vatican Library.

It had eighteen-foot vaulted ceilings, inlaid marble floors, and exquisite crystal chandeliers. There were original paintings scattered all over the place. There were also friezes from the Vanderbilt Manson that once stood one block south. I would have loved to have had the time to explore it all.

The dinner was being held in the reception room. Kellan explained that this was for his company, for his top and medium employees from all departments of Coventry Technologies. Also his top people from other pies that Kellan had his fingers in like the hotels and resorts, and I don't know what else.

This was to thank them for their stellar year and to tell them where they were headed from here.

Kellan introduced me to everyone. He knew all their names and the names of their significant others, even their children if it applied. I was very impressed. When he introduced me as his girlfriend, they couldn't hide their surprise. Or maybe it was shock?

"Come on, baby. Let's go to our table and have a glass of wine." With his right hand resting on the small of my back, he led me to the head table by the podium. Before we reached the table, however, Deric was in front of us with two women. The blonde was Presley Cole, whom I'd seen in New Orleans, the one that Devyn Troyer hurt. The other was one of the most stunning women I had ever seen. She was tall and built like a supermodel with almond-shaped eyes that were so dark that it looked like she had no pupils. Her straight, very dark chestnut hair hung long down her back. She wore a white evening gown that showed off her olive complexion perfectly.

"Kellan," she said huskily, laying a hand on his arm and leaning in to kiss him.

I never thought I had a jealous bone in my body. I was wrong. I balled my fists up by my sides, afraid that if that woman put her lips on Kellan, I would cause an ugly scene and embarrass him. Kellan turned his face to the side, causing her lips to barely graze his cheek. I wanted to fist pump right there in the middle of this elegant gathering. I restrained myself. Barely.

"Asia," Kellan snarled at the woman. "You were never to touch me unless told to. And under no circumstances was their kissing." Kellan was seething. "So why would you do this in front of my girlfriend?"

"That's the reason, Kellan," Deric chuckled. "You changed the game. So Asia is making her move."

Kellan turned cold eyes toward his friend. "I know what you're playing at Deric, bringing two women here. Stay out of my personal life. Or I can change more than I already have."

"Come on, baby." Kellan once again put his arm around my waist, pulling me close into his side. "Let's go get that drink." We sat down at the table and a waiter appeared as if by magic. Kellan ordered a double scotch, and I told him I would really love a top-shelf margarita instead of a glass of wine.

I hated that Kellan was having to go through this with Deric. I wish I had been wrong about how he felt about me and why. Placing my hand over Kellan's that was resting on the table, I wanted him to know I was here for him. He brought my hand to his lips and placed a gentle kiss on my knuckles.

"I'm sorry, Kellan."

"Hush, baby. That's all on Deric."

The waiter returned with our drinks, and a few moments later, other waiters started bringing out the plates. The food was excellent, but I couldn't eat very much. No matter what Kellan said, I hated being the cause of a rift between the two longtime friends.

When the last of the dishes had been cleared, Kellan rose and went up to the podium. Everyone stood up and applauded. Kellan raised his hands, gesturing for silence and for them to be seated.

"No man is an island," his voice rang out. "I have accomplished so much because of the talented people I have working with me. I learned a long time ago that if I gave loyalty to my people, I would get loyalty back. But I have received much more than that. We have not only created a corporation. We have created a family."

I was in awe of Kellan. He was funny, considerate, and thankful. He gave credit where credit was due. Where there wasn't any, he didn't embarrass anyone. He went on to tell them where they would all be heading in the next fiscal year, explaining that they could never become complacent. He ended by thanking all his employees and their families.

There was thunderous applause. I stood up and applauded with the rest. I sat back down, wanting to stay out of the way while Kellan's friends and employees went to him, shaking his hand and patting him on the back.

"India." I looked up to see that it was Deric who said my name. I didn't want any trouble, and I hoped he wasn't going to cause any. "May I sit down?" he asked me.

I nodded and glanced over at Kellan, who was still surrounded. He had already noticed Deric. His eyes narrowed, and his lips flattened into a crooked line.

"I'm sorry, India," he said to me, quietly. "I won't offer any excuses for my behavior. All I will say is that Kellan is like a brother to me, and I really didn't think he would fall for anyone. Because... well, just because. But after seeing him with you tonight? He's happy, and it looks good on him."

I was so surprised. "Thank you, Deric," I said softly. "I didn't want anything to come between the two of you. Including me."

He smiled at me. "I hope you will come to count me as a friend."

I smiled back. "Never can have too many of those."

"I suppose not." He laughed. "Thank you, India."

"What's going on, Deric?" Kellan demanded.

I looked up into Kellan's angry face. "Everything's fine, Kellan. Deric and I were—" I shut my mouth when Kellan held up one of his index fingers. Definitely wasn't staying for the pissing contest.

"Excuse me," I said, standing up. "I'm going to go find the restroom."

"Take your security detail, India," Kellan commanded.

I rolled my eyes and turned to go in search of the bathroom. Catching Bret's eye as I walked toward the entrance of the reception room, he gave me a slight nod. He and Zack caught up with me in the hall outside the room.

There was a restroom right down from the entrance. When I opened the door, there were a lot of women waiting. So I walked on with my two shadows and found one close to the lobby.

A TEMPTATION

Even the public bathrooms in this place were magnificent. Smiling at the attendant who was sitting by the vanity, I went into a stall to take care of business. When I was through, I walked over to one of the sinks. There, to the left of the sinks, was Asia. She was leaning against the wall with her arms crossed.

This should be interesting.

"I want to talk to you," she bit out.

Placing my silver evening bag on the vanity, I turned on the tap. "So talk," I said.

"What do you think you're doing with Kellan?" she demanded.

Turning off the tap and reaching for the hand towel the attendant offered me, I noticed she didn't look happy with Asia. Smiling at her again, trying to assure her that everything would be fine, I handed her a tip along with the hand towel I was finished with. Then I leaned my hip against the vanity, mimicking her pose.

"That's none of your business," I informed her. "Mine and Kellan's relationship is just that. Ours."

"Relationship! Kellan doesn't do relationships. Only what he has within the club. And I, missy, have been with him for ten years."

I was getting pissed. I tried to calm myself down; I didn't want to cause a scene at Kellan's business function, even if I hadn't started it.

"I wouldn't be bragging about it, Asia." I couldn't help rubbing it in a bit. "Do you think I could be jealous of a woman who had remained his sub for ten years? I was never one of Kellan's submissives. You didn't have anything with him but kinky sex."

"I would be worried if I were you. I can give him what he wants. What he needs. He'll get tired of that vanilla shit and come back to me. His future is with me. I can give him everything in all aspects of his world."

I laughed at her. "What makes you think our relationship is vanilla? Have you been hiding in our bed? Oh no. Wait. No one but me has ever been with Kellan in any of his beds, at his homes."

"You bitch!" she screamed.

The attendant left the room when Asia screamed that.

"Hit too close to home, Asia?" I snapped. She called me a bitch; she was going to get a bitch. I smiled. "Kellan left all of that along with you behind. It was his decision. Not mine. Then again, you can always discuss this with him if you don't want to take my word for it."

I knew Kellan. If they had been together even a quarter of the time that she implied, there was no way she would attempt that.

The bathroom door opened, and Bret stuck his head in. "Is everything okay, Ms. Leigh?" he asked me, but stared down Asia.

"What the hell are you doing in here?" she ranted at him. "Aren't you supposed to be following Kellan around like a puppy?"

"Don't you fucking talk to him like that!" That was enough playing around with this witch. "They are my security team, and I'll be damned if you are going to treat him disrespectfully."

"Your security team?"

"Yes, Asia," I snapped. "I'm not a sub, remember? I am someone Kellan cares about and wants to protect." I turned away from her. "I'm ready to go back now, Bret. I need some fresh air."

Bret chuckled and held the door open for me. "Yes, ma'am."

When I walked out of the bathroom, Kellan and Zack were walking toward us. Oh goody. Just what I needed. Kellan was going to bust a gasket. Asia came out of the bathroom door right at that moment.

The attendant, who was standing out in the hall, smiled timidly at me and slipped back inside.

Kellan came right to me. Placing his hands on my shoulders, he looked down into my eyes. "Baby?"

I ran my fingers lightly down his face. "Everything's fine, Kellan."

He looked into my eyes a few moments longer then nodded. Taking his hands off my shoulders, he took my left hand, brought it up to his lips, and tenderly kissed my knuckles. He then entwined our fingers together and turned to Asia.

"You have no business here, Asia. I will make sure it doesn't happen again."

"You can't mean that, Kellan," she entreated. "After everything we've meant to each other?"

"Don't try to make it sound like we had something together in front of India," he lashed out at her. "We fucked, Asia." I winced at that. "We were sexual partners only. And you know it."

A TEMPTATION

Asia gasped. "How can you say that after ten years? I accompanied you to every event with your business and socially. I've been beside you through everything. You've known her for what, five minutes?"

"Listen to yourself, Asia. You weren't with me through anything. You accompanied me. Period. We never talked about anything. You were one of my subs. End of story." Then he got in her face. "You stay away from India. You don't talk to her. Don't even look at her."

Asia took a step back. She had more guts than I did. I would have been gone a long time ago.

"You'll be back, Kellan. I know you," she told him with certainty. "You need what I give you."

"You don't know a fucking thing about me!" he yelled at her. "You only know my commands. I don't need a damn thing from you."

"Come on, baby," he said as he tugged on my hand. "Let's get out of here and go home."

CHAPTER TWENTY-SIX

When we got out of the elevator at Kellan's, he scooped me up in his arms. Holding me close to his chest, he carried me into the master bedroom, slamming the door behind us with his foot.

Kellan slowly lowered me down his body and set me on my feet. He undressed me as though he was unwrapping a present. When I was standing there nude, he walked behind me, kissing me on my neck, right below my ear.

"You trust me, baby?" he whispered in my ear.

"Yes," I answered breathlessly.

"Good." He stepped back from me. "Step out of your shoes." I did as I was told. "Go kneel in the middle of the bed, facing the headboard. Lower your upper body down on the mattress, ass in the air. Extend your arms as far as they will reach, straight out toward the headboard."

I didn't know whether to be frightened or aroused. We had never done anything like this before. But I said I trusted him, so I did as instructed.

Kellan walked over to the side of the bed. He splayed a hand over my back in between my shoulder blades, pressing down, making me go lower still. He turned my head away from him, telling me to lay my cheek flat on the mattress. This position ensured that my ass was straight up in the air. I felt very vulnerable.

"Don't move, India. I'll be right back."

I gave him total control in the bedroom. It was the only thing I did that was remotely like what Asia and the others did for Kellan—*had* done for him, I should say. I didn't like everything we had done, but I was willing to try anything for him.

Kellan came back into the room. I felt him place something on the bed behind me, but I couldn't see what it was. He ran a hand up my thigh, over my bottom, all the way to my left wrist. He wrapped a padded cuff around it and snapped it shut. There was a length of chain attached to the cuffs that he ran through and behind his iron-spindle headboard. He clamped the remaining cuff around my right wrist. I pulled against the chain. There was very little give. This was new. My heart was pounding so hard I could feel it in by ears.

"I've restrained you because I need you to be as still as possible. Okay, baby?"

I nodded my head. I was afraid to say anything.

"No, baby." He ran his fingers through my hair. "Tonight, I need to hear everything from you. I need to know you're all right."

"O-okay," I replied quietly.

"Although I said that I need to hear you, this will be intense. You will tell me to stop, even when I know you can take more. So you will need a safe word. If you say that word, then I will know that you can't take anymore, or you don't want to. Do you understand?"

I nodded my head again—and yelped when Kellan popped me hard across my ass.

"Yes," I corrected. "Yes, I understand."

"Good girl. As much as I want this, I don't want to frighten you. Or hurt you unnecessarily. What's your word, baby?"

My word? Shit. He might not want to scare me, but by saying I needed a safe word, he scared the hell out of me.

"India!" He popped my ass again. "I need your word. Now."

"Dragonfly," I gasped.

He chuckled. "Dragonfly it is."

Kellan climbed up on the bed, kneeling behind me, spreading my legs wide. I felt something cool between my ass cheeks. He started rubbing—lubricant, maybe—firmly on the rosette of my anus. I tensed every muscle in my body, my brain screaming *no!* I had never contemplated anal sex.

"Relax, baby." He leaned over my back and whispered in my ear, "If you tense up, this will hurt more."

"Kellan, no. I don't want this." I pulled my knees under my stomach, which dropped my bottom down, too low for his questing fingers.

"No, India," Kellan said sternly. Kellan lifted me back up on my knees, pushing my upper body and face back down onto the mattress. "We talked about this. I won't make you keep doing something you hate, but I want you to try."

"I can't wrap my head around this being anything but painful."

"I won't mislead you, baby." He started massaging the tight opening again. "There is a lot of pressure, and it does hurt on entering. If done correctly, that pressure and pain blossoms into intense pleasure."

He leaned back over me, whispering in my ear, "And, baby, I want to own this beautiful, tight ass of yours."

One of his fingers breached that forbidden place. Gently, and very shallow, he thrust in and out. Then he went deep, as deep as he could, with that finger. Pulling out, he liberally applied more lubricant as two fingers breached and explored.

"Take a deep breath, baby." He pulled out of my body. "Exhale."

Kellan was trying to enter with three fingers, rubbing firmly around and around the tight rosette. They started to breach. "Your breaths again, India," he commanded.

I breathed in deeply, my muscles let go, and his fingers slipped in. I whimpered with my exhale. This was intense, uncomfortable, with a bite of pain.

Kellan's other hand found my clitoris, rubbing gently in small circles. The feeling changed suddenly. I was being bombarded with new sensations. Needing more, I found myself pushing back against his fingers.

A TEMPTATION

"That's it, baby," Kellan said huskily. He withdrew, and I felt empty. Hearing the foil packet tear, I knew he was putting on a condom. I felt his lubricated plump crown at my opening, rubbing firmly over the entrance. One of his hands was laid firmly across my back between my shoulder blades. The tight pucker flowered open.

"Deep breath, baby," he growled, sounding as if he was holding on to his control by the skin of his teeth.

As I took that breath, Kellan thrust. Hard. "No! Stop!" I screamed. *Fuck. This hurt.*

He froze. "Hush, baby. You're okay."

He unwrapped his hand from around his penis and ran his hands gently over my back and the cheeks of my ass. After a few moments, the burning pain disappeared. It was uncomfortable pressure.

Kellan pulled out partially then rammed back in until I could feel his balls against my pussy. He stilled. My hands fisted around the comforter on Kellan's bed. I tried to get away, but I couldn't move. His hands gripped my hips so tightly I would have bruises tomorrow. Tears were forced from my eyes and falling down my face, my breath coming out in ragged pants.

He leaned over, running kisses all up my spine. "Good girl. That's the worst it will ever be, baby. I promise."

I didn't respond. I didn't trust what would come past my lips. Not safe-wording was a matter of pride.

Kellan started thrusting. Slowly. Gently. One of his hands left my hips, going around the front of my body, finding my sex. He slipped two fingers inside me, pumping, his thumb finding my clit. Pleasure blossomed once again. I was filled with and by Kellan. So full. So deliciously full.

Tension started building. My lungs struggled for air. My body started pushing back and forth on its own validity. I was going to detonate. I was going to be torn apart into so many pieces I would never find them all. Then I shattered, falling down the rabbit hole, sobbing and screaming his name.

I collapsed. Kellan grabbed me by the hips again and rammed into me, over and over. He thrust hard, one last time, freezing deeply inside me, roaring with his release. He collapsed over my back, breathing hard.

A few moments later, he slowly withdrew. I winced. He got up, releasing my wrists, rubbing feeling back into them and my hands. He went into the bathroom and came back out with a warm wash cloth, minus a condom. He gently cleaned me.

Climbing back into bed, he pulled me on top of him, wrapping his arms tightly around me. Taking one of his hands, he pushed my hair out of my face and wiped my tears off my face. "Are you okay?" he asked quietly.

I nodded my head.

"Was it too terrible?"

I had to put my thoughts in order so I didn't say this wrong. "It was awful. And then it was amazing."

I felt him nod his head. "Would you do it again?" he asked tentatively.

"It depends." I hesitated. "Will it always hurt that bad at first?"

"No, baby. That was the worst. It was your first time." He ran his fingers through my hair. "It will always be uncomfortable at first, but nothing like tonight."

"Oh. Okay then." I couldn't keep my eyes open. I was worn out.

"Sleep, baby."

I nodded, too tired to say anything. I thought I heard him say thank you and that I was amazing, but I couldn't be sure.

I woke to glorious bright sunshine. I felt wonderful. Last night was a revelation. What an education I was receiving under Kellan's tutelage. Stretching as far as my body would let me, I found I was extremely sore. My whole body. The only downside on this wonderful morning was that my gorgeous man wasn't still in bed with me. I decided to go look for him before I took my shower.

Hopping out of bed, I went into the bathroom to take care of a couple of things. Wrapping my robe around me, I headed downstairs to find Kellan. He wasn't in the living room, so I followed my

A TEMPTATION

nose to the kitchen. *Mmm, coffee.* Mrs. Parker was the only one in the kitchen.

"Good morning," I greeted her.

"Good morning to you, Ms. Leigh," she said, returning my smile. "What can I get you for breakfast?"

"You already have mine made. Thank you." I took two mugs out of the cabinet and headed to the coffeemaker.

"Mrs. Parker, do you know where Kellan is?"

"He's been in his office all morning. Ms. Leigh, you really should eat. Isn't there something I can get you?"

"No, ma'am. I don't eat in the morning, but thank you."

I prepared Kellan's and my coffee then went to go find him. Halfway down the hall to his office, I heard him. "I don't give a fuck if everyone has to work 24-7. I want this son of a bitch found. Yesterday. No. You're not listening. Our company is supposed to be the best. So why can't your team track this bastard down?"

Damn. Kellan was pissed. For once it wasn't at me. I kind of felt sorry for whoever had been on the phone.

"Kellan," I called out at his opened office door.

He looked up and smiled when he saw me. "Morning, baby."

"Am I interrupting anything?"

He blew out a breath. "No. Come here."

I walked into his office, handing him the coffee I made him.

"Thank you," he said, setting the mug down on his desk. He turned his office chair to the side, taking my mug out of my hand and placing it on the desk also. Pulling me onto his lap, he placed a soft kiss on my lips. "How are you feeling?"

"Wonderful." I giggled. "Sore."

"I'll run you a warm bath. I should have had you soak in one last night, but you were wrecked."

"It's nothing, Kellan. I'm fine. I wanted to see you and say good morning before I took my shower."

"No, you need to soak." He gently pushed me off his lap, stood up, and took my hand. "Come. It's my job to take care of you."

His phone rang. "What?" he barked into it. "Hold on." He took his phone away from his ear. "Sorry, baby. I have to take this."

"It's okay." I raised myself up on my tiptoes and kissed him tenderly on his lips. "I'll see you later." I picked up my mug and started out the door.

"Baby." I stopped and turned around. "Bath, not shower, please. And remember, we have that cocktail party tonight."

I nodded, smiled, and blew him a kiss. *Wow. Kellan said please.*

CHAPTER TWENTY-EIGHT

I was trapped in a five-by-ten cage. I shook the bars on all sides. There was no escape. There were men and women on the outside of the cage. I recognized one. Asia. She came up to the bars.

"How is Kellan's little pet now?" she asked, sickeningly sweetly.

Then she was laughing. All the others started laughing with her. I watched Kellan walk up to her. He put his arm around her shoulder and started laughing also.

"Now you will have to obey me, baby."

No! I woke with that word screaming through my head. I was soaking wet with sweat. It was just starting to get light outside. Untangling myself from Kellan, gingerly so I wouldn't wake him, I went into the bathroom for a much needed shower.

I went down to the kitchen and put on a pot of coffee. When it was done, I went out on the balcony to watch my first sunrise over New York. It was beautiful out here. I hated to admit that this was where I felt the most comfortable at in Kellan's apartment.

This was my third day in New York. Yet I felt as though I had been gone from home for months. I think it was because everything here was so different from what I was used to. Who was I kidding? I was out of sorts this morning, with everything that had gone down with Kellan last night and, to top it off, that damn dream. The dreams always took a toll on me.

I went back into the kitchen and refilled my coffee. Mrs. Parker walked in before I had finished. "You're up very early, Ms. Leigh," she said with a welcoming smile.

"I usually get up before dawn if I'm not out too late. I like to watch the sunrise."

I went into the living room with my coffee. Placing the mug on the end table, I took my laptop off the coffee table. I sat cross-legged on the sofa and lost myself in my book. I was so into it that I jumped when Kellan ran his hands slowly over my shoulders from behind me.

"Hey. I didn't mean to startle you."

"Sorry." I giggled. "I was kind of lost in my story." I turned my head so I could see him. He always looked so sexy when he just woke up, always looked as if he just had great, mind-blowing sex.

"Morning." He leaned down and placed a kiss on my lips. "Are we good?" he asked quietly in my ear.

"Yeah. We're good."

He graced me with a glowing smile. "I have some work to do, baby. I'll be in my office."

I nodded and turned back to my laptop. I heard him chuckling as he walked away. I guess that was because I was so wrapped up in what I was doing. When the scenes were in my head, it was all I could concentrate on until I put it in print. Plus, Kellan was giving me so much ammunition to create these scenes—even if he didn't know it.

I had been working nonstop for a couple of hours when my phone went off. I glanced at the screen. It was my editor.

"Hey, Mallory. What's up?"

"*Fall into Time* has just made the national best-sellers list, India."

"No way!" I'm stunned. I mean, it's my first book! "So what does that mean exactly?"

"It means you are definitely on your way. I told you that you would be famous. On top. But it also means more work. We have to keep you out there."

"How? What do you want me to do?"

"I talked it over with the big guys. We all agreed to bring the other two books out at the same time. By Christmas. If you could come to New York—"

"I'm in New York," I interrupted her.

"Great. How long are you here for?"

"I'm not sure about this time. Kellan, my boyfriend, has to be here all the time. I have to accompany him to his business and social engagements. So I'll be going back and forth."

"Ah. Boyfriend," Mallory teased. "Do I know him?"

"I don't know. Maybe. But I would bet you know of him. Kellan Coventry?"

She must have been drinking something because she sounded as if she choked. "You're kidding! *The* Kellan Coventry?"

"Yeah. Unless there's more than one." I chuckled.

"My God, India! Is it serious?"

"Don't know about him—" I changed the subject. I didn't want to think about how Kellan felt about me. "So what is it you want me to do?"

"Okay. I'll quit being nosy." She laughed into the phone. "We want you to do book signings here, in several locations with the first book, while we strongly promote the following two books at the same time."

"That's cool. No problem."

"All right then. I'm so excited for you. I'll be in touch with the times and locations."

"Okay." I paused. "Mallory, thank you. This wouldn't be happening without you."

I ended the call and just sat there, staring at it. Wow! National best-sellers list and my next two books coming out so soon. It's July now. Only four and a half months. I am living my dream!

I squealed loudly and bounced up and down on the sofa.

"What is it? India, what's wrong?" Kellan belted out, rushing into the room.

I turned around on the couch, kneeling up on the cushion and holding on to the back. Mrs. Parker was behind Kellan. Four of the security guys were behind her.

"Sorry, sorry," I said, smiling at them sheepishly. "Nothing's wrong, Kellan. Everything is great."

"Don't act coy, baby. What's the deal?"

"*Fall into Time* made the national best-sellers list. They're going to release the last two books in the trilogy at the same time because of it. Before Christmas. I'm not only an author, Kellan, I'm a best-selling author."

Kellan walked over to me and reached down. Wrapping his hands around my waist, he lifted me up into his arms. I wound my arms around his neck and my legs around his hips, hugging him to me tightly.

"You've always been a best seller to me, baby."

I raised my head off his shoulder and looked into those beautiful blue eyes. "You're just biased. I bet you have never read anything I've written."

"You think not?" His look was so tender. "I've read every article I could get my hands on. And while we're on the subject, I need you to sign my copy of your book."

"You've read my book?" I looked at him incredulously. "When?"

"Right after I met you. I thought I could find out more about you by reading it. You have great talent, baby. We need to celebrate your success."

The elevator binged, and Bret went out to see who it was. He walked back in with Deric. Deric's eyebrows shot up when he saw all of us in the living room with me wrapped around Kellan.

"Should I come back? Or can I join in?" he asked teasingly.

I let my legs fall away from around Kellan's waist, and he set me gently on my feet. Heat spread up my cheeks. Kellan lifted my face with a hand under my chin. "You have no reason to be embarrassed."

He ran the back of his knuckles back and forth the side of my face. I loved when he was like this. The tender lover.

"You're just in time, Deric. We were breaking open the champagne. India made the best-sellers list."

A TEMPTATION

Mrs. Parker came in with a tray of wine glasses. Kellan went behind the bar, bringing out a couple of bottles of champagne from the wine cooler. He deftly popped the corks and filled all the glasses. Grabbing two glasses, he handed one to me. Mrs. Parker and Bret handed out the rest.

Kellan held up his glass. "To India's success with her first book, and the next two that will follow in the same footsteps, I'm sure."

"Here, here," everyone said, raising their glasses.

Deric set his glass down on an end table after he took a sip. He came over to me and gave me a hug. "Congratulations, India."

"Thank you," I said, smiling up at him.

Kellan's arms came around me from behind, wrapping around my waist and pulling me into his chest. "Get your hands off my woman, bud," he jokingly said to Deric. "Go find your own."

"Oh, hell no!" Deric held his hands up in surrender. "I'm glad you're so happy, man, but I'm cool just how I am." Everyone laughed.

"By the way, India. How do you like being the cause of hundreds of women crying in their beer today?"

"Huh?" I asked, totally confused.

"Have you guys even seen the paper the last few days?" Deric asked.

"Been kind of busy here, man," Kellan said.

Deric went into the kitchen and came back out with the *New York Times*. He found the society section from the first one, handing it to Kellan. Then he did the same with the second one, handing it to me.

Wow. Picture after picture of Kellan and me going into the Sherry-Netherland and coming back out. Same with Le Bernardin. Shots of Kellan holding me tight against him and of him kissing me ravenously. Kellan whispering in my ear. I liked seeing the pictures of us together. I hoped he was all right with it. I looked up at him in silent query.

"This is good," Kellan said, bending and kissing me lightly. "Now everyone will know to stay away from you. Know that you belong to me."

"Oh yeah." Deric pulled something out from inside his sports jacket. "There's this also." He handed it to me.

Unfolding it, I saw that it was one of the tabloids. There were some of the same pictures of Kellan and me. The headline read, "Sorry, Charlies." But when I opened the paper, the next few pages had picture after picture of Kellan with different women. I recognized a few. Asia, Presley, and Alexis. There were a lot of others.

One very big difference between them and me, not in one picture did he have so much as a finger on them. No solicitous hand on the small of their back. No proprietary arm wrapped around their waist. No anything. Kellan was even standing a good foot away from them. A massive difference from how he was with me.

I looked up from the tabloid, my heart, I'm sure, in my eyes. "You okay, baby?" Kellan asked me anxiously.

"Yes," I assured him. "I'm more than okay."

"Deric and I will be in the office. We have some things to talk about." He bent down, placing his lips on mine. When he ended the kiss, he looked into my eyes. "Meet you in the kitchen for lunch?"

I nodded, and he turned and started walking to his office. Before Deric followed him, I looked at Kellan's best friend. "Thank you," I said quietly to him.

He smiled at me. "I thought you needed to see for yourself how Kellan feels about you. No one could say it better than those pictures."

After Deric followed Kellan to his office, I went in search of Mrs. Parker, asking for a pair of scissors. Sitting at the kitchen table, I cut out the pictures of Kellan and me from the *Times*. As for the tabloid, I kept the whole thing.

I placed the cut-out pictures in a book I was reading so they wouldn't get messed up. Then I put the book and the tabloid into my tote that I carried my laptop in.

I went back to work on my laptop. I was so excited about this new series. There was this spark of hope in me that now, quite possibly, there would be a happy ending.

"Lunchtime, baby," Kellan said. He was standing in front of me, holding out his hand. Setting my laptop down, I placed my hand in his. He tugged me up and into his arms. "I'm so glad you're here."

A TEMPTATION

"Me too," I said, barely above a whisper.

His lips descended on mine. He moaned. "Let's go. They're waiting on us." I nodded, and we walked with our fingers entwined into the kitchen.

Lunch was great. The security guys, Deric, Mrs. Parker, Kellan, and I talked and laughed. They all had hilarious stories to tell about Kellan. Kellan, in return, had good ones about them.

I also learned a little about his business, exactly what Coventry Technologies consisted of, what they worked on and for whom. Well, not everything. They did top-secret work for the military and other government agencies.

Kellan was intelligent and innovative. He had started with an idea in college and turned it into a multibillion-dollar company. None of that included his real estate holdings. That was altogether a different barrel of fish.

This Kellan, the one who was talking so animatedly, was dedicated and caring to his employees—from the domestic help and the security guys to all of the employees at Coventry Technologies and the hotels and resorts. They loved him. I heard that he was a demanding employer, but fair and generous.

To me, he was an enigma, one that I couldn't wait to find all the puzzle pieces to.

We then talked about what my publishers wanted me to do, the book signings here in New York, and the intense promoting they were going to do for the last two books of the trilogy since December wasn't that far away. We talked about the new series that I was working on—not what it was about, mind you, but that I was pretty deep into the first book.

Kellan looked at me with pride. The look had chill bumps running up and down my arms, and I shivered.

"If you can get me an itinerary, Kellan, with everything you need us to do, I can schedule the signings and whatever around those."

"Thanks, baby. I will print you out one."

It had been a wonderful day. Hopefully, there would be a lot more like this. If not, I would always have this one to remember.

CHAPTER TWENTY-NINE

*I*t was the end of September. I was getting ready to go to Roman Saunders's office to meet with the committee for the arts program. Only eight thirty in the morning, and I was still exhausted. I had had a harrowing schedule. With my book signings and all of Kellan's functions, we had never stopped. Tonight we had a fund-raiser that was being held at the home of the president of Kellan's bank. What were their names? Wells? Yes. That was it. Wells.

With his work and my writing during the day and all the demands on our time at night, we needed a vacation. Away from everything and everyone, only doing each other. God, that sounded wonderful.

I didn't know when we would be going home, even for just a little while. I had spoken to Kathy, Tim, and Bridgette. Everything was fine there. They missed me, and damn, did I ever miss them. I had even spoken to Noah.

In fact, Noah had called this morning to tell me he was coming home at the beginning of November. I couldn't wait to see him. This had been the longest time in our lives that we had been separated. It had always been Kathy, Noah, and I.

Putting on the pearl earrings that Kellan had gotten me, I went into the bedroom, collected my purse and some literature, and

A TEMPTATION

headed downstairs. It was 9:00 a.m. now, and I was to meet Roman at nine thirty. I had to go.

The people I was going to meet today all knew Kellan. With that in mind, I chose to wear a gray pencil skirt, the length ending right above my knee, a modest but sexy black lace long-sleeve blouse, and simple black heels. I left my long curly hair hanging down my back. I believed my appearance would do Kellan justice.

Arriving at the office building with ten minutes to spare was a good thing. The building was huge, and Roman had the penthouse offices. Bret, Zack, and two of the other guys all got on the elevator with me.

The looks we had gotten from the building's security when we had received our visitor passes were comical. I had become so used to their presence that I didn't think twice about it, but I'm sure the rest of the world would view it as unusual, to say the least.

When we arrived at Roman's offices, I gave my name to the receptionist then had a seat. It was only a few minutes before Roman came out to the lobby, and I stood to greet him. He took both my hands in his. "India, it's so good to see you. You look beautiful."

I felt my blush. I guess I would never outgrow that. "It's good to see you too." I smiled shyly at him.

"Let's go. They're waiting for you." Roman placed my hand in the crook of his arm while he led me to a conference room.

Bret and Zack were right behind us. They always stayed right with me whenever I ventured out. When we entered the conference room, they stood on either side of the door that Roman closed.

There were four men and a woman seated at the conference table. Roman made the sixth person of the committee. The men rose until I took the seat Roman was holding out for me. Mr. Saunders, Roman's father, was the head of the committee.

Roman introduced me to everyone. The woman, who was Asian, seemed to have an attitude toward me. Maybe I was paranoid. I picked up the literature I had brought with me, having made copies for everyone with Kellan's copier. Bret took the copies from me and handed them to the others.

The Asian woman snorted rather loudly. "Does Kellan Coventry trust you so little that he sends his men around with you?" she asked very snidely.

Oh. I get it. *Peterson*. This woman was related to Asia. I looked at her more intently. She looked to be a much older version of Asia. Had to be her mother. Like mother, like daughter, it seemed. Both bitches. And this one just pissed me off.

"I've met your daughter, Asia, Mrs. Peterson. Y'all have the same looks and the same friendly attitude," I spit out sarcastically. I saw Zack and Bret look at each other, and their lips curved up into grins. Yeah. They have come to know me well. "I didn't come here today to discuss mine and Kellan's personal life. Frankly, it's none of your business, and I sure don't owe you an explanation."

I took a calming breath before I continued. "I came here to help y'all start up an arts program. One, I might add, that has produced some highly successful authors, sculptors, and painters. I'm an award-winning author. Between what I have on my plate and Kellan's full book, I'm extremely busy and don't have time for fools." I looked directly at Mrs. Peterson. "In that literature, it states what y'all will need to get started. Anything else, Roman knows how to get in touch with me."

I stood, nodding my head to the men. "It's been a pleasure, gentlemen, Roman. Y'all have a good day."

With my head held high, I started out the door. I heard Roman say he would see me out. Bret and Zack were chuckling behind me. When Roman caught up with us, he was downright laughing as he took my arm.

"Damn, I love Cajuns," Roman said, grinning at me. "That was great. I've wanted to see that woman and her daughter put in their place for years."

"Yeah? Glad you enjoyed the show," I said sarcastically. "But I don't suffer bitches."

At that remark, Bret, Zack, and Roman were laughing loudly. The girl at the reception desk looked at us in total confusion. The other two security guys looked at Bret and Zack as if they had gone mad. After they related what happened at the meeting, I was exiting the elevator with five very large men, laughing like hyenas.

Bret went out to get the SUV; the rest of us stayed in the lobby to wait until he pulled up in front of the building.

"I'll let you know when everything is a go. We will have to wait until we can find a suitable building," Roman said as we waited.

"After that disaster that happened in there?" I asked incredulously.

"Definitely. No one likes Clair Peterson. They will not let her hurt this program. It will be great for this city. So expect my call."

"Good," I said, smiling up at him. "There are so many talented people that would never get anywhere without the knowledge and help that this program can bring them. They don't have the funds or the resources. With their successes, they and their family's lives will be richer. Better education for their children, and hopefully, everything will trickle down. I've seen it happen. Watching it is the greatest reward in the world."

The strangest look came over Roman's face. I couldn't interpret it. "You're amazing. I hope Coventry knows what he has." He ran the fingers of one hand down the side of my face. "I wish things had been different, and I had met you first."

I didn't know what to say, so I didn't say anything. But this made me uncomfortable. I backed up a step, and his hand fell away.

"India. I'm sorry. I didn't mean to make you uncomfortable. I wouldn't do anything to hurt you."

Zack took my arm. "Come on, Ms. Leigh. It's time to go." I nodded my consent and saw the dirty look that Zack gave Roman.

On the way back to Kellan's apartment, I retraced my actions to see if at any time I had given Roman the wrong idea. If I had given off any vibes other than friendship. No. I didn't believe I had. I would keep my distance. Roman hadn't done anything per se, but it had been implied. And I wasn't going to borrow trouble where Kellan was concerned.

I went up to the bedroom as soon as we got back to the apartment. There were things I could be doing, but I had been exhausted before that meeting. Taking off just my shoes, I lay across Kellan's bed.

I was awakened by kisses being rained across my jaw and down my neck. I didn't remember falling asleep. I groaned and reached out, wrapping my arms around Kellan's shoulders. "It's time to get up, sleepy head," Kellan said softly. "You have to get ready for the Wells fund-raiser."

"Aw," I moaned. "I want to sleep for a week."

Kellan chuckled at me. "I know your schedule's been hell, baby. It will lighten up soon." I had turned on my side, trying to get closer to him. He popped me on my ass. "Up now."

"Hey!" I complained. "Your handprint is going to be permanently branded on my behind."

"Don't tempt me, baby." He grinned wickedly.

Kellan's phone went off. He reached in his pocket, and had a confused look on his face when he saw the screen. "I have to take this." He placed a kiss on my forehead then walked out of the room.

I was in the shower. I had already washed and conditioned my hair. My body was all lathered up. My eyes were closed to keep the soap out. I felt Kellan join me. He took the handheld wand and rinsed all the soap from my face and body. Drying my face with the towel I had draped over the glass enclosure of the shower so I could see what I was doing, I squirted shampoo into my hand. Standing behind Kellan on my tiptoes, I gently tugged on his hair. He leaned down so I could reach him. I slowly and thoroughly massaged the shampoo into his scalp. I heard him moan. Everything in me tightened, hearing that arousing sound.

Rubbing his soap between my hands then slowly running them over his entire body, I kept returning to his groin, tenderly cupping his balls with one hand, strongly wrapping the other around his cock. Up and down, I slid my hand over him, the lather making it easier.

Kellan growled and backed under the spray of hot water, letting all the suds rinse away. He stepped into me, bringing his hands to my shoulders. He firmly pushed me to my knees. Wrapping my hand around the base of his shaft, raising my eyes to his, I swiped my tongue across the slit at the top of the plump head. I wrapped my lips around my teeth and lowered my mouth, sucking him in, licking as I went. Taking as much of him as I could. Sucking harder. Then I

A TEMPTATION

unwrapped my teeth and lightly ran them over him. I watched him unravel, saw exactly when all his control evaporated.

He pulled me up by my arms and pushed me until my back hit the marble wall, roughly picking me up and wrapping my legs around his hips. I held on to his shoulders. Bringing a hand between us, he gripped his penis. He backed away enough so that he could position the head of his cock at my opening.

Then bringing both of his hands to my hips, gripping his fingers tightly into my flesh, he slammed into me. I yelped from the bite of pain. He was large and thick, and it usually took a little time to fit all of him into me. I had become very aroused going down on him, but my body had been far from ready. It took just a moment for that bite of pain to turn into incredible pleasure. I whimpered. That seemed to inflame him more. With my back against the wall, he slammed into me over and over. He held my hips still, his hands like bands of steel wrapped around them. He exuded power and authority.

My clit tightened and ached. He rubbed against it every time he pushed back inside me. My pussy pulsed, and my body exploded in pleasure. I threw back my head and screamed. My pleasure so intense it hurt. Kellan kept slamming into me until one last hard thrust. Then he was pulsing inside me, his heated come shooting inside me, and he was roaring my name.

He pressed his forehead against mine. We were both panting, trying to bring much needed air into our lungs.

"What are you doing to me?" I didn't know who he was asking. It wasn't really directed toward me.

He lowered me back down to my feet and got out of the shower. A few minutes later, I heard the door to the bathroom open and close.

What was that about? One minute, he was a raging inferno. The next, cold as ice. For some strange reason, I felt like sobbing.

CHAPTER THIRTY

I went through the motions of getting dressed. Wearing a beautiful emerald-green strapless gown, I put my curls in a waterfall clip, letting it hang down my back. I put emeralds in my ears and around my throat and wrist. I added an anklet and clear stilettos. Wearing the minimum of makeup, I added a smoky green eye shadow and coral lip gloss. My ID, lip gloss, and phone, and some cash went into a matching evening bag. Also a check that I had made out for the women's shelter the money that was raised tonight was going to.

I went downstairs. Kellan was looking out the wall of glass. He must have gotten dressed in his office. Kellan made a tux look good. I stood there at the bottom of the stairs, soaking him in. He took my breath away. He must have felt my presence because when he turned toward me, he didn't seem surprised that I was standing there.

He walked over, stopping right in front of me, running the fingers of one hand reverently down my face. "You are so lovely."

"Kellan, what's wrong?"

He dropped his hand. "Nothing."

A TEMPTATION

"That's not true. I can see it. Feel it." I searched his face, my eyes wandering over his beautiful features trying to ferret out what was disturbing him. "Please talk to me."

"Let it go, India," he snapped at me.

I shook my head. This was one of Kellan's worst faults. He acted. He didn't talk things out. I couldn't fix what I didn't know was broken.

"Shall we go?" he asked, placing my wrap around my shoulders. I shrugged. I really could care less.

Kellan never said a word during the entire drive. I made myself take up as little space as I could, pressing my body against the door of the limo and gazing at the passing scenery.

The Wells lived somewhere north of the city. We arrived at a long, gated driveway. There was a very long line of cars dropping people off in front of a huge mansion. There were standing electric lights every few feet down each side of the driveway. They looked like antique street lights from the 1800s converted from gas. It was stunning.

When we came to a stop in front of the mansion, Kellan came around, opening my door and holding his hand out to me. I put my hand in his and he helped me from the car. As soon as I was standing next to him, he put his arm around my waist and pulled me into his side. There were photographers here also. Not many, but still. I wondered if these people ever felt like bugs under a microscope. At least I didn't have to live like this all the time.

"Smile, India," Kellan whispered in my ear.

"Is that an order?" I bit back.

He sighed and led us through the mansion. It looked like an overstuffed museum. The antiques were wonderful but looked as if they would be more at home in a museum instead of a private residence. We followed the crowd through different public rooms of the house, through french doors, and out into the backyard.

The property was large. Acres. There was a massive tent right in the center, as large as a circus tent. There were white twinkle lights from the french doors to the tent, leading us on. There were also twinkle lights creating paths to and from different destinations.

Inside the tent, at the far back, the flaps were down. A raised stage was in front of the flaps. Tables were placed in a horseshoe formation with three rows through the entire horseshoe; that left a rather large area for dancing.

Kellan found our seats right in the center of the horseshoe; our seats faced the band and sat right on the edge of the dance floor. It was the host table. There were Kellan and I, Mr. and Mrs. Wells, and four other couples at our table. Kellan pulled out my chair, seated me, and took his seat on my left. He was busy talking to the couple on his left a few moments later.

"Excuse me." I heard a timid voice coming from my right. I turned and saw a pretty young woman sitting one chair over. The one between us was empty. "I don't mean to be rude, but my fiancé has been gone a while. I don't know anyone here and feel very out of place. My name is Sabrina. Bree to my friends." She smiled at me and held her hand out.

I shook her hand and smiled back at her. "I'm India. You aren't from here?"

"Heavens no. We're from Chicago. My fiancé travels here all the time and wanted us to attend this fund-raiser. Hence, me begging a stranger to have a conversation."

I laughed. She was delightful. "I'm glad you started talking to me. I don't know very many people here, only the ones I've met through my boyfriend. I'm from Slidell, Louisiana. It's right across Lake Pontchartrain from New Orleans. Kellan has a house there but lives most of the time in Manhattan, where he does the majority of his business."

A waiter came by with a tray of some kind of burgundy wine. Bree and I each took a glass. We said almost simultaneously, "I needed this" and laughed at ourselves. I was very happy to have met Bree tonight.

"What do you do, India?"

"I'm an author. How about you?"

She bypassed my question. "Oh! I love to read. What's the name that you write under?"

"My name." I giggled. "India Leigh."

A TEMPTATION

"Oh. My. God," Bree said so loudly that the others at our table looked in our direction. She lowered her voice. "*Fall into Time* is one of my favorite books. It's great. I can't believe I'm meeting you!"

"I'm just a person, Bree."

"A very talented person!" she exclaimed, her very blue eyes wide. "Do you have any other books out?"

"The next two books of the trilogy will come out right before Christmas. If you give me your address, I'll send you signed copies. I always like making new friends." We exchanged addresses and phone numbers. I really liked Bree. We could become very good friends.

We grabbed a second glass of wine from a passing waiter. Kellan had not talked to me once since we arrived, and her fiancé, Mike, was a no-show. We decided we would get drunk together.

Bree leaned over toward me. "India." She crooked her finger, so I leaned toward her. "Who is that woman hanging all over your man?"

I turned toward Kellan. Naturally, it was Asia. It would have been okay; I wouldn't have gotten bent out of shape because she was talking to him. What pissed me off was she had her hands on him, and he allowed it. He was smiling at her and talking animatedly to her. I had never heard him be pleasant to the woman before. Yet here he was, not talking to me. Why? Only heaven knew. But he was acting that way with her. Fuck that!

I turned away from them and back to Bree. "Bree, I have to find a restroom. Would you like to go with me?"

"God, yes. I've been needing to use the bathroom for an hour, but I didn't want to go by myself."

I laughed. I could understand her discomfort. It's not any fun not having your friends around you. Bree and I started walking off. I heard Kellan call my name. I acted as though I didn't hear him.

"India. Your boyfriend is calling you."

"I know. But right now, he can kiss my ass."

"I like you." Bree said, laughing. "So who is that woman? If you don't mind me asking."

"She's an ex of Kellan's, and a bitch. I don't plan on putting up with either one of them tonight."

"I'm sorry," she said softly to me. "You don't deserve to be treated indifferently."

"No one does, Bree," I told her pointedly because of her absent fiancé.

"No. You're right. No one does."

When we finally found a bathroom, I had calmed down a bit. When we were finished and exited, Bree scooted closer to me and whispered in my ear, "India. There are four men following us. They have been ever since we left the table."

I turned my head and saw my security team. "Oh. It's alright. It's my security team."

Her eyes were so expressive I could see her surprise. "Why do you need security? Are you being threatened?"

"No," I quickly assured her. "Kellan owns a large company and other things. There are always minor threats because of it. He's very overly protective, believe it or not."

We had walked a little ways back toward our table when I heard someone call my name from behind us. I turned around and saw Deric. When he came up to us, I introduced Bree to him.

"I'm sorry to interrupt, but could I talk to you a minute, India?"

"Sure." I turned to Bree. "I'll be right back." She nodded, and I walked a short distance away with Deric.

"What's up with Kellan?" he asked me, looking very serious.

"I don't know, Deric. He was fine when he came home from work. Took a call, and he has been acting like an ass ever since."

"He's being a dickhead to everyone but Asia." He flinched. "Sorry. I shouldn't have brought her up."

"No problem. I'm not blind, Deric." I paused for just a moment. "If I need to leave, would you take me back to Kellan's? I don't want to put you in the middle of anything, but I can only take so much, and I don't have my own car."

"I understand." He shook his head. "I don't know what he thinks he's doing."

I shrugged and rejoined Bree. Kellan wasn't at our table when we returned. He was on the dance floor with Asia. They were dancing the waltz. My heart felt as if someone had seized it. And when

A TEMPTATION

Kellan smiled down at her, I thought they went ahead and ripped it out. He looked up then, right at me.

Without taking my eyes off of him, I motioned Bret over, asking him to find Deric for me. When he went off to do as I asked, I broke eye contact with Kellan and sat down. I felt Bree's hand on my arm, so I turned to her.

"I'm so sorry, India."

"It's all right, Bree. It's his asshole gene coming out. All men have those." I smiled at her even though I wanted to cry.

Deric arrived, and I was so relieved Kellan wasn't off the dance floor yet. "Will you take me to Kellan's please? I need to go pack."

"India," Deric said, "I'll take you to Kellan's, but please don't do anything rash."

"Deric, rash would be doing what I feel like doing right at this moment. But I won't embarrass myself. No one is worth that."

I told Bret that Deric was taking me to Kellan's. He said no, shaking his head and looking toward Kellan on the dance floor. I glanced up. Kellan was watching all of us. He wasn't smiling now.

I looked back at Bret. "I didn't ask your permission. I'm leaving. You can stay here or not. I really don't care."

I got up, telling Bree to call me anytime. Deric led me back out the way Kellan and I had entered not more than an hour before. When we got outside, Deric said he would go and get his car and would be right back. I told him I would rather walk with him. I didn't want to take the chance that Kellan would arrive outside before Deric returned with the car.

When we finally got to his car, he put me in the passenger seat. Tears were falling down my face before he got behind the steering wheel. I heard Deric curse as he started the car when he realized I was crying. He called Kellan some unpleasant names. I didn't know if my security team had followed. I suppose that was moot now.

I didn't say anything the whole way back to the city. Not one sound. I just silently cried with my forehead pressed up against the glass of the window. This was hell. If I had been physically injured, it would have hurt a lot less.

Deric pulled in front of Kellan's apartment building. He opened my door, throwing his keys to the valet as we walked to the entrance. Once in the elevator, I swiped my hands across my face and turned to Deric.

"I hate to impose on you anymore, but if you could give me a ride to the airport, I would appreciate it."

"I don't mind taking you anywhere India." He looked at me closely. "But shouldn't you talk to Kellan first?"

"Why?" I asked him. "Everything looked self-explanatory to me. Or maybe I should just wait until he fucks her in front of me?" Deric looked shocked. All the shit that he and Kellan and whoever were into, and yet I say the F-word and he's shocked? "I'm sorry, Deric. You've been nothing but kind tonight. I'm just so out of my element here. I'm off-balanced."

"It's okay. Go pack, India. I'll wait."

"Thank you."

I hurried up to Kellan's room and changed into jeans, a lightweight sweater, and boots. I packed only what I had brought with me from Slidell. I left everything that he had bought for me.

I was just about to go pack my things from the bathroom when I heard raised voices from downstairs. I walked out of the bedroom and halfway down the stairs so I could hear what was being said.

"You have no idea what she did today!" That was Kellan. What in the hell did he think I had done? Was he so pissed off that I had told off Clair Peterson?

"What the fuck are you talking about, Kellan? I can't see that woman doing anything against you. Not the way she feels about you."

"Well, apparently she is capable of a lot, and not the person I thought she was."

I had had enough. I went the rest of the way down and into the living room. Deric's eyes widened when he saw me. He was facing me. Kellan's back was toward me. Kellan turned when he saw Deric's expression. His eyes narrowed when he looked at me.

"Do you trust your employees, Kellan?" He stayed silent. "If you're acting this way because I told Clair Peterson off, tough shit. I would do it again in a heartbeat since that was the only thing that I did that wasn't the norm. If that's not it, I have no clue. But hey, don't believe me. Talk to Bret and Zack. They never left my side. Deric, I'm almost finished." I turned and went back up the stairs.

I took my small suitcase into the bathroom and packed, once again, only what I had brought with me. I looked at Kellan's massive shower and remembered how callously he had treated me. When I went back into the bedroom, Kellan was standing by his bed, looking at my suitcase. I stopped and closed my eyes against the pain that was beating inside my chest. Tears once again started to fall down my face.

I opened my eyes, squared my shoulders, and faced him. "Don't worry. I only took what I brought from home with me. But if you like, I, I—" My voice broke. "I'll wait while you check."

Kellan walked over to me, taking the suitcase out of my hand and setting it down on the floor. He placed his hands on my shoulders.

"No! Don't you fucking touch me!" I jerked out of his grip, trying to run for the door, but Kellan was faster. He grabbed me around my waist. I kicked. I threw my head back—anything to just get him to let go. I cursed him. I screamed.

"Kellan!" Deric shouted. "Let her go."

Kellan put his back against one of the walls in his room. He let his body slide down until he was sitting on the floor with me in his lap, my back to his chest. He wrapped his arms around my chest, trapping my arms against my body. He wrapped his legs around my legs. I was trapped. I couldn't move. I started sobbing, loud heart-wrenching sobs.

"I just need to talk to her, Deric. I need her to listen."

"Fuck, Kellan. You should have talked to her in the first place. You're doing this shit ass backwards."

"I know," he said quietly. He kissed the top of my head. "Shh, baby. You're going to make yourself sick."

"N-now I-I'm baby again? Now you're concerned? You make my head spin, Kellan."

"Fuck!" Deric cursed. "I'll be right out in the hall."

"I'm sorry, baby. I went nuts when Clair called me saying you were making a fool out of me with Roman. That you and he were hand in hand and…well, other bullshit."

"And you just believed the bitch, Kellan! You didn't talk to me? You didn't ask me anything. You took her word for it. What have I ever done to make you believe I would do anything against you? Look who that woman is. Who her daughter is."

"I know, baby," he said brokenly. "I go crazy even thinking about someone touching you. It's not an excuse—"

"No. It's crazy is what it is. And how you acted with Asia tonight? You humiliated me. You broke my heart."

"I know. I know." He started rocking me. "Can you forgive me, India? I'll do anything."

"I don't know, Kellan," I said quietly. "I have never felt the way I did tonight. It would have been kinder if you would have shot me."

He flinched. "I am so sorry, baby. I would never hurt you on purpose. I understand that I have," he assured me. "But I swear, I would rather cut off my arm than to cause you an ounce of pain."

"But you did, Kellan. You hurt me. I asked you before to talk to me. You not doing so is going to destroy us. How can I trust you when you don't trust me?"

"I do trust you!"

"How can you say that, Kellan? You took that woman's word! You didn't believe any differently until you talked to Bret and Zack."

"I—" He blew out a breath. "You're right," he sighed. "That is exactly what I did. I didn't understand the implications until now. I'm sorry, baby. You have never done anything to make me not trust you." He was silent for a moment. "I will see someone, India. A therapist if you like. I don't want to hurt you ever again."

"I need you to talk to me, Kellan," I said emphatically. "We need to be able to discuss any problems so we can solve them. One more time, Kellan. It happens one more time, and I'm done."

"Thank you." He let out his breath. "There won't be another time."

He stood up with me in his arms. He walked over to the bed and laid me down reverently. "I'm going to go talk to Deric, and I'm

A TEMPTATION

sure some of the guys are out there too. I'll go tell them that you are all right. I'll be right back."

I just nodded my head. I was so exhausted. Kellan exhausted me. I curled up around a pillow and was asleep before I knew it.

CHAPTER THIRTY-ONE

I was sitting in a chair on a dance floor. The lighting was dim. Kellan had Asia in his arms. They were dancing, around and around my chair. He was looking down at her tenderly, smiling his wicked smile that I loved—except now it was for her.

I tried to get up, but I couldn't. Looking down, I saw that I was tied to the chair. My arms were tied to the arms of the chair, my waist to its back, and my legs to its legs. I tried to say something to Kellan, but nothing came out.

Then there were other couples dancing around me. They disappeared just as fast. Only Kellan and Asia remained. They weren't dancing anymore. They were standing still, right in front of me. Kellan leaned his head down, tilting it to the side. His lips descended on Asia's, his mouth devouring hers. I kept trying to shout, to scream, but still nothing came out. I couldn't sit here and watch this. I closed my eyes, but then I could hear them.

No! I opened my mouth wide. With every bit of air in my lungs and every bit of strength in my body, I willed the scream to erupt. The sound that escaped was the cry of a wounded animal. I was a wounded animal.

A TEMPTATION

I woke up to Kellan shaking me by the shoulders. "It's just a dream, baby. A bad dream. I've got you. I'll never let you go."

He pulled me over on top of his chest. I started crying. I was shaking so hard I was afraid I would break something. He kept telling me everything was all right, rubbing soothing circles on my back. I cried so much; I cried myself back to sleep.

I was lying in Kellan's bed the next morning, not wanting to move. I had a monstrous headache. Closing my eyes once again, I placed a hand over them. Feeling a weight sink down next to me on the bed, I peeked out through my fingers. It was Kellan with a cup of coffee.

"You okay, baby?"

"Headache," I moaned out to him.

"Here. Sit up." I sat up on the side of the bed as he asked. He got up, set the coffee on the nightstand, and plumped some pillows and placed them against the headboard. "Sit back, baby." He patted the pillows. "I'll get you something for your head."

He walked off into the bathroom. When he came back, he handed me two tablets and the coffee.

"Thank you." I gladly swallowed the tablets down with the first sip of coffee.

It was Sunday, the first of October. This was my favorite time of year. October, November, and December.

Kellan sat back down on the edge of the bed next to me. "How about we stay in today and just relax?" he asked me.

I smiled at him. "Best offer I've had in a long time."

My phone went off. I looked at the nightstand, but my phone wasn't there. Kellan got up from the bed and walked over to the dresser. He picked up the evening bag that I used last night and brought it over to me. My phone was still in there. I took it out and looked at the screen. It was Bree. *God*, I thought, *the way I left her last night*. I shook my head and took the call.

"Bree. Hey, I'm glad you called." Kellan sat back down next to me.

"India, are you okay?" Bree asked.

I sighed. "Yes. Everything is okay now. I'm sorry that I had to desert you last night." Kellan placed an apologetic hand on my thigh.

"Oh please. Don't think anything about it. I wouldn't have been able to handle that as gracefully as you did. In fact, I didn't."

"What?" I raised a hand over my mouth. "Your absent fiancé?" I lowered my hand. "Did he come back?"

"No. He didn't. But I went looking for him. I found him in a compromising position on the dark side of the Wells mansion. I ranted so loud that it brought others over to where we were. Then I slapped him so hard I left my handprint. I took the limo back to the hotel. I don't know where Mike went. Don't really care. I'm at the airport now, waiting for my flight back home."

"I'm so sorry, Bree."

"Don't be. I really knew he was playing me. I just didn't want to believe it." She paused. "When you asked me what I did for a living last night, I didn't answer because I was embarrassed. I have a degree, but I use it at my father's company. That's where I met Mike. He works for my father. My father is the one with all the money. I realized that the company and the money was why Mike was with me."

"You have nothing to be embarrassed about," I stressed. "That's all on Mike. You're smart and beautiful. Outgoing and kind. You'll find someone who deserves you."

"Yeah. Well, I'm not going to go looking anytime soon. But hey, I would like to stay in touch with you if that's okay?"

"It's more than okay, Bree. You could come to Louisiana. You would fit right in with my friends and have a great time."

"That sounds great. I will certainly take you up on it. I've got to go now, India. They're calling my flight."

"Sure. I'll talk to you later. Have a safe flight." I ended the call and glanced over at Kellan.

"Do you want some more coffee?" he asked me.

"Of course," I teased him. "But I want to take a quick shower first."

"Okay. You get your shower. I'll get your coffee." He started walking to the door, but turned his head toward me when he reached the threshold. "I'm really sorry about last night, baby. More than you will ever know."

"I am too," I said quietly. "I hope you can start opening up to me. I can't do any more."

"I know. You don't need to. I do." He continued out of the room.

I was standing under the hot water in the shower, letting it relax all my tense muscles. *Kellan must have some mean demons.* That's all I could think of that would have someone run so fast from hot to cold. I wondered if something in his past was so detrimental that he only had the D/S, er, relationships because of it. Then I came along, and he didn't know how to deal with it, with the passion, with the emotions. *He doesn't quite know where I fit.* He was afraid I'd realize, afraid of what I could do to him emotionally—afraid of me ripping his heart out.

I turned off the water, stepped out, quickly dried off, and wrapped the towel around me. When I walk back out to the bathroom, Kellan was placing another cup of coffee on the nightstand. His eyes met mine. I froze. That look in his magnetic gaze? Everything in me melted.

He stalked over to me. He flicked the knot on the towel, and it fell to the floor. With one arm going behind my knees and one behind my back, he lifted me, holding me against his chest. He carried me to his bed, laying me upon it reverently. He climbed up, straddling my waist.

Kellan tenderly kissed my lips then rained kisses down the side of my face, down my neck, on my shoulders, collarbones, to my breast. He suckled my nipples. First one then the other. I arched my back to bring me closer to him.

He was being so gentle. So loving. So very different from how intense and commanding he usually was. He continued down, over my rib cage, down my belly. He settled between my legs, spreading my thighs wide.

Kellan raised his eyes to mine. He smiled. It was sexy and adorable, not a smile I was familiar with from him. He placed a soft kiss on my mound. Then his tongue found me. He flicked my clitoris with it, running his tongue around and over that pulsing bundle of nerves.

He circled my opening then speared that talented tongue inside me. I moaned, squirming. He held my thighs tightly so I couldn't move any longer. He was fucking me with his tongue. His mouth found my clit again. He lathed it then suckled it, and I erupted. It was wonderful. It was frightening. I was afraid I was going to crash and burn. He continued licking softly, bringing me gently down.

Kellan crawled up my body. He softly brushed my lips with his. Looking into my eyes, he slowly filled me. This was my favorite part, when he was inside me, the connection so strong between us. We became one. I moaned, closing my eyes.

"Open your eyes, India," he demanded quietly. "Watch me. I want you to see me."

I obeyed, opening my eyes. Kellan made love to me. Not rough, demanding sex. He was telling me he loved me the only way he knew how. No words. I didn't know if Kellan was capable of saying he loved me, but I felt it. Deep and strong. I felt cherished and safe, wrapped up in his love. Tears came to my eyes.

"I love you, Kellan," I whispered to him. I had to tell him. I needed him to know what he meant to me. That he was a part of me. He froze.

"Oh, baby," he rasped out. "I will treasure your love. You? You're everything to me."

He moved slowly in and out, swiveling his hips, hitting that spot inside just right. He knew my body well. His pelvis rubbed my clit every time he pushed back in. I unraveled, my orgasm sweet. He came with me. Together. We were one.

"India," he whispered in my ear, "I can't even think about being without you."

"You don't have to, Kellan. I'm right here."

That Sunday started a new chapter in Kellan's and my life. That day? I will remember that day as long as I live. A new side of Kellan Coventry emerged, one I had never thought to see.

He never said the words "I love you." Not once. But he showed me in a million different ways. He was much more demonstrative.

A TEMPTATION

Not just in a sexual way. He showed me how much he cherished me. Needed me. Wanted me.

The only times that we were apart was during the day when he was at his office. I never trespassed on his time at work, knowing how busy he was with all the responsibility he had. I didn't want him to worry about me at those times.

I had all of his nights and every spare moment of every day that he had. Every day, I fell harder and deeper in love with Kellan. Soon I would not be able to survive without him. Without his touch. His looks. His smell, even. It was all being branded deeper and deeper into my soul.

All of New York were used to the phenomenon of Kellan and me as a couple. I went to all the parties and functions that required his attendance. We went out to clubs and restaurants, walked in Central Park, and even went sightseeing.

I was happier than I could ever remember being. My heart was light, and I had not had another nightmare since the night of the Wells fund-raiser. All in all, life was good.

CHAPTER THIRTY-TWO

*I*t was the third week of October, and I was getting ready to go meet Roman. A building had been donated for the arts program. I winced, thinking about the discussion Kellan and I had about it last night.

At first, Roman was going to pick me up and take me to see the site. Kellan said absolutely not, that the security team would drive me there and back.

"Kellan, they can follow like they usually do. That will give Roman and me time to discuss a lot of other details that need to be covered."

"I. Said. No." The look that Kellan directed toward me was warning enough. I knew not to tread this path any longer.

"Okay!" I threw my hands up. "You win. I go with the security guys."

"Thank you," he said and kissed me lightly on the lips.

I shook my head at my reflection in the bathroom mirror. My Kellan had come a long way, but when it came to my safety or another man being around me, he went all caveman. I picked up my purse on the way out and went downstairs to meet the guys so we could head out.

A TEMPTATION

"Oh wow. This is great," I said excitedly to Roman. "It will be perfect."

The building turned out to be a small warehouse. We would need to clean and paint, and build some sort of walls to separate the different areas. We would also need shelves built. We needed tables, chairs, and supplies.

"I think so," Roman said with a smile. "But you know more about that than I do. What do you say to lunch? We can go over everything then."

"I appreciate the offer, Roman, but I have a book signing at one." I held up a finger. "Can you excuse me for a minute?"

I took my phone out of my purse and scrolled down to Kellan's number. I never called him at work. I never wanted to intrude there. I walked away from Roman so I wouldn't be over heard.

"India, what's wrong?" Kellan's voice came out frantic.

"Nothing! I'm sorry. I didn't mean to worry you. I wouldn't normally call you at work, but I needed to ask you something."

I heard him release a relieved breath. "You can call me anytime, baby. No matter what I'm doing. Now what do you need?"

"I was thinking that since we're staying in for dinner tonight, if you wouldn't mind if Roman joined us. That way, we can go over the plans for the building and the supplies they'll need to start the classes." I also thought that Kellan would rather I meet with Roman with him present. I kept that thought to myself.

"That's fine, baby. What time did you have in mind?"

"I have my book signing at one. That will end at five. So around seven? I would like a shower when I get home."

"That sounds good. I'll call Mrs. Parker and let her know. Have a great signing, and be careful please."

"I will, Kellan. Thank you." I ended the call and went to ask Roman about dinner. He said it was a date. He locked up the warehouse, and we went off to our separate days.

The bookstore was on East Ninety-Second Street. It was a privately owned bookstore and was called The Book Nook. It was owned by a husband and wife, Robert and Cheryl More. They were in their thirties and had one of the best relationships I had ever witnessed. They teased and joked with each other, and there were still quiet touches and intimate looks.

The store itself was set up as a full bookstore and coffee shop. There was internet connection and cozy sitting areas with love seats and big cushy, comfy chairs. There were also bistro tables and chairs. It was a quaint, comfortable place.

I couldn't have asked for a better signing. A lot of fans showed up. I thought we just might run out of books. It was 4:45. The store closed at 5:00 p.m., but there were still people waiting. The More's said they would stay open until they were all seen.

I had just finished signing a book for a bubbly teenage girl. Looking up at the next customer, I froze. It was Devyn Troyer. I got up so fast that I knocked my chair over. I would have tripped over it if Bret hadn't grabbed my arm. Looking up at Bret, my bottom lip trembled, and I was shaking all over.

"India, are you sick? Do you need a doctor?"

"Get him away from me!"

As soon as the words left my mouth, all hell broke loose. Bret and Zack grabbed Devyn. The other two guys grabbed me and pushed me behind them. Devyn started screaming that he wanted his book signed by the whore. Bret decked him once, and he was out cold on the floor. Robert called the police. I went hysterical. Zack called Kellan.

The store was filled with police. I was sitting in an overstuffed chair with all four of my security guys surrounding me, blocking me from everything.

Bret and Zack stood directly in front of me. I was facing their backs. Even though Devyn was outside in a police car, I could still hear him screaming, calling me all sorts of vile names.

Suddenly, Bret and Zack parted, and Kellan was kneeling on the floor in front of me.

"Baby, look at me." I automatically looked up at his command. He ran his thumbs under my eyes, wiping my tears away. "Are you hurt, baby?"

"Shit," Kellan spat out. "India! I asked you a question. Answer me. Now!"

A TEMPTATION

I jumped. It was like coming out of a fog. I shook my head. "No, I'm not hurt, Kellan. He didn't touch me."

"Thank God!" Kellan stood up, pulling me up and into his arms, holding me tightly against his chest.

Bret relayed to Kellan everything that happened. This time, charges were pressed against Devyn Troyer. The police had also said that I should take out a restraining order. Kellan said he would contact his attorney tonight and have him handle it.

Kellan had his driver pull up to the back door of the bookstore. He put me in the backseat and slid in behind me. He pulled me onto his lap, holding me close to his heart. He placed a kiss on the top of my head.

"I'm not used to feeling fear, India," he murmured. "I was terrified."

I turned and laced my arms around his neck. "I was too, Kellan. But I'm not afraid when you're with me."

He wrapped his arms around me so tightly I could hardly breathe. His chin rested on top of my head. We stayed that way until we arrived at Kellan's apartment building.

Kellan went to his office to call his attorney as soon as we entered the apartment. I went up to take a quick shower. Roman would be here soon.

I threw on a pair of jeans and a Saints T-shirt and put my hair in a ponytail. Barefooted and with no makeup on, I got back downstairs.

Roman was already there. He and Kellan were sitting on one of the sofas in the living room with drinks in their hands. I went over to Kellan, leaned down and kissed him, then said hi to Roman and asked if they would like another drink. I got them both another Jack on the rocks, and me a glass of wine.

Mrs. Parker announced dinner, and we went into the dining room. Over dinner, Kellan asked questions about the building and everything we would have to do with it for the arts program. He seemed very interested.

When we finished dinner, I went into Kellan's office for paper and a pen. Back in the dining room, over more drinks, I wrote down what I knew would be required, adding that the individual artist would have to let him know about the rest. I looked up at one point and saw Roman staring at me.

"What?" I looked down at my shirt. "Did I get something on me?"

Roman laughed. "No. Sorry. It's just that you look like you're in your teens when you're dressed down."

"Thank God she's not!" Kellan exclaimed. And we all laughed.

An hour later, Roman took his leave. Kellan said he had some work he had to finish, but that he wouldn't be long. I headed up to bed. It had been a long, crazy day.

I was sitting in The Book Nook, but I was all alone. One minute, no one was in front of me; the next, Devyn Troyer was there. He snapped his fingers, and the table that was in front of me vanished. I was so afraid that I couldn't move. Devyn grinned an evil grin. He brought both his hands up to the neck of my shirt. He ripped my shirt in two. It fell open. He reached for me, and I screamed.

The next thing I knew, light was blazing in my eyes and Kellan was wrapping me in his arms. He rocked me, saying it was only a bad dream. He whispered soothing words. Told me how much I meant to him and how happy he was to have found me. Told me about all the things he wanted us to do together and all the places he wanted to take me to see. He continued until I fell asleep again, safe in his arms.

I woke up extremely late the next day. Kellan was no longer in bed beside me. I had no doubt he was at his office. It was eleven in the morning, and he usually left for work at seven. I washed up, got dressed, and went downstairs for much needed caffeine.

Taking my coffee out on the balcony, I noticed that it was quite nippy out. Then again, it was nearing the end of October, and this wasn't southern Louisiana. I realized how cold it would get here in the winter. I shivered. I hated the cold. Heat was in my blood—Gulf Coast heat.

Noah would be getting back home next Thursday. I spoke to Kathy, and we were planning for all of us having one of our New Orleans weekends. Not only could I not wait to see Noah, but my

A TEMPTATION

friends and I hadn't had one of our weekends since, well, since the weekend I met Kellan. That was almost six months ago. Man, how strange, and how fast had my life changed. Also, how wonderful.

I went back inside and went to work on my book. I was so lost in the story that I worked through lunch. I felt and saw hope now in my pages. I just prayed that this dream wouldn't turn into one of my worst nightmares.

It was six in the evening when I finally closed my laptop. I went into the kitchen. The guys were in there with Mrs. Parker. They were getting ready to eat dinner. I asked if anyone had heard from Kellan. No one had. He was usually home by now. Mrs. Parker asked if I was ready for dinner. I said that I would wait for Kellan.

At 8:00 p.m., Kellan still wasn't home, and I was worried. This wasn't like him. I picked up my phone and called him. He finally answered on the third ring.

"What?" he practically yelled into the phone.

"Kellan? Is everything all right?"

"Yes, India."

That's it? "Yes, India"? "It's just that it's getting so late. I was worried about you."

He sighed. "Sorry, baby. I have a lot going on."

"Okay. When do you think you'll be home? I was waiting for you to eat dinner. I—"

"Damn it, India! Things come up. I don't know when I'll be there. Don't wait for me." And he hung up.

I looked at my phone. Something was wrong. Very wrong. Like normal, though, Kellan would get angry about whatever was going on and not talk to me. *I don't know. Maybe I shouldn't jump to conclusions.* But I couldn't shake the bad feeling I had.

I went upstairs, took a shower, and put on pajama pants and a T-shirt. Pouring me a glass of wine when I got back downstairs, I sat on the sofa waiting for Kellan. I really should eat. But I was so worried about Kellan that the thought of food turned my stomach.

I was on my second glass of wine. It was after nine when I finally heard the ding of the elevator. I stayed seated on the sofa. Kellan came into the living room and went straight to the bar, pouring himself a Jack. He downed that one and quickly poured him another.

I went to him. Standing behind him, I wrapped my arms around his waist. He put one of his hands over mine.

"What's wrong, Kellan?" He shook his head. "Talk to me, Kellan, please? Maybe I can help."

"Damn it, India." He jerked out of my hold. "Talking does not solve everything." He ran his fingers through his hair. "I'm sorry. I don't mean to take this out on you."

"It's okay," I said quietly. "I'm just worried about you."

"Don't worry, baby." He pulled me into his arms. "We're going back to Louisiana tomorrow. Why don't you go up and pack now because we are leaving early. Pack anything you think you can use there. Hell. Pack it all. I don't know when we will be coming back. You can always bring it back when we do. I have to go talk to Bret. I'll be up when I'm finished."

I nodded and went upstairs. Something was very wrong. The things he had bought for me were supposed to be so I didn't have to pack to go back and forth. Pulling out my suitcases, I once again packed only what I had brought with me.

CHAPTER THIRTY-THREE

*I*t was Saturday, midmorning, when we arrived at New Orleans International Airport. Bret and Zack made the trip with us. Kellan had spoken to Bret last night, telling him he would feel a lot more comfortable if he and Zack would be part of my permanent security detail. They agreed.

Daniel was waiting for us when we landed. It was great to see his grin. Two other guys from Kellan's security team were there also with the big, dark SUV. The trip from the airport to the mansion on St. Charles was made in silence. In fact, Kellan hadn't said a word since we left New York. I felt him pulling away from me, distancing himself. I felt bereft.

When we arrived at Kellan's house, he told me he had work he had to finish and shut himself in his office. After a couple of hours with no sign of him, I had had enough. I asked Bret to get my suitcases from Kellan's room. I hadn't unpacked. Then I went to Kellan's office and knocked on his door. When he didn't respond, I turned the knob and walked in. He was on the phone.

"I have to call you back," he said gruffly into the phone and quickly hung up. He looked up at me, running his fingers through his hair. "What is it, India?"

Damn. It was as if we were strangers. "You're busy and distracted, Kellan. I'm going to get out of your hair and go home."

He looked at me intently as though he was trying to memorize my features. "All right. Yeah. Okay. Bret, Zack, Toby, and Tim are to be with you at all times. No exceptions, India."

"I'm not stupid, Kellan," I said snidely.

"Watch it, India," he said in his warning tone. "I'm not in the mood for any of your smart-ass comments. I have to go out of town, and I need to know you're safe."

Out of town? We just got here. "Do you need me with you? I can go check things out at home and come back."

"No," he said abruptly. "You stay here. Have your weekend next week with your friends. I would rather you and your friends stay here instead of the hotel. It would be safer and a lot more convenient."

I looked closely at him. This was not my intense lover, nor my caring, considerate, tender boyfriend. Something was terribly wrong. I felt as though he didn't want me anymore, like he was relieved I was leaving.

"Heaven forbid I cause you any inconvenience," I responded sarcastically then turned on my heel, leaving his office.

He followed me to the SUV. I turned to him before I got into the backseat. "You're pushing me away, Kellan, and I don't know why."

He took my face in between both of his hands. "No matter what anything seems like. No matter what anything looks like. Know that I don't feel any differently. You are mine. You're my everything."

I gazed into his beautiful cerulean eyes. Tears came into mine. "Perception is important, Kellan. Feeling secure, even more so." I shook my head. "You're doing it again. You're not talking to me. I know something is very wrong. I feel it. You and me? It's up to you if it stays that way. I've been committed for a while now. Everything's in your court now."

I kissed his wonderful lips softly. Tenderly. Reverently. Then I pulled out of his grasp and climbed into the backseat. Kellan looked at me through the window. He stayed in the driveway watching the car. I turned in my seat and watched him until the house was out of sight. I felt as if something shifted in our relationship again. Only this time, not in a good way.

When we pulled up to my house, Bridgette and Tim met us on the front porch. I hugged Bridgette, and then Tim grabbed me in a tight bear hug, sweeping me off my feet. Damn, I had missed them. I had missed my home. My sense of belonging.

I went straight to the kitchen, grabbed a cup of coffee, and went out to the back porch. I stood at the railing, looking out over the bayou. This was where I belonged. There weren't any terrible women wanting Kellan here. There wasn't a deranged man trying to hurt me.

But then again, Kellan wasn't here. He wasn't with me, and I had no idea when I would see him again. No idea where he was going. After being together constantly for almost three months, this sense of loss was devastating. It would be different if he was going away, and everything was fine with our relationship. This was in no way like that. Something was wrong, and he hadn't even said he would be in touch with me. There was nothing I could do. It really was all up to him.

I called Kathy, letting her know I was back. She wanted to know if I was going to be tied up with the pervert.

"Don't call him that!"

"Okay. Just for you, I won't," she chuckled as she said that. "So are you going to be busy with him?"

"No. I'm home. Alone." *Well, as alone as I could get with Tim, Bridgette, and the three security guys,* I thought to myself.

"For how long? I can't see Mr. Control Freak letting you out of his sight for any length of time."

"I don't know, Kat. I don't know when I'll see him again," I told her, barely above a whisper.

"What's going on, India?"

"I wish I knew. He's going out of town. I don't know where or for how long. He didn't even say he would be in touch. He was so cryptic. I don't know what's wrong." I pause. "I can't breathe. It hurts so bad."

"That asshole! I knew he would do something like this."

"That's just it, Kat. I don't know that he has done anything. Everything was great until yesterday. I guess I'll let everything ride until I definitively know otherwise."

"I'm coming over, and you're going to tell me everything. I'll bring the Jose."

An hour later, Kathy and I were doing shots, sitting at my kitchen table. I related just about everything of Kellan's and my time in New York.

"Is he bipolar, India? I mean, from what you tell me, he runs so hot and cold."

"No. He's not mental, Kat. He might be too intelligent. Too driven. I believe he has some dark secrets and that those are why he only had…a certain type of relationship. I don't think he knows how to be in a normal relationship, and that's why he holds so tight."

"How can you stand it? You don't have any freedom. Even when he isn't with you, you have babysitters."

"I agreed with the security so he wouldn't go nuts. That really doesn't bother me anymore. What bothers me is how he's acting now. For him going from one extreme to another. I feel so lost. It's like a death. I'm going to be driven insane before I even know what's going on."

"I don't like what he's doing to you, India. He's messing with your head. And I'm afraid how it will end." I couldn't disagree with her. I couldn't defend Kellan's present behavior.

The next week, I buried myself in work. I had a list of artists that lived in New York who, quite possibly, would volunteer for the arts program there. My friends that volunteered here with me had given me the names. I placed all the calls and set up appointments with them for next week. Roman was going to send his private jet for me, and his company kept a suite in the Sherry-Netherland. I would stay there whenever I had to be in New York.

I worked in my yard and took care of all the plants. I walked along the bayou, wondering what Kellan was doing, where he was. I hadn't heard from him. I felt as though I was missing my heart. You couldn't live without a heart, right?

A TEMPTATION

I worked tirelessly on my book. I wanted to get it out as soon as I possibly could. Every word I wrote was wonderful and terrible at the same time. Even with the names of places and people being changed, this was the story of us. Kellan and me. Last week, I had hopes of it having a happy ending. This week, I didn't even know if there was an us. It didn't feel as if there was.

On Wednesday, I received the renderings that would be the covers for my next two books, if I approved. They were magnificent. I immediately called Mallory and told her I loved them. I would take these and have them framed to hang in my office, next to the one for *Fall into Time*.

Noah was getting in tomorrow night at six fifteen. I asked Kathy about staying at Kellan's, only because I wasn't going to be the first to break my word. She said that it was fine with her if it wouldn't be too difficult for me. Kathy was taking off from work Friday so we three, Kathy, Noah, and I, could have time by ourselves without our other friends.

We walked into the mansion on St. Charles—Kathy, Noah, and I—Thursday night. As happy as I was to be reunited with Noah, it didn't stop the incredible stab of pain in my chest at being here without Kellan.

He must have talked to Mrs. Carter about all of us being here this weekend because she was beyond prepared. The dining room and kitchen were loaded down with food. Alcohol of every type covered the sideboard. Kellan had spared no expense for my friends and me. But this wasn't what I wanted from Kellan. This was just stuff.

Since there were going to be so many people here this weekend, I had to stay in Kellan's master suite. If I would have had any other option, I would have taken it. When I walked into his room, I was hit with such an oppressive sense of loss. Why had I thought I could do this?

There was a note and a small box sitting on my pillow—well, it was the pillow I used when I was here—on the side of the bed I slept on. I rushed over and picked up the note. It said simply "I miss you." *That's it?*

I opened the box. It was the most magnificent ring I had ever seen. It was platinum, Kellan's metal of choice. The ring had a large princess-cut emerald in the center, which had to be at least three karats, surrounded by diamonds. It matched all the other emerald jewelry Kellan had gotten me. I had that jewelry with me in Louisiana, only because I had been wearing it when we returned home. I didn't want jewelry. I wanted Kellan! I threw the box on the bed. Tears were running down my face.

"India, you have to tell me who this place belongs to. And why would he open it up to us? I mean, damn—" Noah noticed my tears, came over to me, and pulled me into his arms. "Kitten. What is it? What the hell is wrong? I've never known you to cry."

Kathy walked into Kellan's room. She took one look at me then looked around the room. She picked up the note and the ring and started raining curses down upon Kellan's head.

"Okay. That's enough. You two are going to tell me what's going on right now," Noah demanded.

I guess, in retrospect, it was a good thing all our other friends wouldn't be here until tomorrow night. This was not something I would get into with anyone but Kathy and Noah. We decided to go downstairs to have some liquid courage to aid in this discussion. I let Kathy fill Noah in while I just kept refilling my wine glass.

"Shit, India. I don't know what to say. We are all straightforward. We say what we mean and mean what we say. I wouldn't know how to deal with someone who wasn't. On the other hand, I can't see the man doing all of this if he wanted it over between you two."

Kathy snorted. "Kellan Coventry has more money than God, Noah. It doesn't mean the same thing to him as it does to us."

"All I know is that this is driving me crazy. I don't know what will happen next. It's destroying me."

"Well, that's your answer, Kitten. Fuck whatever is going on with him. No one is worth going through this shit."

"Yeah. It wouldn't be worth it, Noah," I said miserably, "if I didn't love him."

"Fuck!" Noah bit out.

"My sentiments exactly," I said to him.

CHAPTER THIRTY-FOUR

I had a hangover from hell. I washed my face, brushed my teeth and hair, and then went down to the kitchen. I was sitting at the kitchen island with my head hanging over my cup of coffee when some of the guys walked in.

"Morning, India!" Bret called out.

I winced. "Shh. Not so loud." I grabbed my head.

He chuckled, walked over to a cabinet, and brought me some much needed pain reliever.

"Thank you."

"Anytime." He smiled down at me. Then his expression grew serious. "If there's anything you need, I hope you know you only have to ask. We live in close quarters, so we can't help but know what's going on. The guys and I have become very protective of you. Just know that we're here."

"Y'all shouldn't get involved in this, Bret. He's your boss. I have a whole network of people to help me." I shrugged. "As much as anyone can help with something like this."

I was thinking about Kellan while I sat in his kitchen. I still hadn't heard from him. He knew I was here in his house, but still, he didn't reach out to me. I wasn't worth a phone call. Wasn't worth a conversation. And yes, I was being extremely stupid where Kellan was concerned. It was as though I was waiting to see if a two-by-four was going to hit me upside the head. The way things were going, it was a matter of when, not if.

Noah, Kathy, and I, along with all the security guys, were in the kitchen eating lunch. Noah and Kathy were regaling them with exploits of ours.

"Okay, okay," I interrupted. "Believe me, Bret and Zack know firsthand what a walking disaster I can be. Y'all don't have to add fuel to the fire."

It was nice to laugh again. My friends and the security guys were making sure not even Kellan's name was brought up.

We all decided we were going to play hearts to pass the time. I ran into Kellan's office to get some paper to keep score. Seeing the copies of the *New York Times* sitting on his desk, I thought he must get it delivered here. Duh. Of course he would. That's where the majority of his business was conducted.

I picked up the first one. It was from Wednesday. Pulling out the society section, I was curious to see what had been going on for the last week. And the two-by-four landed. It hit so hard I saw stars. I couldn't breathe. I couldn't feel anything but the most debilitating pain. I brought the paper with me when I went back into the kitchen.

"Did you have to go out of state for that paper, India?" Kathy asked, laughing and looking up at me. She stood up abruptly. "What's wrong, India? You look like you've seen a ghost."

Before I answered her, I picked up my cell phone from the kitchen table and called Tim. "Hey," I said into the phone. "Look, I'm sorry, but I need you to come to Kellan's and pick us up. And, Tim? I don't want you to get in an accident or anything, but please get here as soon as possible."

After I ended the call, I turned to my friends. "Y'all need to get your stuff. We're leaving."

"That's fine, kitten," Noah said, coming over and putting his arm around my shoulders. "But you need to tell me what's wrong. You're as white as a sheet."

A TEMPTATION

Kathy had taken the paper out of my hand. After seeing the pictures and reading the captions, she turned so red in the face I was afraid she would have a stroke. "That fucking asshole!" she spat out furiously. "Who is this bitch, India?"

"That's Asia Peterson. I didn't even know he was in New York. To see him escorting her, one of those women?" I shook my head and turned to Bret. "I don't want to bring trouble to your door, but I won't be needing security anymore."

"Yes, India. You do," Bret said emphatically.

"No, Bret. I don't. I only needed it because I was with Kellan. As of right now, I'm done. He can send y'all to protect Asia."

"India. Don't do this, please," Bret tried to reason with me. "I don't care what's going on with him. We don't want to leave you unprotected."

"I appreciate the sentiment. Really I do, Bret. And I thank y'all for everything. But I don't want anything to do with…anything that is Kellan." I turned to Kathy and Noah. "Let's get our stuff, okay?" I took the paper out of Kathy's hand. I had a place in mind for this.

"Yeah. Let's get out of here, Kitten," Noah said, taking my arm and leading me upstairs.

"I think he broke me, Noah," I whispered.

"That motherfucker!" Noah was pissed. "It won't be like this forever, Kitten. It won't feel like this forever. I promise."

Forever didn't matter to me though. I knew me. There was something broken inside that no amount of time would heal. My grandmother had been right after all. But unlike my mother, the one whom I had finally fallen for didn't love me in return. So there would be irreparable damage.

I was just finishing collecting my stuff when Bret knocked on the opened door. "India, Mr. Coventry wants to talk to you. He said he couldn't reach you on your phone."

"That's because I'm not taking his calls, Bret. And I don't want to talk to him."

"Yeah. Okay," he said into the phone. "He said if you don't get on the phone, he—"

I interrupted him with a laugh. It wasn't a pleasant sound. "He doesn't have the right to demand anything of me anymore. You can talk to him all you want, but I don't have to. I don't plan on talking to him ever again. If you want to help him, Bret, tell him that. Tell him to stay away from me."

When I was finished packing my stuff, I did the last thing I would ever do in Kellan's house. I laid the picture of Kellan and Asia on the pillow with the ring and the note.

As we climbed into the SUV, Tim held his phone out to me. I shook my head. I wasn't talking to Kellan. But Kathy was a different story. She grabbed the phone out of Tim's hand.

"I'll talk to the son of a bitch. I have a lot to say."

"No, Kat," I said, taking the phone out of her hand. "It's done. It's over. Let it go. I don't want to hear anything. I don't even want to think about it anymore."

I heard Kellan screaming on the phone "India! Baby! Please talk to me!" when I handed the phone back to Tim.

"Tim, I hate to do this to you and Bridgette. Both of you have become like family to me, so I would like y'all to stay. But in order to do that, y'all will have to terminate the employment with Kellan. I will pay what he was paying and cover health insurance. The SUV will have to be returned to him. I'll get you something else. It is strictly up to you and Bridgette."

"I called Bret, India. I know what went down. As far as I'm concerned, I'll stay with you. I can't speak for Bridgette. I'll call the company when we get back to your house and give them my resignation."

"I'm glad you're staying, Tim. Thank you."

"What can we do, India?" Kathy asked me softly.

"Y'all can come out with me tonight. We are going to kick off the next chapter of my life."

I didn't even remember the time between that Friday and today, which was the following Thursday. The only reason I could think of that I had any cognitive recognition was because I was back in New

A TEMPTATION

York. I didn't want to run into Kellan, so I had to stay aware. I didn't know if he was here, but I wasn't taking any chances.

Roman picked me up from the airport when his jet touched down. On the drive to the Sherry-Netherland, Roman turned to me.

"India. I'm sorry. I don't mean to get into your business, but I can't help but notice that you don't have your security people, and Coventry has been hanging out with his old crowd."

"You're saying nicely that he's hanging out with the women that there's all the rumors about. Besides the rumors of them, what he and the other men do with them."

He flinched. "I didn't know you knew about any of that."

"Hell, Roman. I live in Louisiana, not Siberia."

"I didn't mean it like that."

"I know. I'm sorry, Roman. I didn't mean to take my shit out on you." Roman didn't deserve my snippy self.

"It's over between Kellan and me. It's none of my business if he has gone back to…whatever. I don't want to see him, and I don't want to talk about him." As if on cue, my cell went off. I looked at the screen, pressed send, then end.

"I take it he didn't get your memo." He tipped his head toward my phone.

"I'm sure he'll get tired of calling a hundred times a day. He'll realize I'm never going to talk to him again."

"I don't know what to say, India, except you don't look happy about it."

"I'm not, Roman. I had to end it because I couldn't put up with his crap any longer. I didn't want this. I thought…never mind what I thought." I sighed. "I really don't want to talk about any of this."

We had about thirty minutes until the artists met us at the suite in the Sherry-Netherland. We were pushing it to get there in time.

Everything went well. The artists were excited about the program and were all on board. Their personalities were such that they would be good teachers. We set up the time that they would meet with Roman at the warehouse, and they could make out the lists of everything else they would need.

Then the second week of December, we would all be at the fund-raiser dinner for the arts program.

I would not be back in New York until then. If it wasn't for the arts program, I wouldn't voluntarily come here at all right now.

When everyone left except Roman, he asked if I would like to go to dinner. I told him I would, but I would rather not venture out of the Sherry-Netherland. I didn't know if Kellan was in New York. I just didn't want to take the chance of running into him.

Roman and I were seated in the Harry Cipriani restaurant in the hotel. We were having a glass of wine waiting for our orders and just talking.

"So what else is going on in your life, India?"

"My next two books will be released the second week of December. I will have some functions that I will have to go to with that, but not like the first one. They believe the books will sell themselves because the first one went over so well. That the fans will want the next two books of the trilogy. I'm almost finished with the first book of my next series."

"You deserve all the recognition. You're very talented."

"Thank you." I smiled at him. "I just like making up stories."

"India, I need to speak to you."

I looked up to see where that harsh voice had come from. It was Kellan. Deric was with him. I looked away from him. "There's nothing to say, Kellan. I don't want to talk to you. I don't want to see you."

"I can't help what you don't want, baby. But we are going to talk." He grabbed my upper arm and brought me up out of the chair.

"Hey!" Roman exclaimed, rising out of his chair. "You heard what she said, Coventry. You need to take your hands off of her."

"Stay out of this, Saunders. I see you wasted no time trying to step in."

I jerked my arm out of Kellan's grip and turned on him. "You asshole! I'm here for the arts program. We had appointments with the artists today. Roman isn't doing anything. But you know what? If he were, it would be none of your business. It's"—I shook my head—"I'm nothing to you."

A TEMPTATION

"Anything that concerns you is my business. You damn well know that."

"Kellan. Come on, man. You're causing a scene," Deric said and tried to take Kellan's arm to lead him out.

"Back off, Deric," Kellan growled. Deric raised his hands in surrender.

"I'm out of here," I spit out. I made it as far as the lobby.

"India. Don't do this. Think about the last thing I said to you in New Orleans before you left to go home."

"Kellan. Talk to her, man," Deric stressed to his friend. "Tell her what's going on. You're not handling this right. If I were her, I would be thinking and feeling the same way."

"I told you before, Kellan. You not talking to me was going to destroy us. If you're not going to explain what's going on and why you're spending time with Asia, I don't want to hear anything you have to say." I tried to walk away from him, but he stopped me again. Only now his expression was closed off, telling me he wasn't going to talk to me about those things.

"Fuck, Kellan!" Deric snarled. "You're going to lose her."

"I'm already gone, Deric, so he doesn't need to worry about that."

"India. Please keep the security team. I need—"

"I don't give a fuck what you need, Kellan!" I yelled at him. That shut everyone up. "Roman, could you contact your pilot please? I want to get back to New Orleans as soon as possible. I won't be staying the night here."

"Of course," Roman said and pulled out his phone to take care of it.

"India, think about what you're doing," Kellan pleaded. "If you would think about what I was saying—"

"Cryptically, Kellan. How am I supposed to solve your puzzle? You had your chance to talk to me. To tell me what was going on. Since you can't do that, I only have what I can see."

"India, the pilot's waiting. Whenever you're ready. I already sent someone after your things."

"Thank you, Roman."

"You haven't eaten, and you really need to. Do you want me to go get you something? You can take it with you."

"No. That's okay. I'm really not hungry anymore. Thanks for being such a good friend, Roman."

"Baby, you really need to eat. You're losing weight. Remember what the doctor said."

I looked at Kellan after he said that. He really had no clue. "Don't call me that! You don't get to call me that anymore. Whatever is going on with me is no longer your concern."

"India, you're still mine. You will always be mine. Whatever you go through is damn well my concern."

"Think again!" I snapped at him. "You don't get a vote. I'm nothing to you anymore. Stay away from me."

The boy brought my bags down. When I turned to go out the exit with Roman, I heard Deric.

"You're being stupid, Kellan. This is all on you."

I didn't make it to the car before the tears started falling.

CHAPTER THIRTY-FIVE

It was the second week of December. I was leaving tomorrow, Thursday morning, for New York. The fund-raiser dinner for the arts program was tomorrow night. Kathy and Noah were going with me because of what had happened with Kellan the last time I was there. If Kellan kept his distance, we three were going to stay the weekend in New York and do our Christmas shopping. I prayed that if Kellan was in New York, he would not go to the arts dinner. If there was any decency in him, he wouldn't attend. He would know that I had to be there.

Tim took Noah, Kathy, and me to the airport early Thursday morning. After we were in the air, the stewardess brought us champagne, saying it was from Roman.

"The people you know, India," Noah said, chuckling. "Damn. Look at this jet."

"Shut up, Noah," Kathy growled at him.

"It's okay, Kat. I'll tell Roman you're in love with his jet." I smiled at Noah.

Roman was waiting for us at the airport when we landed. I made the introductions when we got into his limo. Before we got to the Sherry-Netherland, they were all good friends.

In the suite, Kathy turned to me. "He is halfway in love with you, India."

"Huh?" I asked, totally confused.

"Roman. Anyone could see it."

"No, Kat. He has become a good friend. That's all. We've never even been able to finish a meal together."

"Be that as it may, India. I'm telling you, he's interested in a lot more than friendship with you."

"Who is?" Noah asked when he came out to the living room.

"Roman," Kathy told him.

"Oh, him." Noah chuckled. "Yeah. That man has it bad."

"It wouldn't be a bad thing, India," Kathy said to me. "He's a nice man. I like him."

"Do you know he went to school with Will?" I asked her.

"Yeah. Will told me that the other day. I had never met him though. Will also said that he was the most honest person he has ever known."

"Are you trying to sell me on Roman, Kat?"

"I just want you to be happy again, India. But if I had to handpick someone out for you, it would be someone like Roman Saunders."

"Kat, I don't even want to think about another relationship right now. I don't know how I could ever trust another man."

We stayed in and ordered room service for lunch. We joked and laughed, and I finally relaxed. Maybe everything would be okay this time. Maybe Kellan wasn't in New York.

I stepped out of the shower, dried my hair, and piled it on top of my head, leaving a lot of curls cascading down. I put on my makeup and got dressed.

I had bought a new gown for tonight. Having lost quite a bit of weight because of the Kellan fiasco, my clothes didn't fit anymore. It was a beautiful gown. It was emerald green and sparkly with sequins over the entire thing. It was sleeveless, cut low in the front, but not indecently; showing sexy cleavage, not slutty. It was cut superlow in the back, right past my waist. There was a thin strap running shoulder to shoulder, tying behind my neck, that kept the whole thing together.

A TEMPTATION

I brought my mother's emeralds to wear with it. My grandmother had told me a long time ago that my father said emeralds reminded him of my mother's eyes. And I had my mother's eyes. Kellan had told me almost the exact same thing not so long ago. *Stop. I will not think about him.*

Kathy and Noah were already in the living room when I entered. My friends were gorgeous with Noah in his tux and Kathy in form-fitting red.

"You look great, India," Kathy said. "If any of those bitches are there, they'll be eaten up with jealousy."

"Shit, Kitten," Noah chimed in. "I think I can wrap my hands around your waist. It's so small."

"Does it look bad?" I asked him.

"Hell no! It's hot."

We went down in the elevator to the lobby and walked over to the reception room where the fund-raiser was being held. We were seated at the table with Roman and the rest of the arts committee. Clair Peterson was conspicuously absent, I was happy to see. Roman stood and took my hands in his.

"You look lovely, India."

"Thank you. So do you," I teased, and he chuckled.

Roman introduced my friends to everyone at the table. Then he stopped a waiter and handed Kathy, Noah, and me a glass of wine. He held up his glass.

"To you, India. For everything you've done for this program." Everyone at the table stood and held up their glasses. Roman tapped my glass with his. I took a large sip. I needed this. I was so afraid Kellan would show up.

After we had dinner and desert, Mr. Saunders, Roman's dad, went up to the podium. He thanked everyone for coming out and said that with all of the money that had been raised tonight, it would be more than enough to get the arts program going. Then to my horror, he spoke of a great young woman who had put it all together for them, just like the one she had put together in New Orleans, where she was from. And would everyone give a hand for Ms. India Leigh.

I wanted the floor to open up and swallow me. I had wanted to keep a low profile tonight.

"Come on up here, young lady," Mr. Saunders said in a booming voice.

"I don't want to go up there, Roman," I said in his ear. "That's not what this is about."

"I can't help what my father does, India. But he's right."

I turned to Kathy and Noah. "I don't want to go up there. Kellan could be here."

"There's nothing for it, Kitten. But we're here, and we will not let him cause you any grief."

I shook my head and took my embarrassed ass up to the podium. When I was next to Mr. Saunders, he gave me a light hug and presented me with a plaque.

"Thank you," I said into the microphone. "This was not necessary. I believe in this program. I have seen firsthand the excellent results that have taken place in my city. Now I would like to introduce you to the artists that will be the instructors here in your city. Y'all come on up."

After getting and giving hugs to the instructors, I sneaked away, back to my table. When I was up there, I saw that Kellan was indeed here. He, Deric, Asia, and Presley. Seeing that picture in the paper was one thing. Seeing Kellan once again with those women in the flesh? I couldn't handle it. I told my friends that Kellan was here, and that I had to get out. All four of us left.

We were in the middle of the lobby when I heard my name called. I pretended not to hear and continued to the elevator. The only luck I seemed to have lately was bad. Before the elevator could open, Kellan was facing me.

"Congratulations, baby. I know how hard you worked."

I didn't say a word. Didn't even raise my eyes. I kept them trained on the floor. How could he do this to me?

"You have a lot of nerve," Kathy told him. "What are you going to do for an encore? Shoot her?"

I knew Kathy wouldn't be able to keep her mouth shut. Not that I blamed her. If circumstances were reversed, I would have done

A TEMPTATION

some damage protecting her. But I just wanted to get out of here with as little trouble as possible.

"You don't know the circumstances," Kellan said to Kathy.

"Apparently no one but you knows what those are, and you aren't talking," Kathy bit out.

"This is between me and India."

Noah faced Kellan, placing his arm around my shoulders. "Not anymore it isn't. She doesn't contact you. She doesn't try to see you. You're doing your own thing. Leave her alone."

Kellan's look became furious. He didn't like Noah touching me. "Who the fuck are you?" he growled.

"Noah Bure. India's friend. I do give a shit about her, and I'm not going to let you hurt her anymore."

Asia, Presley, and Deric came walking up. "Kellan, darling," Asia simpered, "we are ready to go the club." Kellan gave her the coldest look I had ever seen.

I couldn't take anymore. "Don't keep her waiting, Kellan," I said to him.

"It's not like that, India," Kellan snarled.

"I really could give a shit what it's like. Just go."

"You need to quit messing with his head," Asia snarled out at me.

"I think you've got that all wrong. I'm not the one going after him," I said that knowing it would really get to her to be reminded that it was Kellan doing the pursuing.

"You wish he was after you. He's back with us now, where he belongs."

"Asia! Not another word." Kellan commanded her.

"Who is this bitch, India?" Uh-oh. Asia got herself noticed by Kathy.

"No one, Kat. She's nothing. Let it go."

"India, you need to watch your mouth," Kellan commanded me.

That did it. He thought he could command me like one of his subs? Fuck him and the horse he rode in on. I turned to him and got right in his face.

"You don't get to talk to me like that. I'm not, nor have I ever been one of your subs. That's what Asia is for, and those other women. I can say whatever I damn well feel like saying. Y'all came after me, not the other way around. And I'll be damned if I'm going to keep my mouth shut after the shit y'all have been saying tonight. Run along. Your subs waiting for you to take them out."

"Why, you cunt!" Asia screamed. "How dare you say that in front of all these people?"

"I dare because it's the truth. If you can't live with the truth being broadcasted, then I suggest you change your lifestyle."

Asia took a step toward me, but Kellan grabbed her. "Oh, don't stop her, Kellan. Y'all have gotten me royally pissed. I'll beat the shit out of her. You know as well as Kathy and Noah I don't scratch and pull hair."

"Some of India's friends will be with her whenever she has to be in New York. Y'all are in for a rude awakening," Kathy warned them.

"Let's go," Kellan spoke to Asia, Presley, and Deric. "This isn't over, baby."

"Yes it is, Kellan," I threw back at him. "For a while now."

Kellan went toward the exit with Asia and Presley. Deric came up to me.

"I'm sorry, India. This isn't what it looks like."

"I really don't care what it is, Deric. But since you brought it up, this looks exactly like it did before Kellan and I started seeing each other."

"I know what it looks like, but I swear it's not."

"It doesn't matter anymore, Deric. Do you understand me? He's done and said too much."

The elevator doors opened. Roman, Kathy, Noah, and I got in.

"If I could tell you, India, I would," Deric called out.

"It would be too late, Deric."

The elevator doors closed. I hadn't thought I could hurt any more than I had been. But I was wrong. Seeing Kellan like that, with them? What had I ever done so wrong that I would have to pay for it like this?

A TEMPTATION

"Well, Kitten," Noah said. "It's good to see you didn't forget your roots."

I started crying. My heart was breaking all over again. I put both hands over my face while sobs were wrenched out of me. Roman wrapped me in his arms, and I buried my face in his chest. He rubbed a soothing hand up and down my back.

"Those people aren't worth the dirt you walk on, India," Roman spoke to me softly. "You're beautiful and kind. Giving and caring. I know you're hurting because of how you feel for Coventry. But it was his loss, not yours."

"That doesn't stop my heart from feeling like it's being ripped out."

"No, it doesn't. But it does mean that the person that is truly meant for you is still out there."

We went up to the suite and decided that we would sit around and get drunk. I went and changed into a pair of sweats and a T-shirt. I washed my tearstained face and took my hair down.

Roman had a lot of alcohol sent up to the room. Jack Daniels, Jose, Fireball, and wine. He had taken off his jacket and tie, pulled his shirttails out of his slacks, and rolled the sleeves up to his elbows. Kathy and Noah had changed like I had. We were going to do some heavy-duty drinking, and we needed to be comfortable.

We talked. We played drinking games. We called down to room service and ordered a lot of finger foods so we wouldn't get sick. One by one, we passed out.

The next day, *morning* being a relative term, I woke up while the other three were still passed out. Roman and I had passed out on the couch, Kathy and Noah on the floor. I put coffee on and went searching through my bags for the Excedrin. I washed my face and brushed my teeth, trying to get the tequila taste out of my mouth.

I went back into the living room and grabbed a cup of coffee. I curled up in the corner of the couch that Roman wasn't lying on. I shook my head, looking at my two oldest friends and my new one. It had been fun last night. They did their job well, keeping my mind off Kellan and what went down last night.

Unfortunately, I couldn't play and stay drunk forever.

Life is a funny thing. It changes in the blink of an eye. We like to believe that we have control over our lives, our destiny. But there is no control because there are other people, places, and things that border our destiny. Those change all the time, which in turn changes the phases of our lives constantly. So no control. We just float along, praying that the changes won't destroy us. That it will not take away who we fundamentally are. That it won't turn our hearts to stone and turn us into unfeeling drones.

I heard Roman groan. I got up and fixed him a cup of coffee. I held it out to him with the bottle of Excedrin.

"Thank you," he mumbled and grinned up at me. "I haven't had that much fun since I was in college."

I curled back up on the end of the couch. "The trick," I said to Roman, "is to remember how you feel the morning after so you don't do it too often. Those two?" I gestured with my hand toward Kathy and Noah. "They have cast-iron stomachs and selective memory. They could do this every night."

He chuckled then raised a hand to his forehead. "Ow. That hurt."

I laughed. "Sorry. I feel the same way, but you did look funny."

"Hey. If it makes you smile, I would do it every minute of every day."

"Thank you, Roman. I really value and appreciate your friendship."

"It's not a hardship, believe me, India. You're easy to like. Easy to care for."

"You need to come down to Louisiana. I can promise you would have a great time, and you would love the rest of our friends." I looked down for a minute. "I won't be coming back to New York anytime soon."

"I can understand that. And I will definitely take you up on your offer." He sat up and scooted closer to me. He took one of my hands in one of his. "But don't let him ruin your life. Don't give him the power to keep you from where you want to be or what you want to do. Don't let what he did define who you will be for the rest of your life. The person you are is wonderful. Don't let him take that away."

A TEMPTATION

"I'm trying very hard, Roman. It's okay until he makes contact. When he pushes his way back in for a minute. I have to keep him from doing that. One of the steps is to stay away from here. Not forever. Just until he tires of this game."

He nodded, and we started laughing when Kathy and Noah started moaning.

Roman took off, and we got dressed and went Christmas shopping. We found great things that we knew all our families and friends would love. We also had to indulge, since we were in New York, in clothes for ourselves. We went to Gucci and a lot of other places on Madison Avenue and Fifth Avenue.

I didn't like being that close to Kellan's apartment. This familiar real estate made me twinge and brought back memories that I wanted to forget.

We went out for lunch and had a good time. Noah regaled us with stories of the people he met when he was gone for so long with his job.

We made it back to the Sherry-Netherland and filled half of the living room with our purchases. Kathy and Noah wanted to go out to a club. I told them to go and have fun, but I didn't want to even smell alcohol, nor did I want to take a chance and run into Kellan. They tried to insist that they stay in with me, but I wouldn't hear of it. I wanted them to go and have fun. I was very appreciative of them coming here with me. I wanted them to do something they really wanted to do. Before they left, they stressed for me to call them if I needed them. I promised I would then told them to get out and dance for me.

I soaked for forever in the huge sunken tub. I had laced the water liberally with my favorite vanilla/jasmine bath oil. I lay back in the water, reading, until my body pruned, and the water cooled. Getting out of the tub, I put on another pair of sweats and a T-shirt. I went into the living room, curled up on the end of the couch, and continued to read my book.

It was around 10:00 p.m. when there was a knock on the door. I assumed it was Roman because he would be the only other person who knew we were in this particular suite. Kathy's, Noah's, nor my name, were registered anywhere in this hotel.

I opened the door with a big smile on my face that promptly fell. Kellan stood on the other side. I tried to shut the door, but he grabbed it, holding it open until he forced his way into the suite. He closed and locked the door behind him.

"You need to go, Kellan. We have nothing to say to each other."

"You're wrong, baby." He grabbed me by my upper arms and dragged me into his arms. "You feel this, India? This thing between you and me? It's too strong. It will never be over."

I balled up my fists and started hitting Kellan's chest, banging and banging against the body that not too long ago I so lovingly caressed. I started crying, begging him to go away, to just leave me alone.

"I can't do that, baby. I could never be without you. You need to trust me with this. It has to be the way it is right now."

"You don't have a choice, Kellan. I'm telling you to stay away from me. I could never trust you again. Time after time, I tried to walk away from you. But you wouldn't let me. You made me love you then betrayed me. There can never be any trust between us."

"You will understand when this is all over, then everything will be okay." He lifted my head with a finger under my chin. "You looked beautiful tonight in that gown. The emeralds I got for you would have been perfect with it."

"I left the emeralds for you at your house on St. Charles."

"Why? They're yours. Everything that I bought for you is yours. Everything that I have is yours."

"I don't want any of it, Kellan. It doesn't mean anything. All that we went through? All that we were to each other? In the end, didn't mean shit."

His mouth descended on mine. He devoured me, forcing his tongue past my reluctant lips, fucking my mouth with his tongue. "Does this feel like nothing, baby? Does this feel like what we have together is over? We will never be over." He ran butterfly kisses from my mouth, over my jaw, and down my neck. He bit gently, that spot under my ear.

A TEMPTATION

My traitorous body betrayed me. It melted into him. He picked me up and carried me into one of the bedrooms. He laid me gently down on the bed. Slowly, he removed my sweats, T-shirt, and panties. He quickly did away with his clothes and climbed onto the bed, settling over me. On his knees, one on either side of me, he tenderly kissed my lips, running his tongue and lips from there down to my breasts. Raining kisses all over them then landing on my nipple, he laved then sucked it into his mouth.

My back arched. I quit thinking. He transferred to my other nipple, and drove everything that happened away. He kissed down and over every inch of my body. Worshiping it. Making it once again his.

He ended at the juncture of my thighs. He raised his eyes, watching me as he flicked his tongue over my clit. I jumped. I couldn't remain still. He reached his hands under me, lifting me by my ass, raising me to his mouth. He ravished me with that brilliant mouth and tongue.

"You're mine, India. This is mine. Only mine." He sucked my clit into his mouth, and I left the planet. He licked, gently bringing me back to earth.

Kellan climbed up my body, settling between my thighs. He plunged, fully seating himself with one hard thrust. I cried out. It was wonderful. It was awful. It was going to destroy me. He was destroying me.

He moved powerfully over and in me. "You feel this, baby? You feel me? This wonderful, powerful thing that ties us together? I have never felt this with anyone. Will never feel it with anyone else. And you never will either. We are one and always will be."

Tears silently ran down my cheeks. My broken heart didn't matter, however. Kellan's expertise found that spot inside me, and his pelvis rubbed against my swollen clit. I spiraled out of myself again, my orgasm milking Kellan into his. When he stopped pulsing inside me, he slowly pulled out. Rolling onto his back, he took me with him and laid me over his chest. I fell asleep, crying silently on his chest with his fingers running through my hair.

I woke to an empty bed. An empty room. I took a hot shower, washing away all traces of Kellan. When I was dressed, I went in search of Kathy and Noah.

They were in the living room, sitting on the couch. They both looked up at me when I walked in. Kathy gave me a wicked grin; Noah, a knowing smile.

"I'm happy to see you hooking up with Roman. I have a good feeling about it," Kathy said.

I didn't smile back at my friends. Their smiles died. I'm sure they could see the pain in my eyes. "That wasn't Roman last night, and I don't want to talk about it. Let's get out of here. I want to put New York behind me."

We were ready in record time. I refused to think until we were high in the air.

I couldn't let Kellan keep doing this to me. What? Did he think he would come around every now and then to fuck me? So not happening. He wouldn't be able to get to me in my house. I was going to close myself in, not let the rest of the world touch me. I was going to lose myself to my writing and my home.

But it felt so empty, thinking of being without him. If time heals all wounds, I hoped to hell it would go at warp speed. I would see what fate had in store for me next. I just prayed it would be kind.

CHAPTER THIRTY-SIX

As soon as I arrived home from New York, I started getting ready for Christmas. I loved Christmas, and I always decorated over the top. I had decorations for every room of my house and added to it every year. Then there were the decorations for outside, including four Christmas trees for the wraparound porch.

Tim took all the decorations down from the attic. Bridgette and I piled them up in the rooms that they belonged in.

The next day, Tim decorated the outside while Bridgette and I tackled the inside. We put on Christmas music and started getting into the Christmas spirit.

I wanted to have a huge dinner on Christmas Day. All of my close girlfriends and their families, Noah and his family, Roman, Mr. Saunders, and Bree were all going to be here.

Friday morning, Mallory, my editor, called. She said that my two new releases, *All Out of Time* and *It's About Time*, were flying off the shelves. I let her know that I would have the manuscript ready in January, for the first book in my new series. She was thrilled with how fast I was putting out my books. I wished her a Merry Christmas and a happy New Year then ended the call.

I kept my days extremely busy and wrote whenever I had a free minute. Hoping, if I was lucky, I would be so exhausted I would pass out as soon as I fell into bed. If that didn't happen, my mind traveled to Kellan. My body missed him. My heart missed him. I felt like an empty shell.

Thankfully, there was an endless round of parties with my friends. It was wonderful spending so much time with them again. I hadn't seen them in all that time that I had been in New York with Kellan, and I had missed them.

Noah and I went to the movies, out to dinner, or just hung out. Kathy and I went to lunch, the spa, and did some shopping. I think my two best friends didn't want me spending too much time alone.

Christmas Eve morning, the house looked and smelled fabulous. The outside looked like a winter wonderland on the bayou. Tim was at the airport picking up Roman and his father. Bree's flight would get in tonight. Noah was in charge of collecting her. All three were staying at my house for the holiday.

It was 10:00 a.m., and my doorbell rang. It was a florist delivery, a beautiful Christmas arrangement. I thanked the man, took the flowers, and read the card. It was from Kellan. The card read simply, "Thinking of you." I left the arrangement on the porch and went back inside.

After that initial delivery, there was an endless barrage of deliveries. All from Kellan. There were baskets of food, candy, cookies, fruits, and just about everything you could think of. There was even a case of wine that he knew to be my favorite, a small live Christmas tree, and a Christmas bear with this year's date. I left it all on the porch. I didn't want it. Didn't even want to see it.

At noon, Tim was back with Roman and Mr. Saunders. I met them outside. It was really nice to see the two men, and I was very happy they were going to be here for Christmas.

"Hey," I said when they walked up on the porch. "I'm so happy that y'all are here."

Roman grinned at me when he saw all the deliveries sitting on the porch. "Santa run out of room inside?"

A TEMPTATION

I snorted. "These aren't staying." I looked at Tim. "Would you mind running all this stuff to St. Genevieve's for me. I'm sure the priest could find a use for it."

"That just told me who sent all this stuff," Tim said, smiling at me. "I'll take care of it."

"Thanks, Tim." I turned to my guests. "Come on in. Coffee's on."

"It's beautiful here, India," Roman said, looking out over my yard to the bayou.

"Thank you." I smiled at him. "This place means a lot to me."

I led them into the kitchen and introduced them to Bridgette. We sat at my kitchen table with our coffee.

"Roman," I said as I turned to him, "have things calmed down at your firm since it's the end of the Christmas season?"

"As far as the mad rush, yes. But I acquired a few more very big accounts. Those are keeping me hopping."

"How about you?" he asked with interest. "How are your new releases doing?"

I went into the details that Mallory gave me then excitedly told him and his dad that I would be sending the manuscript in for the first release of my new series next month.

"It's a total 180 from my other books. I have to admit, I'm a little nervous to see how my fans will react to it." I gave a little shrug. "Regardless, it was something I needed to do."

Roman gave me a curious look. I could see he had questions but knew he wouldn't voice them with the others around.

When Tim returned from the church, we all had lunch around the kitchen table. Roman regaled me with all the gossip from New York. He very carefully kept out anything to do with Kellan and his set, which I was thankful for.

"I miss seeing you, Roman. But I have to be honest and tell you that I don't miss anything else."

"It would have been different, India, if all that shit hadn't happened with Coventry."

"Yeah. I know you're right. That's his corner of the world, however."

After lunch, Mr. Saunders went up to his room for a nap. Roman and I took coffee out on the back porch. He was leaning on the railing next to me, looking out on the bayou.

"It's so peaceful here," he said, turning to me. "I can see why you love it so much."

"It's home," I responded. "I like seeing everything else out there, and I haven't even made a dent in all of the places I want to go. But at the end of the day, this is where I will always come back to. It's a part of me."

He nodded. "Your new series, India. Why are you changing genres?"

I looked at him for a moment. "I had a whole new world opened up to me. One that I didn't understand. So I researched. Then when...things started pulling me in? Well, I released it the only way I knew how."

"Makes sense," he said. "How are you doing with all of that?"

I shrugged. "Getting by. I try to stay busy. Being home helps."

"I hope you know if you need anything"—he looked at me intensely—"and I mean anything, all you have to do is ask."

"Thank you, Roman. The same goes for you."

The greatest thing about Roman had nothing to do with his great looks. It was the type of man he was. He was kind, friendly, and funny. He loved life and people. I was honored to call him a friend.

Noah and Bree got in at eight that night. She looked good, a lot better than she had at the Wells fund-raiser.

"Bree!" I squealed. "I'm so glad you came."

She came over to me and gave me a big hug. "I wouldn't have missed it, India. It's so good to see you."

"You look great," I told her, holding her at arm's length. "What's your secret?"

"I got rid of Joey." She smiled. "When I told my father what had happened in New York, he fired him. I hadn't realized how uptight I was because of him. He made me self-conscious of who I am." She shivered. "Made me feel as if I were somewhat less."

"Fuck," Noah spit out. "What's with these assholes in those circles you have been running in, India?"

A TEMPTATION

"You know damn well I'm not anything in that circle, Noah, and I don't have anything to do with anyone in it, other than Roman. And he's not an asshole," I replied heatedly. "There's good and bad everywhere, Noah. You know that."

"Beating down women emotionally is not cool. Physical injuries heal. Not always so with mental ones. Everything that Kathy caught me up on that happened with you while I was gone?" He shook his head. "Those people were all from one social circle. They believe they're entitled. I'm glad you're back where you belong."

I hugged Noah. "I am too. We just have to adopt Roman and Bree."

"I'm down with that," Noah said, sliding a sidelong glance toward Bree.

"Oh. While I'm thinking about it," I said, changing the subject. I walked over to the sofa table in my living room and picked up four books. I checked out the inside of the front jacket. "Like I promised." I held out two of my new releases, first to Bree then to Roman.

They opened the front cover, reading the inscriptions I had written inside.

"This is great! Thank you!" Bree exclaimed. "I told everyone I know in Chicago about meeting you, India, and that I was coming here for Christmas. I don't think they believed me. But now," she said as she held up the books, "they will have to."

"Good God, India," Noah said grinning. "You're famous."

"Or infamous." I smirked back at him. "Depends on how you look at it."

"You're talented is what you are," Roman cut in. "Now you're getting the recognition. Thank you for this." He held up the books. "It means a lot to me."

I felt the blush. Its heat started at my neck, spreading on to my hairline. "You're quite welcome. I'm thrilled to count you and Bree as friends."

We all sat around the fireplace in the living room with glasses of wine, talking until the early hours of Christmas morning.

Noah ended up staying the night. He was always at Bree's side. I watched with interest, the shy interested smiles she sent him. I know

Noah. Usually, he bulldozed his way through women. He would put himself blatantly out there. If they wanted what they see, great. If not, their loss. Very few, however, turned away from Noah.

This? This was different. Noah was gentle with her. Tender. Affectionate. I hoped they would get together. Bree deserved to be treasured. And I would love to see Noah happy with someone as sweet and kind as Bree.

I was watching the sunrise over the bayou after only a couple of hours of sleep. This was not how I had pictured this Christmas. It would have been Kellan's and my first. I had visualized Christmas in New York with him. There would have been endless functions and parties we would have had to attend.

Instead, Asia was with him. And I, I was here without him. One day, that thought won't hurt so intensely. Until that time, I prayed that I would survive. If Kellan stayed away from me, didn't try to contact me, it would make it easier.

"Good morning."

I turned at the greeting and smiled at Roman. "Merry Christmas."

"Same to you, India."

We stood at the railing of my back porch. In companionable silence, we watched the brilliant colors slowly emerge over the water.

"This place reminds me of you," Roman said softly. "Beautiful and wild. Soft and fiery. Strong yet delicate." He turned to me. "Don't let the fiasco with Kellan Coventry change who and what you are. I want to see the happy, vivacious women that I met."

I nodded. "I'm still the same person, Roman. I can't help how I feel or how long it will take for me not to seem so incomplete. But it's easier being here."

"Okay," he replied, smiling at me. "I just didn't want that bastard to have stripped away whom I have come to care a great deal for."

Christmas dinner turned out to be exactly what I needed. With the people that I cared deeply about seated all over my dining room, I knew I had been blessed in this life.

After dinner, we exchanged gifts in the living room. There were lots of oohs and ahhs along with a lot of teasing and joking.

A TEMPTATION

My phone had been going off for about an hour. It was Kellan, and I refused to answer.

Tim came over to me. "India, Kellan's been blowing up my phone. He said that he won't stop calling both of us until you talk to him. He also said that if we turn off our phones, he will drive over here."

Oh, hell no! There was no way I wanted Kellan over here. My phone went off again. *Fuck! What does he think he's doing?* I got up abruptly, grabbed my phone, and went into the kitchen.

"What do you want, Kellan?" I almost yelled into the phone.

"I needed to hear your voice," he said in his low, sexy voice. "To tell you Merry Christmas. To see if you're okay."

"Why do you do this? Do you hate me that much?" I asked him quietly. "I'm not a masochist, Kellan?"

"I'm not doing any of this to hurt you, baby. In fact, quite the opposite. You're an intelligent woman. If you would only use your other senses, not just your eyes, you would know that for truth."

"You're insane, Kellan. Stark raving mad. If, as you say, there's something else at play, you should have talked to me. Should have let me know what was going on. Either way? It's a betrayal."

"No—"

"I'm hanging up now, Kellan. Leave. Me. Alone."

I ended the call and laid my head down on the kitchen table. I was so tired. I didn't sleep because of thoughts of Kellan, or I would have nightmares that starred him. His vague comments drove me crazy.

"India?" I opened my eyes to see Noah kneeling on the floor by my chair. I hated to see the worry in his eyes.

"I can't take this anymore. If I didn't love him, it wouldn't be a problem. He betrayed me. Yet he won't leave me alone once I walked away. I would change my cell, but he would be able to get the number because of who he is. I feel like I'm trapped in a box. There's danger inside of it and out. I don't know what to do."

Noah took both of my hands. "I don't know what game he's playing, but from now on, Kitten, no matter what, don't talk to him. It doesn't matter what he or those sluts he hangs with say. Not even if it hurts. Don't acknowledge it. Walk off. Get on with your life even through the pain. It's the only way to make him back off."

My phone went off. With my heart in my throat, I looked at the screen. Tanner. It was my friend Tanner. Thank God!

"Tanner," I said excitedly into the phone. "Merry Christmas. How are you? Where are you?"

"Hey, India." He chuckled. "Merry Christmas to you too. I'm great, and I'm in Baton Rouge having Christmas with my family."

"Oh wow. You're home. I hope that means you're going to come see all of us. If not, I'll have to hurt you."

"Do you think I could be this close and not see you? I thought you knew me better than that."

I giggled, got up, and walked into the living room. "Hey, everybody. It's Tanner."

All of my friends squealed and yelled greetings and Merry Christmas out to him. "I'm sure you can hear how much everyone wants to see you."

"Yeah. It's great to be loved," he said cockily. "How's tomorrow? Is that okay?"

"Of course it is. You don't have to ask. You know you're always welcome."

"Great. I'll see you then."

"Can't wait."

I ended the call and let all my friends know. We made plans for all of them to come back tomorrow so they could see Tanner.

All too soon, everyone left, except Bree, Roman, and his father. Roman and his dad were flying out tomorrow. Bree was staying through New Year's.

Roman came and found me outside in my favorite spot. He sat down beside me, on the steps of my back porch.

"I've really enjoyed being here, India. I wish I could stay longer."

"I know you have to get back. I hope you'll come down here often. I can't go back to New York just yet, but maybe it won't be too long before my mind-set is in a better place, and I can go back."

A TEMPTATION

"I wish Coventry wasn't being such an asshole, then you could come to my New Year's Eve party. I host it every year. It won't be as much fun knowing you're down here."

"That's a very nice thing to say. But please have a good time." I dropped my eyes to my lap. "I am going to forget Kellan. Noah had some very good advice tonight."

"I'm happy to hear that. I would like the chance to know you better."

I raised my head and looked into his eyes. "I can't promise you anything, Roman."

"I know. You wouldn't be who I'm fascinated with if you could move on that fast. But I need you to know that I'll be waiting when you're ready."

CHAPTER THIRTY-SEVEN

The next morning, after Tim took off to the airport with Roman and his father, Bridgette, Bree, and I got busy making hors d'oeuvres. My friends would be returning, and we were going to spend the late afternoon and night drinking and eating, enjoying having Tanner among us once again.

Later that afternoon, Tim was putting beer on ice in coolers in the kitchen. Bridgette, Bree, and I were setting all the food in the dining room when my friends started to arrive.

Noah was the first. He stayed glued to Bree's side as soon as he came through the door. The girls and their guys started trickling in after that. Finally, Tanner arrived at five.

Everyone piled out on the front porch. They were all talking at once, hugging and shaking hands. I was standing right outside my front door. When Tanner finished greeting all our friends, he walked over and stood right in front of me.

"India," he said huskily.

I hugged him tight. He wrapped his arms around me and lifted me off my feet.

A TEMPTATION

"You look good, girl, so don't take this the wrong way." He set me back down on my feet. "You've lost too much weight. A lot since I saw you in Washington."

I shrugged. "I've been really busy, Tanner."

Kathy snorted. "It's because of an asshole."

"Coventry," he growled. And it wasn't a question.

"Look. Everybody." I ran my gaze over each one of my friends. "It's over. I don't want to hear his name. I don't want to hear a word about him. Do I make myself clear?"

I heard "Yeah, okay" and "I'm sorry" from the lot of them. But not Tanner. He just looked confused and as if he had a lot of questions.

"Okay. The party awaits." I grinned. "Hand over your keys, and I mean everyone. Give them to Tim, and y'all can drink until you pass out if that's your wish."

They all traipsed back into the house, turning their keys over good-naturedly to Tim. He placed them in a basket and put that where only he knew.

I had made gallons of daiquiris. Between all the food and liquor—and all of my friends' shenanigans—I laughed more than I had in half a year.

By eleven that night, I had friends draped all over the furniture and floors of my living room. Some were out for the count. Noah and Bree were tangled up together on the love seat. Tanner and I were lying on the floor. We had been catching up on our careers.

Tanner turned from his back to his side and propped himself up on his elbow, his head resting on his hand.

"I know what you said out on the porch, India. But I haven't been around. You know I've been worried since I saw you in Washington because of him. I can see the difference in you. Not just your weight. The shadows in your eyes. The sadness." He paused. "Talk to me. Please?"

I mimicked his position, turning to face him. "What do you want me to say? That I played and lost? That I didn't listen to my instincts and keep running? That my stupid heart finally fell in love but with the ultimate wrong person?"

"I want you to tell me that whatever number he pulled on you, you'll be okay. That you won't let him win by letting what he did fundamentally change you."

"I can't tell you that, Tanner. With everything that I saw and experienced, it has changed me. I have always liked people. In his world, I met so many devious...cutthroat people that I don't think I will ever be able to trust anyone outside of our circle again.

"And then there was Kellan himself. I trusted him with everything that I am. I gave myself to him. Body, mind, and soul." I shook my head. "He took what he wanted and gave what he wanted. And then when I couldn't breathe without him, he threw it all away. He was gone. Back to those...relationships that he was in when we met. Back to the lifestyle that apparently he doesn't want to give up."

"He can't be what you judge all men or relationships by, India. He's not the norm. He and his lifestyle are too far out the box."

"Yeah," I snorted. "What does that say about me? After twenty-four years, he is who I fall for. It wasn't a crush, Tanner. I had no say in the matter."

"You are one of the best people I know, India," Tanner stressed. "It doesn't mean otherwise because you fell for him. You weren't part of his lifestyle. You're not one of those devious people you spoke of. It might take a while, but you'll find your way again. Those shadows will go away, and your heart will mend."

I sighed. "If he would leave me alone, it would be a lot easier to try to forget. To feel something other than numb. But I've decided it is my life, and he isn't going to control it anymore. Not even from the sidelines. So now I need to rewrite my life."

"And you will. I know you. Everything that you want, that you think you've lost? You'll find."

"Thanks, Tanner. I don't know what I would have done without all of my friends." I looked up at him. "What are you doing for New Year's Eve?"

"I don't have any plans. Why?"

"You want to be my date?" I asked him, wiggling my eyebrows.

He laughed. "Yeah. Whatever all of you are up to, I'm in."

A TEMPTATION

Nine o'clock on New Year's Eve found all my friends and me at the Marriott on Canal Street. The party was being held in the massive ballroom. It looked magical, all decorated in silver and gold. There was a band set up against one wall in the middle of the room with tables upon tables of food against the wall on one end and a bar set up on the other.

I couldn't help but remember all that had happened the last time I was here. Devyn Troyer attacking me. Kellan rescuing me. That event led to the relationship that I had had with Kellan. I couldn't stop the shiver that ran down my spine.

"Hey. Are you cold?" Tanner asked me, putting an arm around my shoulders.

I shook my head. "Just something walking over my grave," I muttered to myself.

"Have I told you how sexy you look tonight?"

"I believe that has tumbled out of your mouth once or twice."

"Good," he said close to my ear. "Because you outshine everyone else here."

I had taken special care getting ready for tonight. I wanted to look good, feel different. I was wearing a short black velvet cocktail dress. It rested off my shoulders and draped low between my breasts. It was very short and clung sensually to my body. Kathy and Bree did my hair and makeup. I felt sexy, and for the first time in quite a while, I felt in control.

"I'll go grab us something to drink," Tanner was saying.

"Just a glass of wine for me please. I can't hang with all of you. I'm liquored out."

"Lightweight." Tanner chuckled.

Kathy, Bree, and Noah flanked me after Tanner walked off.

"The band's good," Kathy said.

"Yeah. They are," I agreed. "I say we get back to old times, and get out on that dance floor."

We all went out on the dance floor. After dancing as a group for one song, Noah grabbed me for the next. As kids, we pretended that we were the main characters from the movie *Dirty Dancing*. As a result, we became very good dancers.

We performed a PG version on this dance floor. Very sensual; suggestive, but not vulgar.

When the song ended, almost everyone in the room applauded. Our friends whistled and catcalled.

Noah wrapped his hands around my waist, lifting me off my feet. I wrapped my arms around his neck, holding on as he spun me around. When I found my feet, Noah and I took a bow.

Tanner was standing at the edge of the dance floor, holding our drinks and wearing a shit-eating grin. "Who says playacting as kids doesn't lead to great things?" he asked, handing me the glass of wine as I walked up to him.

I thanked him and laughed. "If you only knew how long we would practice, you would say we were obsessed, not playing."

"It doesn't matter. The results are amazing." He leaned into my side and whispered in my ear, "And hot as hell."

I turned to the side to make a comeback to Tanner. Before I could open my mouth, my eyes fell on a furious Kellan; even furious he had my heart pumping. He was my dark, brooding, and arrogant fallen angel. Well, not mine. Not anymore.

He was wearing a tux. It was tailored for him and showed off his amazing body to perfection. He had let his jet-black hair grow out some. It had that sexy just-fucked look. Ha! For all I knew, he probably had just gotten laid.

"You and Noah knew he was here," I accused Tanner. "That's the reason for that dance."

"Yep," he said bluntly.

I watched Deric say something urgently to Kellan. Alexis rubbed her hand in what looked like a soothing motion up and down his arm. He angrily shook her hand off and barked something out at her. Her hand fell immediately to her side. He never took his eyes off mine through all of that.

All my friends surrounded Tanner and me, cutting off my view of Kellan.

"He's just another guy here, Kitten," Noah said, putting his arm around my shoulders.

A TEMPTATION

Tanner put one of his arms around my waist. "Just an ex," he whispered in my ear.

"He should be in New York," I addressed all my friends. "He would have a lot of places he needed to go to tonight. It's weird how he always shows up where I am, when I'm out in public."

"That's probably not a coincidence," Tanner mumbled.

"What?" I turned to him.

"What does his company do, India?" He looked at me, exasperated. "He didn't become as rich as he is because he's mediocre at what he does."

"My phone," I gasped.

"Yeah," Noah said. "That's what we think. You need to get another cell, Kitten. Get rid of the one you have."

Before I could answer, someone pushed through my ring of friends. A furious Kellan stood in front of me. I had never seen him so mad. Deric came right behind him, grabbing his arm.

"Kellan. Come on, man. You don't want to do this."

Kellan ripped his arm out of Deric's grip. "Stay the fuck out of this, Deric."

Oh shit. I thought. *This was not going to be good. Okay, remember what Noah said. Don't say anything. Don't respond.*

Bret and Zack stepped up behind Kellan and Deric. Alexis and the other woman walked up beside Deric. Alexis had a smart-ass smirk on her face. Bret and Zack caught my eyes, apologizing with their looks.

"It looks like I taught you too well, India, if you can start fucking your make-believe brother."

There were gasps from all of my friends, and I felt Tanner and Noah tense beside me.

"Kitten," Noah said. I looked up at him, praying the tears in my eyes would not spill over. I wasn't hurt over what Kellan said, believe it or not. I was angry. Angrier than I had ever been in my life.

"What I said in the kitchen on Christmas?" Noah continued. "Forget it. I was wrong."

I nodded. I brought my hand back and slapped Kellan across his furious face as hard as I could.

"You didn't deserve her," Tanner spit out at Kellan, getting into his face. "And you sure as hell don't know her if you could say something like that."

Bret pushed Tanner back, out of Kellan's face.

"That's my point," Kellan said, never taking his eyes off me. "With what I saw, she definitely is not what I thought she was. I don't know this person at all."

"You asshole," Lucas broke in. "India and Noah—"

"No, Lucas," I interrupted him. "He doesn't deserve an explanation. I don't owe him a damn thing."

"Damn straight," Kathy said. "Don't think your bodyguards frighten us, Mr. Coventry. We were brought up on the bayou. We take care of our own and don't give a shit who we have to go through to do it."

Then everything happened at once. Out of the corner of my eye, I saw Alexis reach for me. Before I could do anything, Bree got in front of Alexis, wrapping her hand around her wrist.

"Don't even go there, bitch. I will mop the floor with you." I couldn't believe that came out of sweet Bree.

Tanner pushed me behind him, and all of my friends stepped forward into the personal space of Kellan and company.

"Go back to your sluts, Coventry," Noah growled. "Stay away from India. We won't let you hurt her again."

I couldn't see Kellan with Tanner standing in front of me, but I could hear his condescending tone loud and clear.

"Trust me. I don't want anything to do with her. You're welcome to her."

"You motherfucker," Tanner growled and drew back his fist.

"No!" I shouted and pushed my way in front of Tanner, effectively stopping the punch. I stared right into Kellan's eyes. "Stop. Everyone. It's not worth it. This is over."

"Yeah, it is," Kellan agreed. I knew he wasn't talking about the almost fight.

I watched as Kellan turned away, putting his arm around the shoulders of the blonde woman I didn't know. Damn. I hope that sight wouldn't hurt this bad for long.

A TEMPTATION

"India." Deric broke through my pain. "I'm sorry. What he said was wrong. He just goes crazy where you're concerned."

I looked up at Deric and gave him a small smile. "It doesn't matter why Kellan does or says what he does, Deric. There are no excuses. After tonight, I'll make sure we don't run into each other anymore."

"Ms. Leigh—" Bret started.

"It's okay, Bret," I assured him. "This is all on Kellan. I don't feel anything but friendship toward you and Zack."

Bret looked into my eyes for a moment then nodded. Then he, Zack, and Deric turned and followed Kellan and the blonde.

"Do you want to leave, Kitten?" Noah asked me softly.

"No," I told my dear friend. "We came here to chase the New Year, and that's what we are going to do. Our life is here. His is in New York. I will not let him drive me away from where I want to be."

"That's my girl," Noah said proudly.

"Bree," I said, getting her attention. "What you did with Alexis—" I stopped, unable to find the words.

"Hey. I might not have been raised on the bayou," Bree said, "but I didn't grow up in Chicago for nothing."

Everyone laughed. With that laughter came relief. For the first time in a long time, peace settled over me. I looked over all my friends. I may not have Kellan anymore, but I was richer than most with everything that I did have.

"Ready to get this party started, gorgeous?" Tanner asked me.

"Definitely," I said to him. "But I think it's time to invite Jose."

There was agreement from everyone. Tanner wrapped his arm around my shoulder. Noah wrapped his around Bree.

As we headed back to our table, I heard Noah say to Bree, "Come on, Joe Lewis, I'll buy you a drink."

"What?" Bree asked.

And we all laughed. I was happy that I had met Bree that night at the Wells fund-raiser. She and Roman were the only good things I came away with from my relationship with Kellan.

We all piled up at a large table. We had two shots of Cuervo when Noah turned to me.

"Come on, Kitten," Noah said. "Let's go do our best dance."

I knew why he wanted to do that. Kellan had been on the dance floor with that blonde since that argument. They were dirty dancing also—except it was sleazy, not talented. Either that blonde was a new sub, or she was more to Kellan. He usually did not even touch a sub in public. He had been all over this female all night. And I really mean all over. If she was a sub, he was doing this to try to get at me.

"It's okay, Noah. I don't care what he's doing," I tried to argue.

"I do. That's another one of his sluts. I say we go show him what talent and class is."

Everyone agreed with Noah, and Kathy walked up to the band. Noah took my hand. I looked at him, shook my head, rose, and let him walk me onto the dance floor.

When Noah stopped me in the middle of the dance floor, all the other couples left the floor and turned to watch us. That made me nervous. Noah placed me in front of him, my back to his front.

"Don't be nervous, Kitten," Noah whispered in my ear. "This will have him eating his heart out and also show him how wrong his assumptions were. We're not holding back this time, Kitten."

The strands of "Time of My Life" started, and I let everything go, letting the music wash through me. I thought of happier times when Noah and I danced this dance. We were so in sync with each other from years of executing these dances and years of knowing each other so well.

Before I knew it, the song and dance ended. There was thunderous applause and shouts of encore. The band went into another song from the movie. The dance to this one was more risqué. Noah looked down at me, one brow raised in question.

I nodded my consent, and he leaned down, his mouth to my ear. "Remember, Kitten, no holding back." And we were off.

When the music ended, the applause started again. When the crowd started shouting for more again, I turned to the band, shaking my head. I needed a drink and to sit down. I was out of breath. Noah threaded our fingers together and led me back to the table.

All of our friends were standing, waiting for us. Noah let go of my hand and wrapped Bree up in his arms. I walked over to Tanner. He put an arm around my shoulders.

A TEMPTATION

"You were beautiful out there, India," Tanner said.

"Hey. She wasn't dancing by herself," Noah teased.

"Sorry, big guy, you were beautiful too," Tanner joked back.

"You guys are so good," Bree said.

"They should be," Kathy added. "They practiced every day for a year when they were eleven. Do y'all remember the show we put on for our parents when we were twelve?"

"Yeah. I didn't know my grandmother could turn that red." I chuckled. "I need some more tequila. I danced mine away."

"Even with the natures of the dances, all the parents said y'all were great," Lucas chirped in. "So they didn't stop y'all from doing them."

"Come on, Noah," Tanner said. "Let's go get Jose for everyone."

I watched the guys walk off, and my eyes met Kellan's. I hadn't known they were so close to us. There was no way he hadn't heard our conversation. He no longer had his hands on the blonde.

I felt a light touch on my shoulder. When I turned, I saw it was Bret.

"Zack and I were amazed, Ms. Leigh. You were great."

I grinned up at him. "Thanks, Bret. We've practiced since we were little kids. What's with this Ms. Leigh shit? What happened to calling me India?"

"I didn't know if you would still want to have anything to do with us," the big bodyguard replied.

My smile disappeared. "I don't hold anything Kellan does against y'all, Bret. That has nothing to do with you."

"Okay. I'm glad to hear that." He smiled at me. "Remember, if you ever need me, you have my number."

"Thanks, Bret. Happy New Year."

He nodded and went back to his post.

Noah and Tanner returned. We did more shots, laughing and talking about times past and dancing more as a group. None of my friends left me alone at any time.

I felt Kellan's eyes on me all through the night. But he never came back over to me. Never tried to talk to me again. I must be a masochist—because even though I couldn't take Kellan's crap anymore, love doesn't disappear overnight. And this still hurt like hell.

At midnight, hundreds of white, silver, and gold balloons fell from the ceiling. The band played "Auld Lang Syne" while we were all hugging, kissing, and wishing each other Happy New Year. I prayed 2015 would be a great year for all of us.

I saw Kellan, Deric, Alexis, and the blonde walk toward the exit. Kellan stopped, turned, and looked right at me. This look was different. It was sorrowful. He gave me a slight nod, turned, and walked out. I had a feeling I wouldn't need to replace my phone now.

Two days later, I was in my office, working. The house was so quiet. Bree had gone back to Chicago yesterday, Tanner back to Washington this morning. It was back to just Bridgette, Tim, and me.

I hadn't heard from Kellan. No more phone calls. No more flowers.

I had worked day and night on my new book. *Temptation* would be going out to my publishers on Monday. It was so much more than a novel because it wasn't fiction—though no one would know that. It was me. My emotions. My feelings. My life—for just one moment in time.

A peek at the second instalment of the Discover Trilogy:

POSESSION

CHAPTER ONE

*I*t was Sunday evening, and I was boxing up my manuscript when my phone went off. I looked at the screen. I didn't recognize the number.

"Hello," I said hesitantly into the phone.

"Yes," A woman's voice, that I didn't know, answered my greeting. "Is this India Leigh?"

"Ah…yes."

"My name is Ellen. Ellen Harrow."

It was Kellan's aunt. I couldn't imagine why she would be contacting me. I hadn't ever met the woman. Kellan had mentioned that he wanted to take me to meet her. But we hadn't lasted that long.

Then my heart jumped into my throat.

"Mrs. Harrow. Is…is Kellan okay?"

"Oh yes. He's fine dear." She went silent for a moment. "I was hoping that I could convince you to come and visit me."

"I don't understand?" I shook my head. "Mrs. Harrow. Kellan and I are no longer seeing each other."

"I was afraid it was something like that. Would you please humor an old woman? It would mean a lot if you would come and see me."

"Mrs. Harrow," I sighed. "I don't think Kellan would be very happy about that."

She laughed into the phone. "You let me worry about my nephew."

"Yes ma'am."

I had errands to run tomorrow, so I asked her if it would be convenient after that. She agreed, and gave me her address.

I sat for a while after I ended the call. Kellan must be very different with his aunt. I didn't think she understood how angry he would be when he found out about us meeting.

Two p.m. the next afternoon, found me on my way to Mandeville. I was very nervous. Nothing good could come of this.

When I pulled into Mrs. Harrow's driveway, one of Kellan's security guys-I couldn't remember his name-met me at my car, opening the door for me.

"It's good to see you Ms. Leigh," he said sincerely. "Go on in. Mrs. Harrow is expecting you."

"Thanks," I nodded to him, and walked up to the front door. Kellan was probably already on his way, I thought, since his security team knew I was here.

Before I could knock on the front door, another one of Kellan's security guards opened it from the inside. He led me through the house to the large, bright, kitchen in the back.

"India!" Exclaimed this very petite, white haired, sixtyish woman. Instead of shaking my hand, she gave me a huge hug. "I have so wanted to meet you."

"It's nice to meet you to, Mrs. Harrow."

"Call me Ellen dear." She walked over to the kitchen island. "Please come have a seat. Do you drink coffee?"

I laughed. "It's my favorite food group."

"Woman after my own heart."

She was delightful. This was so not the type of person I thought I would be meeting.

After exchanging some pleasantries, I turned to her. "I don't mean to seem rude, but with your security team knowing I'm here, Kellan does. We will not have a lot of time."

"Oh no. I made it clear when the guys first came here, that nothing that transpires privately with me, gets reported back to my nephew. If that happens, I will not keep a security team."

"Whoa," I said surprised. "I didn't get a say in anything. But I agree with you. Everyone has to have some control in their own life."

"I know my nephew has control issues India. I'm not making excuses for him, but he had no control in a very tragic childhood. I believe his personality, his dominance, I guess you could say, is a result."

"I won't pretend I know anything about his past. Hell. I don't know anything about his present." I shook my head. "All of that is beside the point. There is nothing between Kellan and me any longer. What is it that you want from me Ellen?"

"Kellan has always kept his distance from people. Except for Deric and me, he has never allowed himself to form close attachments. But then he met you." She reached across the island and put her hand over mine. "For the first time in that boy's life, I saw and heard an excitement for the next day. For the next step. For the next time he would be with you again. Then last month it wasn't there anymore."

"I don't know what to tell you. I don't know what happened. One minute Kellan wanted this...major relationship. The next he was gone.'

"He didn't give you a clue?"

"No ma'am. Everything was wonderful, and then he just pushed me away. He's back to hanging out with the women that he and Deric used to hang out with. But at the same time he says cryptic things, like it just has to be this way right now. That I'm supposed to wait until I don't know what. I can't do that."

"But that sounds like something fishy is going on. It doesn't sound like he wants it over between you two."

I took my hand out from under hers. "If that's the case, he should have confided in me, not pick up with old lovers." I looked into her eyes. "I love your nephew. But even loving him? I can't handle what he's doing. The reasoning does not matter."

"I don't believe that any woman, if they were truly in love could handle that India. It would hurt to much."

The front door opened and slammed shut. We heard men's voices raised in anger. Kellan had arrived.

Kellan, Deric, and some of the security guys, stomped into the kitchen.

"What the fuck are you doing here?" Kellan growled, standing over me. "Would you go through any lengths to get at me India?"

I stood up and got right in his face. "I didn't come here for…"

"This is going to far," he bit out, interrupting me. "You stay away from my aunt."

Tears stung my eyes. I wasn't hurt. I was pissed and embarrassed.

"Kellan!" Ellen shouted. "I called and invited India here. You have no right talking to her like this."

Kellan took a deep, calming breath, then spoke gently to her. "I don't want her anywhere near you.

You'll have to trust me on this."

"Ellen," I addressed his aunt with as much dignity as I could muster. "It was very nice meeting you. I'm sorry I couldn't help you. I guess I shouldn't have come here until I got a new phone so he wouldn't have known where I was."

I saw the surprise on Kellan's face. "Yeah. I figured it out, and I will break this last tie between us." I turned to go.

"India." Ellen's voice stopped me, but I didn't turn around. She walked around to stand in front of me, taking both my hands in hers. "Please remember what I said," she whispered and looked intensely into my eyes. "He wouldn't be acting this way if he didn't care."

I gave her hands a slight squeeze. "Thank you. But if this is his way of caring? I don't want any part of it. Good-bye Ellen."

ABOUT THE AUTHOR

Mary E. Buras Conway is a wife, mother, and grandmother. A native of New Orleans, LA, she now resides in northwest Florida with her family. Becoming a published author has been a life-long dream.

CPSIA information can be obtained at www.ICGtesting.com
Printed in the USA
LVOW10s0256011015

456472LV00003B/5/P